THE RACE OF FIRE

Revealing Rexa

ALSO BY THIS AUTHOR

The Race of Fire
Book 2: Awakening Sand
Book 3: Rekindling Truth

The Curse of Mycenae

Crystal Runes

Ella Mortimer

The Race of Fire

Revealing Rexa

MY THANKS TO

My mother, who first nurtured this book when it was merely a seed in my mind's eye, and who awaited each instalment eagerly, no matter how long it took.

AUTHOR'S NOTE

I was born and raised on the Central Coast of New South Wales on the east coast of Australia. This book has been with me for most of my life. The first tentative scenes were written down as a young teenager. I graduated from University as Bachelor of Arts with Honours in 1994. Then I picked up the book again. The first draft was complete by the end of 1996. The novel went through several edits until the fourth draft was complete at the end of 1999. Then life took over and the book was put on a shelf.

Ten years later, I stumbled across the Amazon Breakthrough Novel Award via a post on Facebook. There is a certain satisfaction in coming back to a book after such a long time. I was able to improve on the lives and loves of my characters in ways that I would never have been courageous enough to do when I was younger. So, I sat down to undertake this final edit. I discovered that I had in fact written two novels. So the book was split and I began work developing both halves separately. This volume is the first.

The first edition of Revealing Rexa was published in 2011 under the pen name Ella Stradling. It was the name I invented as a teenager, and I never considered using my real name. The name Ella was given me by my father in honour of his favourite singer, Ella Fitzgerald, and the name Stradling was used in memory of my 4th Great Grandmother, who was the last of her line. Now, I am reclaiming my books under my legal surname.

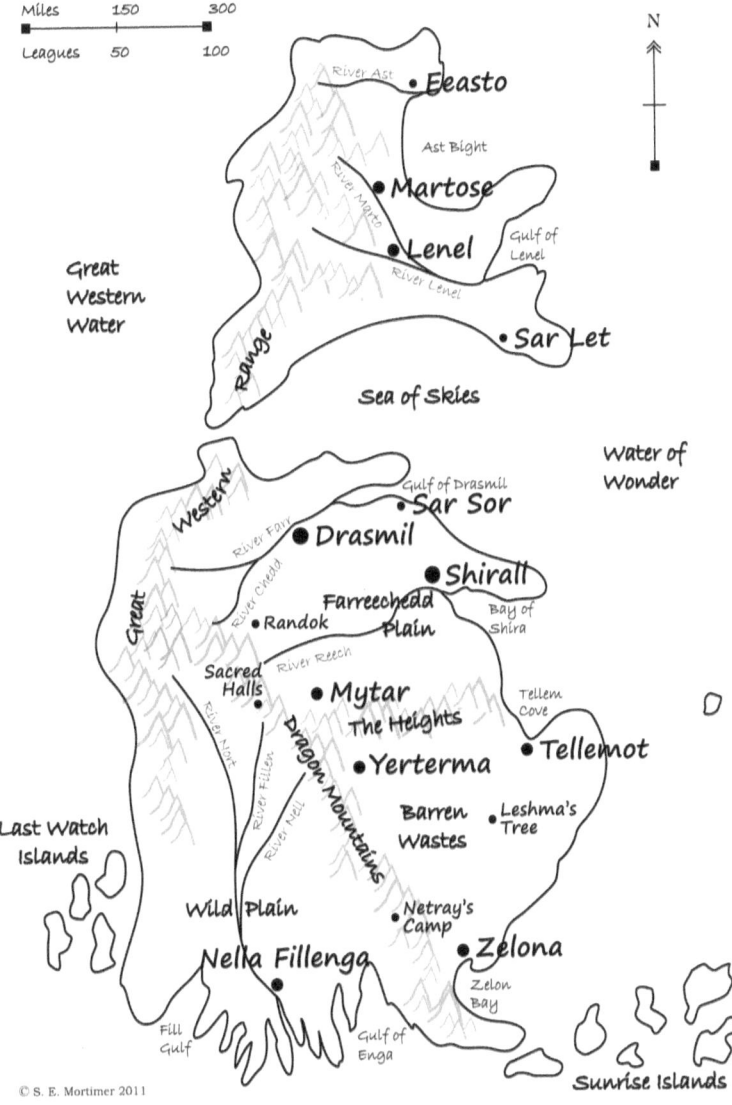

Miles 150 300
Leagues 50 100

N

River Ast •Eeasto

Ast Bight

•Martose

River Mato

•Lenel

River Lenel Gulf of Lenel

Great
Western
Water

Range

•Sar Let

Sea of Skies

Water of
Wonder

Western

River Farr Gulf of Drasmil

•Sar Sor

•Drasmil

River Credd

•Shirall

Farreechedd
Plain Bay of
Shira

Great •Randok

Sacred River Reech
Halls •Mytar

The Heights Tellem
Cove

River Niet •Yerterma •Tellemot

Dragon Mountains

River Fillen

Barren •Leshma's
Wastes Tree

River Nell

Last Watch
Islands

Wild Plain •Netray's
Camp

Nella Fillenga •Zelona

Zelon
Bay

Fill
Gulf Gulf of
Enga

Sunrise Islands

© S. E. Mortimer 2011

PROLOGUE
THE SONG OF REXA
(Abridged)

When time was young, this land was won,
A land of splendour, bathed in sun.
The people lived in a land that was new,
With hope for the future and troubles few.

But a hostile race of black intent,
Who all their lives in darkness spent,
Claimed for themselves this glorious land,
Left nothing behind but dust and sand.

The dark ones used the people as slaves,
Till a leader emerged, his people to save.
With the loyal help of many a friend,
Rexa escaped, the oppression to end.

Descended from one who once was king,
This man was possessed of an ancient ring.
When paired with a golden amulet,
The power released could free them yet.

Alone, both necklace and ring held magic.
Together, the fate of the dark ones was tragic.
For here was a power so full of might,
It could forever defeat the men of the night.

The enemy, reduced to a fractured few,
Turned tail and fled, spread wings and flew.
Rid was the land of the terrible foe,
Who had taken their freedom, so long ago.

With peace returned and freedom restored,
Rexa found the babe he had mourned;
His only grandchild, an orphaned girl,
Whose beauty is said to have rivalled the pearl.

Rexa summoned the soul of his wife,
And gave the spirit eternal life.
Her spirit he sealed in the pendant of gold,
Naming her Leena, beautiful and bold.

He took his ring, its weight he measured,
And mixed with items of gold he had treasured.
With the last of his life he caused them to meld,
Formed a new charm, in his dying hand held.

This Rexa instructed the girl to give
The man with whom she was destined to live.
He named it Naali and with a grin,
His own life force he fused within.

In the course of the years Naali was lost,
But Leena remains at any cost,
In the hands of queens, hidden from strangers,
Giving protection and warning of dangers.

The people now prosper and live in joy,
And this story holds wonder for many a boy.
Cares are forgotten and bells will chime,
In a land of wonder 'till the end of time.

ONE

Darkness surrounded her and darkness was hunting her. All of her awareness was filled with the sound of footsteps and heartbeat pounding in unison. Her mind screamed in silent pain as the golden amulet about her neck radiated the heat of a furnace, sending messages to her ravaged brain, warning "danger, danger," urging her to go ever faster.

Her trembling hands clutched at the chain, but knowledge hidden deep within her mind prevented her from tearing the amulet away. The acrid smell of singed grass wafted on the night air and assailed her nose as she tried to draw breath. She could hear the sizzling of burnt leaves with each thud from the heavy footsteps following ever closer.

She ran barefoot through the dense undergrowth, having lost her flimsy slippers long ago, feet scratched and bloody. Long, spindly, wooden fingers had clutched at her skirts so many times that her dress was torn and tattered. Each branch and twig seemed to drag at her, hindering her progress, bringing the enemy closer to her heels.

Her breath came in gasping sobs and panic thudded in her heart as the branches clutched at her ankles, threatening to land her on her knees. She shivered as her dress was snagged again and again, shrinking from the thought that one of those clutches might not be a branch.

After what seemed an eternity of blind running, her

small cabin came into sight and a wave of relief swept over her. At last, hitting the front door, she scooted inside, hurriedly sliding the bolts home. She collapsed against the solid wood, trembling uncontrollably, her body racked with sobs.

When gentle hands were laid on her shoulders, she tried with little success to stifle a scream. Then, as the warmth of the room finally began to seep into her battered consciousness, she realised that she was safe and turned into her husband's comforting arms.

"They have..." she gasped, "found us... Ordel."

* * *

The revealer and his companion approached the imposing fortress at a fast trot. He gazed up at the formidable stone wall, rising high above as they rode into its shadow, and was glad. Whenever he stood beneath those massive walls, they always took him back to the first time he had stood there looking up in awe.

As a young boy of ten years old, he had come as a supplicant seeking admission into the secretive College of the Art, to begin training as a revealer. He had lived and trained there for almost twenty years, learning to use stealth and the powers of the mind to reveal information. He had become the youngest ever to reach the rank of artisan, the top of his profession.

But, looking up at those impressive stone walls, that first day was as vivid as yesterday. At the huge barred gate, a challenge echoed from the dimness under the arch and the old gatekeeper glared through the stout iron rails.

Evelar dismounted in one fluid movement, and led his stallion closer, his companion silent on its back. He spoke in a low voice to the guard, and the heavy gate lumbered slowly open to reveal a dark passage and bright sunlight beckoning from the inner courtyard. Evelar hesitated, savouring this moment.

Once he stepped through the gate he would leave his worldly identity behind and become Sand, the artisan revealer. Here you were known only by your deeds, and any fame would come by skill alone, the accident of birth meaningless in the College of the Art.

He shrugged as he shouldered the cloak of anonymity, taking on the Art name which had become as much a part of him as his real name. Sand led his stallion through, and the gate clanged shut behind them. The gatekeeper noticed the young woman seated on Lumen's back, and stiffened.

"Who is that?" he asked suspiciously.

"A friend."

The stout, weathered old man stared doubtfully at the girl in the dimness. She smiled and named him with a laugh of confidence, using his Art name.

"What's the matter, Worm? Don't you know me?"

The old man jumped in surprise, peering at her with his aging eyes, then gave a joyful shout. "Miyam?"

Sand's practiced mask hid his surprise, and his eyes flicked from one to the other. "You know each other?"

"Of course," said the old man with glee. "You'd best hurry through, child. The Maestro will be delighted!"

With a quizzical look, the revealer took an abrupt step between the two of them to swing up into the saddle behind Miyam. He looked down and raised an eyebrow at the grinning gate keeper. He had thought he would never get Miyam past the guard, fully expecting to leave her alone in Eeasto, outside the College. Instead, he found she was known to the guard, and he wondered what else she had hidden from him.

Sand took the reins in his hands and touched his heels to Lumen's flanks, annoyed at himself for being taken off guard. They cantered across the yard, heading around the main building to the stables behind, where a young novice ran out to take the reins as they dismounted.

"Take care, lad," said Sand to the boy. "He has been a faithful friend for many a day and he's very tired. See that he's treated well."

"Yes, Sir Artisan."

Sand watched as the boy focused on the name badge that fastened his cloak, trying to read the secret characters that only a member of the College could understand. Reading the badge of a fellow revealer was an important skill, serving as a failsafe identification tool, and preventing criminal spies from posing as revealers. The boy mouthed the sounds, his brow furrowed as he tried to remember the meanings of the symbols.

"It says..." Sand began.

"Please, Sir. I want to read it myself," the boy said.

He studied the badge again, then he smiled. "Sand!" he said triumphantly. Then his jaw dropped as he realised what he had said.

"S... Sand?" he stammered.

"How old are you, lad?"

"I'm ten," said the boy. "Nearly eleven!"

Sand chuckled. "Keep practicing, lad, and you'll do well."

"Thank you, Sir!"

They collected their meagre baggage and turned to leave, but the tall, stocky stable-master saw them and hurried forward.

"Sir Artisan," he said with a bow. "Welcome home, Sand."

The stable-master looked at the young woman with him and his eyes opened wide.

"Miyam! This is wonderful!"

Sand blinked in surprise, his mask faltering for a

moment as he stared at his companion.

"He knows you?"

"Why yes," she replied. "Hello, Tack."

"I expect you'll be wanting to hurry in to see the Maestro," said the stable-master. "Don't let me keep you." He grinned again at the girl. "He will be so surprised!"

Sand had thought he knew this woman, even though her past had always been a mystery. She had known his tricks, had helped him in his work as well as any trained revealer could. He shouldn't have been surprised that she was welcome in the College, knowing her mother had been a revealer. But even children of the College were excluded at age ten if they chose not to join the ranks of the novices. He realised with a sinking heart that her secret past was much more complicated than he had dreamed, and he didn't know her at all.

He forced himself to remember what he did know. She was beautiful, intelligent, a talented fighter and gifted in the arts of the mind. She was everything a revealer should be, without the formal training. His heart swelled with pride for this amazing woman and he realised that this discovery went a long way towards solving the mystery that was Miyam.

The Maestro sat behind his desk, the white scarf of his rank tied about his head and his formal revealer's cloak, midnight blue with a white border, hanging on a hook by the door. Hearing a knock he grunted absently, and as the door opened he saw a flash of red at the edge of his vision.

Looking up he saw a man, still fully cloaked, with the red border of an artisan. He smiled in recognition and rounded the desk to welcome his favourite. There was a flicker of movement, and the Maestro stopped as he noticed a young woman standing quietly in the doorway.

He recognised her at once and beamed with pleasure. The last time he had seen her she had been a shy teenager subjugated by the will of her over protective father. Now she stood before him a grown woman with a quiet confidence and a spark in her green eyes. He grinned and crossed the room in three strides.

"Miyam!" he exclaimed, grabbing her in a bear hug. "This is a most delightful surprise!"

Sand sat down hard in a chair, his eyes open wide.

"What ails you, Sand?" said the Maestro in surprise. "You look like you've seen a ghost!"

"You know her?" he asked, incredulous.

"Why of course! Miyam was once one of my finest novices. Didn't you know?"

Sand looked from the Maestro to the girl and back again, shaking his head in confusion.

"My dear Sand, are you slipping?" the Maestro asked, and then chuckled at his joke. "I'm shocked!"

Sand went very quiet, his eyes showing his astonishment. The fact that she had once been a member of the College was obviously a revelation. It was not often the Maestro got to see his star pupil bested, and he silently applauded Miyam for her skill in keeping her past a secret. The fact that she had successfully kept this hidden from the most accomplished member of the College showed what an amazing revealer she could have been.

"Why didn't you tell me?" Sand asked her.

"You didn't ask," she replied.

"I told you she showed promise," the Maestro chuckled in glee, adding to the poor man's confusion.

"What?"

"You have met before," said the Maestro, enjoying the game. "You were, I think, about sixteen at the time. You came to see me about something and I had just concluded a meeting with a new novice." With a flourish, he indicated Miyam. "You passed each other in the doorway."

Miyam looked at the revealer, who completed the story. "And you said to me 'that little girl shows great promise'."

The Maestro chuckled again as they looked at each other in surprise. Sand grinned, acknowledging that Miyam and the Maestro had both outwitted him.

"It's good to be home," he said with a chuckle.

"You are both very welcome," said the Maestro. "I'll have an apprentice prepare a room for you, Miyam and then I would be delighted if you would both join me for the evening meal."

"No need to bother an apprentice, Sir," said Sand with a smile. "Miyam will be staying with me."

The Maestro watched them leave with a raised eyebrow. Better and better, he thought. Now there was a story he couldn't wait to hear.

Chuckling, he returned to his desk and the many documents awaiting his attention.

Sand's apartment was much nicer than Miyam remembered of her time in the College, when she had shared a dormitory room with four others, but back then she had been a novice. As a member of the highest active rank, Sand's rooms were elegant and spacious. It would take some time to grow used to her new status.

Miyam hoped she would have a chance soon to see her younger brother, who was now a novice here at the College. She wondered how Sand would react to yet another revelation.

She hadn't intended to keep so many secrets from him, it had just happened. College training made secrecy a way of life, and he had kept plenty of secrets of his own.

Refreshed and relaxed after a private bath in Evelar's

apartment, Miyam and her revealer made their way to the large dining hall. Miyam gazed at the assembled members, the symbolic borders of their ranks flashing out against a sea of midnight blue, grouped in their colours just as she remembered. She felt almost naked, the only person in that immense hall not wearing a revealer's cloak.

The years of following the strict rules of the College still held true, and they quickly took their place at the Maestro's table. Their entrance was watched with curiosity by many of the younger Art members. Hearing a shout, Miyam looked towards the voice in time to see her young brother being led back to his seat by the hall master, head craned over his shoulder.

"Mym!" the child called.

The Master sat the boy down and Miyam watched as the boy was disciplined for breaking the rules. She could not hear, but she could imagine what the Master was saying. "You know you don't leave your seat at meal times, boy. Now eat your supper and stop causing mischief."

She saw the boy open his mouth to complain, but at a look from the Master he thought better of it. Instead, he waited until the Master had gone and turned in excitement to his friends.

For the rest of the day, Domyn was preoccupied, a head full of questions. He wondered when his sister would come looking for him. He had seen her at dinner, talking and laughing with the Maestro and that artisan. The boys at his table had looked to where he pointed and whispered together, stretching their necks to see the man in the red bordered cloak.

They had hardly believed his excited assertion that his sister was indeed sitting at the Maestro's table. When he finally convinced them, they had been envious of Domyn, whose sister seemed to be so well known to the most important member of the College, and was friends with an artisan.

Domyn had never met an artisan revealer before. He was desperate to see Mym so he could ask her who he was. People of that illustrious rank were more than good at their job, they were legendary. He seemed to know Mym so well, but where had she met him, and why had she come to the College?

His ears were tuned for the sound of his sister's light footfall, and he glanced often toward the open doorway. He began to wonder if she wasn't coming.

Then Miyam finally appeared, with a letter for the scullery master. Domyn was careful to continue with his sweeping, but he glanced sideways as the Master broke the Maestro's seal and read the note. When he called Domyn's name the boy took care to lean the broom against the wall and approached them.

"You're dismissed boy," said the Master.

Domyn bowed in respect to the Master, and Miyam held out her hand. With a grin he put his hand in hers and together they left the scullery. Once out of earshot of the Master, the boy bubbled over with the questions he had been dying to ask, most especially about the artisan revealer.

"Who is he?"

"A friend," Miyam laughed.

"Can I meet him? Where is he now?"

"He's making his report to the Maestro."

When he realised that she was not going to tell him anything more, Domyn shifted focus and bombarded her with excited chatter about his lessons as they walked. He especially loved history, where he could lose himself in the adventures of bygone days. He talked with avid detail about the legend of Rexa and his quest to save his people from the evil ones.

"Do you think Leena is still around somewhere?" he said.

Miyam smiled. "I have it on good authority that she still guards the royal house of Shirall."

"Really? How do you know?"

"Because I've seen her. My friend Netta is Leena's bearer."

Domyn gasped. "When did you see her?"

"I've just come from there. Her and Naali were getting reacquainted."

"Naali? I thought he was lost!"

"He was. We found him."

"Who's we?"

"Netta and myself, Prince Atwin of Drasmil, and my artisan friend."

Of course, he had to hear the whole story then, but Miyam hushed him.

"All in good time, Dom."

They were at the end of a long corridor in a part of the College he had only ever seen once before. He looked up and let out a surprised gasp, as he saw the name plate on the door, which simply said "Maestro". He had been so involved in his excited chatter he hadn't noticed where they were.

"This is an informal gathering, Dom," said Miyam with a light tap at the door.

She advised him to remove his yellow bordered novice cloak and hang it by the door, then helped him tie the matching yellow sash about his head. When the door was opened, the mysterious artisan stood in the doorway, cloakless with the red scarf around his brow holding back his long dark hair. Domyn went silent, mouth agape.

At the boy's reaction, Miyam turned with a radiant smile, offering her hand to the man. He took it in his and kissed the back of her hand, a twinkle in his eye. Domyn looked from one to the other, surprised by the familiarity. With a smile, Miyam looked at the boy.

"Domyn, I'd like you to meet Sand."

His jaw dropped and he stared at the man, eyes wide.

"Would you like to join us?" said the Artisan to the boy.

Awestruck, Domyn nodded, and the Artisan led them into the room, keeping hold of Miyam's hand in both of his. The boy stared, unable to speak.

"What ails you, Dom," said Miyam.

"It... it's Sand?" he whispered.

"Yes, Dear, that's what I said."

"But... he's famous! We learned about him in class!"

Sand looked over to where the Maestro sat by the fire. "What have the masters been saying about me?"

The Maestro just chuckled.

Domyn bubbled over. "Well... you're a legend, Sir... I mean... you're the perfect revealer!"

"I am?" he said.

"What you did when Mist... you know... well it was exactly what a revealer is supposed to do!"

"What do you mean?" asked Sand, with another look at the Maestro. "Tell me what they've been teaching you."

"You... you fought well... I mean two of you killed ten of the enemy... you faced death without fear... you brought your partner home and saved the information... you showed courage and dedication and you learned from defeat..."

Miyam was laughing, and Sand looked at the boy with a panicked expression.

"Can you tell me everything now, Mym?" said Domyn eagerly, his curiosity getting the better of him.

"Yes," said the Maestro from his large soft chair by the hearth. "Now that we're all here, come join me and we'll have a nice chat."

*

Miyam sat with Domyn on the soft rug, bathed in the orange glow of the flames which danced in the fireplace, while Sand chose to sit with his back to the wall in the shadows beside the hearth.

"I must admit I was very surprised when the two of you turned up here together," the Maestro laughed. "I never dreamed that my two best students would ever fall in with each other like this, but it seems right somehow. It must be a fascinating story."

"It's a long story," said Sand with a grin.

"Good, I love stories!"

Sand gestured for Miyam to speak.

"As you already know, Sir," Miyam began. "When our father died a year ago, I gave Domyn the choice of taking over the family business or of coming here to the College. He jumped at the chance to come here, so I sold the business and sent Domyn off with a guardian and the money to pay for his tuition. And I sat there in Martose with my whole life stretching before me and nowhere to go."

"You could have come here too," said the Maestro in regret.

"I know that now, but things would have turned out differently if I had," she replied. "I think I prefer it this way."

She glanced to where Sand sat in the shadows, sharing a tender smile with the Artisan.

"I made up my mind to go somewhere, anywhere," she continued. "So I gathered up my most treasured possessions and began my journey."

* * *

TWO

Something was terribly wrong. As I rode out of Martose I was shocked by the most incredible stench. I had never smelled anything like it, and I wondered what could have caused it. Then, as I approached Netta's farmhouse, I saw that the whole property was crawling with kalkar, the ground sizzling about their feet.

I stopped in surprise. For a moment I worried that they might notice me, but the sun had just peeked over the trees, and the kalkar were dormant. It was a small pack, about ten in all, but it was enough to have inflicted dreadful damage on the scenery. The grass was blackened, the leaves had shrivelled on the trees, and the air was full of smoke.

They stood frozen and steaming, absorbing the sun's energy. I crept closer to examine one. I had never seen kalkar up close, and in that moment all the childhood horror stories came flooding back, feeding my fear.

They appeared to be human in shape with a dark grey cloak draped about them, but as I approached I realised they were not human at all. What I had thought was a cloak was in fact a fleshy membrane wrapped about them, looking almost like wings folded in the manner of a bat. The head was covered by a fold of skin membrane similar to the rest, growing from the neck but pulled over the head like a hood. A light rain had begun to fall, and steam rose in little puffs where the raindrops hit the creature's flesh.

All I could see of the creature itself were the long

powerful toes on skeletal feet, with sharp claws, and scales that repelled what little rain reached them. I stretched out one tentative hand to pull open the cloak of skin and look underneath but quickly drew it back again. The creature was radiating enough heat to cause a nasty burn.

With a shiver, I eased my way through the pack, careful to not touch any of them, and headed to the house. I pounded frantically on the thick wooden door, which was covered in scorch marks.

"Who is it?" said Netta's father, in a voice I barely recognised. Ordel was the strongest man I knew, but his voice was somehow stretched and thin, as if he was close to breaking.

"It's Miyam. Let me in, quickly." The door opened the merest crack and I pushed my way in, hearing the door slam behind me and the bolts slide home.

"What's going on out there? I barely got past those kalkar."

"We're leaving, Mym," said Netta.

"Are they the cause?" I asked, indicating toward the door and the evil forces outside.

Netta looked a question at her mother and, at a nod from Delsi, began to explain.

"They have been out there since last night, pounding against the door and trying to get in."

No wonder Ordel had been so reluctant to open the door. The sun had barely begun to lighten the sky and the dark ones must only have stopped their hammering moments before I arrived.

"Why are they after you? Who are you?" No ordinary family could have engendered such hostility from the evil ones. Netta hesitated but I urged her to tell me.

"My mother is the Queen of Shirall. I didn't know myself until this morning."

"Ah."

"You're not surprised."

I shrugged. I was only a child, living with my mother in the College, when they had arrived in Martose some twelve years before. Nobody knew where they had come from and they had settled into a quiet, unobtrusive lifestyle. They had stood apart from society.

I remembered meeting Netta as a teenager when I first came to live with my father. She had been lonely and isolated, desperate for companionship, and I had needed a friend. Netta's parents had always seemed a little out of place on their small farm, teaching their daughter to be cultured and aloof, and Netta had been constantly berated for forgetting her manners.

There were many rumours about them, not least of which was that they were nobility who had fallen on hard times. No, I was not surprised to find they were exiled royalty. It explained a lot.

"The trouble began long before Mother took her place on the throne," Netta continued. "The evil ones thought they could gain control by overthrowing the ruling houses. Mother says they needed to protect me from harm, since I would eventually take her place. So we came here. Now, we plan to return to Shirall."

I looked at Delsi with new respect. Only then did I notice her dishevelled condition. She was battered and bruised, covered in small scratches. There was a panicked look in her eye and about her neck were red scorch marks where her necklace lay as if it had burned her flesh.

The charm itself pulsed with a white-hot aura, and her pain was barely hidden beneath a serene expression. Her fine hair was wildly tangled, and she sat slowly combing it out.

"So you're really going?" I had intended only to see my

friend Netta to take my leave, but now... "Would you let me go with you?" I said.

"What of your father?" Delsi asked. "Would he allow you to go?"

I hesitated, my grief still raw. "My father is dead."

"I'm so sorry, Mym," said Netta. "When?"

"A few days ago. I've sold father's business and I sent Domyn off to Mother's people this morning."

"Will you go back to your mother's people too?"

"I don't know. That's why I want to go with you. Maybe a change of scenery will help." I looked at each in turn. "Please take me with you."

Delsi nodded. "Of course, Miyam, you are more than welcome. But it will be dangerous."

"Thank you," I said, feeling good to have somewhere to go and not caring what perils I might face.

We gathered up our possessions and carefully opened the door. The kalkar stood all around, quietly sizzling, darkly malevolent, but oblivious now to our presence. Netta took one last look around the room, her parents waiting in silence as she took her leave of the only home she knew.

We made our way to the stables and saddled up the horses. We rode through the day, eating in the saddle. It was vital that we get ourselves as far away from the kalkar at the farmhouse as possible, before they became active again after sunset.

The moon was high by the time Ordel called a halt. We snatched a few hours sleep before rising again at dawn to continue our flight, aware that the dark ones were closing the distance while we slept.

The people in the villages through which we passed stopped in their daily chores to stare as we thundered by. We travelled at this pace for several days, but still Delsi could feel the kalkar gaining on us every night.

Early in the afternoon of the fifth day we slowed to pass through the bustling city of Lenel. As we approached the southern outskirts a little girl ran out of her house and stood in the middle of the road, watching us approach. When we stopped, she stood there in front of us, hopping nervously from one foot to the other.

"Speak, child," said Delsi with a kind smile.

"My Lady..." the little girl hesitated. "My mama sends a message. She can... see things. She says you're going into danger. She says you should be wary." With that she ran into the cottage and hastily closed the door.

We looked at each other in consternation. The woman foretold danger ahead? Were there more kalkar waiting for us on the trail? If so, we were indeed in trouble, but how? Surely the dark ones could not have sent a message ahead. That would have been out of character with everything we knew of the kalkar; they always stuck together in their packs. There could only be one explanation; kalkar were not our only worry. There had to be some other danger on the road to come.

The south road was a busy thoroughfare, used to transport valuable trade goods to and from the sea port of Sar Let. We crossed the river Lenel by way of the only stone bridge on the entire course of the river. The kalkar would be trapped on the north side of the river, since they could not pass openly through the town to use the bridge.

We hoped they would avoid any other, wooden bridge because it would burn under their feet and drop them in the water, which would quench the internal fire that kept them alive. I remembered the kalkar's fleshy cloak I had seen at the farm house and I wondered if it really was bat wings, or simply a protective membrane to shield the water sensitive flesh underneath.

We rode at a hard pace through the afternoon and into the evening. For the first time since leaving Martose we decided to stop early and get a full night's rest, while we had the safety of the river between us and the enemy. The water would not hold them forever. We had no doubt the kalkar would gain access to the bridge somehow.

In the half light of dawn, something woke me and I glanced about the camp. The fire had gone out, but the sun would soon warm the campsite. The Queen and her husband were still sleeping soundly. Netta's bed roll, however, was empty. I could hear faint noises from behind me, where the horses were tethered.

I sat up cautiously and looked around, in time to see the Princess's cloaked figure swing up onto her horse and guide the animal away from the camp. I cursed. She should have realised it was too dangerous to slip out of camp and explore, but Netta had always taken solace in riding when she felt stressed or out of sorts. I quickly saddled my horse and followed her, hoping she wouldn't run into trouble.

Soon the Princess was cantering along the quiet road. The air was crisp and refreshing, and flitter birds welcomed the morning in their sweet trilling voices. Ancient simpa trees lined the way, casting their dappled shadows over the stones of the road. Somewhere a bell could be heard tolling the morning.

I could hear her humming happily to herself. In her carefree mood, the Princess did not notice two riders quickly approaching until too late. I kicked Cheena forward to catch her and pull her off the road, but Netta resisted.

"What are you doing, Mym?" she said with an angry look.

"What are you doing riding out by yourself? Don't you

realise how much danger there is out here on your own?" I indicated the approaching riders, who had now noticed our raised voices.

The cloak hid most of her face, and I prayed that she would think of the danger in revealing her golden hair and fine features which would mark her as a noblewoman. Mercifully, she kept her head bent as one of the riders kicked his horse forward and came toward us.

The other man held back, and I noticed his distinctive cloak, midnight blue with a red border, indicating a revealer of the highest rank. The red around the edge of the hood framed his face, and the red sash at his brow held the hood in place, proclaiming his rank as artisan. For a moment the sight of the revealer sent me reeling as memories of my mother, five years dead, came flooding back.

She had been an artisan too, but she was killed on duty, and my life had changed forever. I was there again, a fragile teenager, forced to leave the life I loved as a novice, pulled from the College of the Art to live with a father I hardly knew.

I could still hear the screams of my brother Domyn, then five years old, as we were ripped away from our home. I had begged to stay, but my father had been determined to remove us. He said he would not let his children be put in danger and possibly killed the way our mother had been.

I stared, tears blurring my vision. I forced the memory down and made myself think of the implications of the revealer's presence there. Not only did it suggest covert dealings afoot but it also implied that the young man who now approached was wealthy and probably of noble birth.

"Is there a problem here?" The suspicious stranger asked.

I groaned inwardly, holding back to study the man. He was a handsome young nobleman, with short-cropped sandy hair. He was dressed expensively and sat comfortably on his horse, a steed which showed remarkable breeding. Though Netta did not seem to notice, the stranger was studying her with interest, noting her clean smooth hands and cultured manner.

"No problem, Sir," Netta said.

"What are you doing out on the roads at this time of the morning?" the stranger asked suspiciously.

"I didn't realise I needed permission to take a morning ride!"

"Do you not know that you should bare your head when speaking with the nobility?"

Netta lifted her head and her eyes flashed. "I have no desire to bare my head to the likes of you!"

"You should treat the nobility with more respect. You should dismount and bare your head. I command you to do so."

"You command me? Noble or commoner, you must earn my respect, not command it!" Netta spurred her horse and spun away, leaving him staring after her with great surprise. Then, before I could do more than watch in concern, he kicked his horse after her and blocked her passage.

"You have not been dismissed."

"I need not your dismissal!" She tried to move her horse around him, but this time she was trapped.

"Nevertheless, you must wait until I dismiss you."

I held my breath, but thankfully Netta held her tongue.

"Good," he said with satisfaction. "You may go."

Netta fixed him with a stern glare and retorted, "As you were."

The two sat there, staring each other down, Netta haughty and confident, the young man calm and arrogant. Finally he gave an amused chuckle, clicked to his horse and moved off.

His silent companion followed, his enigmatic gaze capturing mine as he passed, sending a delicious shiver up my spine and leaving me gasping for breath. Then he spurred his stallion to catch up to the other young man, and together they galloped away. Netta smiled to herself, as if she had just won a great victory.

"I hope you enjoyed that," I said, putting a stern tone in my voice. She jumped and looked at me. "Do you realise the peril you could have brought down on us all?" I admonished.

"I guess I was a little silly, wasn't I?"

"You could say that." I looked up at the rising sun through the branches. "I think we'd better get back to the camp."

Finally, we arrived at the little port town of Sar Let, where we would board a ship to cross the Sea of Skies. Delsi warned us that the amulet was beginning to burn again, and we knew that the kalkar had once more picked up the trail.

In a little tavern near the dock we bought a hot meal, and Ordel left us to seek passage on the next possible ship. He was gone for some time, and night fell while we waited. As the minutes crawled by, Delsi became increasingly anxious.

The amulet was burning white hot, and she was in a panic by the time Ordel returned. With one look at his wife he said "Let's move," and we hastened down to the dock where a small ship waited with sails full.

While Ordel took the horses and had them quartered in the hold, Delsi led the way onto the deck. Netta and I watched the darkened shore, where a commotion was stirring. We could see several dark figures, and the acrid smell of kalkar wafted over the brief span of water between us and the dock.

Long thin limbs showed, mottled with markings of green and yellow and brown, where the cloak-like membrane had been swept back off their shoulders in their hasty pursuit. Delsi whimpered as the amulet burned her, and when Ordel joined us he took her in his arms. The two watched breathlessly as the enemy came closer.

The ship cast off, and there were shouts from the dock as the kalkar swept all from their path in their attempt to reach the ship. We pulled away from the wharf as the kalkar began to cross, not realizing that they had left the safety of the stone dock and were now on the wooden jetty.

The structure gave way in flames beneath the foremost of the pack, which perished in a cloud of steam on contact with the water. Those remaining dockside came to an abrupt halt and stared across the deadly water to the escaping ship.

I wondered why they did not spread those wings and come after us, but the fleshy membrane hung loose like a cape so maybe it was not wings after all. I glanced about and noticed we were being watched. To my surprise and dismay the strange young man we had encountered on the road was on board with us.

He seemed very interested in our plight, and I sensed another observer somewhere nearby. For a moment I wondered if there would be more danger on board that ship than out there with the kalkar.

THREE

Shaken from their close escape, Delsi and her husband headed below. Before we could follow, Netta was halted by a shout, and to our dismay we heard the sound of approaching footsteps.

"It is the haughty little farm girl!" said an arrogant voice. "What are you doing on a ship to Sar Sor? With such an enemy in pursuit?"

The young man caught Netta's arm, and she spun to give an angry retort.

"I know not why I should tell the likes of you!"

He eyed her with suspicion. "A farm girl you are not." He said in a dangerous, quiet voice.

"How observant of you!" Netta said, voice dripping sarcasm. I hissed at her to be careful.

"Tell me your name," he ordered.

Netta looked to me with a plea in her eyes, but all I could do was shrug my shoulders.

"Very well," said the Princess. "It is... Dayna."

"And your friend?"

I breathed a sigh. "Miyam," I said.

"I am Atwin," he said.

Now why was he being so friendly? Perhaps he was trying to put us at ease, so we would give something away. Whatever the reason, it was making me nervous.

"Pleased to meet you, I'm sure," I said, "but we really must go."

"And why, pray tell?" he said, looking about. "We are on a ship with nothing to do and nowhere to go."

"That's none of your business!" said Netta in anger.

I took Netta by the arm as we quickly moved away, and thankfully we were not followed. But he called out to our retreating backs.

"Take care, Dayna," he said, and we turned to look at him. "The dark ones are gathering, their numbers increasing. You need to learn who your friends are."

Netta shivered as we turned away.

Late in the night, the four of us came together in the tiny cabin. We had decided to wait until the rest of the ship's complement was asleep to avoid distracting noise. Under Delsi's guidance we gathered in a circle and joined hands.

"I need your help now, Netta," Delsi said, hushing her questions. "We are going to send a message to my sister in Shirall. You will just have to concentrate on holding the link. Ordel, will you feed strength into the circle, please." He nodded.

The Queen began to recite a strange charm in the ancient language and Netta, at first hesitantly but stronger as she gained confidence, joined her voice with her mother's. Her sweet voice seemed to fill the room, and the powers of the ancient language worked their magic as the spell was woven about us. As the room was filled with the power, there was a strange falling sensation, and I felt Netta jump when the voice came, inside our heads.

HELLO SISTER, WHAT BRINGS THIS COMMUNICATION? IS SOMETHING AMISS?

KALKAR HAVE BEEN CAUSING TROUBLE. I AM WORRIED.

DO YOU MEAN THAT THEY HAVE FOUND YOU?

YES. I BARELY ESCAPED THEM.

I don't know what happened then, but I heard something slipping into the circle, a menacing presence listening in, and a sound like faint, faraway laughter, and suddenly the circle was broken.

Netta fell to the floor with a cry of pain, clutching her head in her hands. Delsi, too, had begun to sink to the ground, but Ordel caught her. My head felt like it was going to burst.

Delsi, breathing in ragged gasps, struggled against weakness and staggered to her daughter's limp form. Delsi placed her hand on the girl's forehead and mumbled a few ancient words. Finally, Netta struggled fitfully back to consciousness.

"Where am I?"

"You are safe, angel. Rest for a moment."

"I'm alright," she said.

"What happened?" I asked.

"I couldn't hold the link. Something was listening!"

"Get some sleep," said Delsi. "We can try again tomorrow."

"No, it's alright. We should finish it now."

"Are you sure?" asked Ordel, concerned for her.

"Yes, I'm fine. I know what to do now."

Reluctantly, and with some persuasion from Netta, Delsi agreed to try again. The second attempt was difficult, but this time the link was strong, and soon Delsi was again addressing her sister.

IS ALL WELL THERE, AVERIL?

YES, SISTER. WHAT HAPPENED JUST NOW?

WE ARE FINE. JUST SOME... DIFFICULTIES.

ARE YOU SAFE?

FOR NOW. WE ARE CROSSING THE SEA OF SKIES, BUT OUR ENEMIES KNOW WHICH SHIP WE ARE ON.

PLEASE BE CAREFUL, DELSI. WHAT WILL WE DO IF

YOU DO NOT ARRIVE SAFELY?
WORRY NOT, SISTER. WE SHALL SOON BE WITH YOU.

Early the next morning I awoke before the sun with a headache. The communication spell we had used was cumbersome and messy, prone to leaking psychic noise, with none of the finesse of the mind speak used by the revealers. The breach had caused a mental shock wave that left us all aching.

As I climbed up onto the deck for some fresh air I suspected that Delsi and Netta, less practiced in mental technique than I, would both be worse off than me. I longed for some peace and quiet, so I walked along the rail to the bow.

Most ships have a wonderful little spot over the rail where the gunwale tapers off, where you can be almost hidden from anyone walking along the deck. As I climbed over I froze momentarily in surprise.

Was it my imagination, or had I just seen a dark cloak with a flash of red disappear over the side? Had I inadvertently flushed the revealer out of his spy-hole, hindering his work?

I sent him an apologetic thought and considered retreating, but a wave of reassurance washed over me. I knew then that he had already closeted himself in an even better spot without even breaking concentration. An artisan revealer would never be worried by my blunder. So, I settled myself down, enjoying the cool breeze across the bow.

I took a deep breath and calmed my mind, readying myself for some deep relaxation exercises. I needed to clear my head and explore a nagging sense of foreboding that I could not shake.

But as I let my thoughts fade and let the meditation state take hold I sensed an unusual background noise. I could not concentrate to continue the exercise, distracted by the feeling of intrusion.

I opened my eyes and scanned the horizon, noting the faint glow that heralded the sun even as I searched for the source of the mental noise. It was too far away to be on board with us, but there was nothing on the water and only one lonely bird high in the moonlit sky above.

I squinted, trying to see it better. With a cold shiver, I realised it was not a bird. I sent out a careful finger of thought and encountered... something strange. A sense of many minds focused on this one as it flew above, watching. Tracking us, I thought.

I wondered why they did not attack the ship. Somewhere out of the consciousness above I heard my answer. The water. They were afraid, aware that the ship would burn and knowing that the water would kill. As I watched, the scout turned and flew away, heading back to land as the sky lightened with the approaching dawn.

As the ship rode gracefully through the water I could see several beautiful gildas surfing on the spray. The Princess would have been enchanted as the sleek animals glided through the waves. I was surprised then to suddenly hear her voice raised in anger.

"What do you want?"

"I only wish to talk. May I join you?"

"But, Sir!" she exclaimed. "You are asking permission?"

"That is what I wish to talk about."

"Talk, then."

"I do not blame you for being angry," he began. "I was very arrogant."

"Of course. You have never lived among commoners," she said mildly. "We do have our pride, you know."

"It is not only that. I wanted to know why you are dressed as a farm girl."

"Oh? And what makes you think I'm not as I dress?"

"Come now, I have eyes. Your hands are clean and your hair gives you away."

Carefully, I rose up until I could peek over the rail.

"What about my hair?" she asked, one hand going involuntarily to the large bun on top of her head.

As I watched in chagrin, he reached out and carefully loosened the bun, letting the long braid fall down her back.

"No farm girl would dare grow her hair so long for fear of angering some noblewoman by besting her in length. Even you must know that."

Netta lowered her eyes. She said nothing.

"There was a communication last night," he said triumphantly.

Netta and I both jumped in shock.

"You were there, were you not?"

"How did you know?" asked the Princess, beaten.

"I sensed it, of course. I have communicated myself. There was a great mental noise when your circle was breached."

Netta turned away and gazed out toward the horizon. I ducked down out of sight. I heard the Princess breathe a sigh.

"Who are you, Dayna?" he asked then.

"I cannot tell you. Please don't ask me."

"I must know."

"No. You must not know. If I tell you, I will be endangering my own life and the lives of my family and all that I hold dear."

"What do you mean?"

"We have enemies, following close behind. Perhaps ahead as well. I cannot risk betrayal."

"Is it the kalkar?" he asked. "What do they want with you?"

"I cannot tell you!"

"I have enemies also. I will not inform on you."

"I'm sorry. I cannot take that risk."

As I listened I heard her footsteps retreating, and I slowly stood up. Atwin was standing at the rail, staring out over the wide expanse of blue, deep in thought. He started as I slipped over the rail back onto the deck.

"Why couldn't you have just left it alone?" I asked.

I followed after Netta, giving him no time to answer with more than a strangled "I..." and I thought to myself, a trifle mischievously; another time, another place and those two could have made a match!

I felt a powerful sense of being watched, and glanced back instinctively to find the revealer had appeared as if by magic at Atwin's side. He was staring at me, dark mysterious eyes hiding unseen depths behind a placid mask.

My steps faltered as a compulsive thrill hit me and I wanted nothing more than to open my mind to him, but I struggled out of the pull of his eyes and continued on, shaken by the intensity of that compelling gaze.

The ship neared port early in the afternoon on a dull day with a lowering sky. Netta and I stood on deck watching as the ship approached the little port town of Sar Sor. Netta's parents stood not far away, Ordel with one arm comfortably about his wife's shoulders. Netta, who was sensitive to her mother's emotional state, commented on the worry and fear she saw in the Queen's eyes.

"What is wrong, Mother?"

"Danger awaits us in Sar Sor. The amulet burns already and my dreams are filled with the burning thoughts of kalkar. I fear that our safety is far from sure."

The Queen's face showed her pain as the amulet lay hot on her flesh. Together they looked anxiously out over the water, searching for signs of kalkar. Netta was the first to see a dark shape. Then the Queen gasped in horror and covered her eyes as her husband held her close. As I scanned the shore I could not believe what my usually reliable eyes were telling me.

The activity dockside was choked and subdued and nobody stood on the pier ready to catch the painter which a crewman had ready to throw ashore. The jetty was entirely cut off by frozen black shapes sizzling along the line of the dock, preventing passage. All business had come to a standstill, since ship to shore transfer of goods and personnel was impossible. Grim faced, Ordel went to speak to the captain.

As the sun inched toward the horizon, Ordel and the Captain scanned the shore for a possible landing. When debarkation had proved impossible at Sar Sor, Ordel had persuaded the captain, with the help of a little coinage, to sail into the gulf of Drasmil in search of another place to land. Unfortunately, the impassable cliffs along that stretch of coastline, which made Sar Sor the only port to the north of Shirall, were offering no chance to put ashore.

As the Captain and the Queen's husband stood at the helm, we three women sat astern, saying little. We had begun to despair of ever finding a break in the towering cliff face. Our only hope was to find some tiny stretch of sand.

Having spent the past five years under the roof of my crooked father, I knew instinctively this captain would certainly have been employed at some time or other in the trade of illegal goods, and would know of any number of hidden beaches all around the Sea of Skies.

At last, the Captain found what he was looking for. A tiny gleam of yellow sand almost swallowed by two towering headlands caught the sun, shining out for just a second before being hidden again. We stood and joined Ordel and the captain.

"I'll get the ship in as close as I dare," he said, "but it's low tide and this coast is treacherous. I'd rather not turn my ship into a wreck. We'll have to swim the horses across and use the punt for yourselves and the baggage."

As the ship dropped anchor about five hundred metres from shore we gathered our belongings and stowed them in the punt before it was lowered over the side. On the cliffs above the beach, small even at low tide, I could see dark shapes silhouetted against the setting sun.

At high tide there would have been no sand at all, and thankfully the kalkar had not blockaded the beach. We climbed over the rail and down the rope ladder into the little boat. Once we were under way, the horses were harnessed one by one and lowered into the water, where several crew members were waiting to remove the sling-like harness and point each animal toward the shore. All was proceeding smoothly until the pack horse panicked.

Before the sailors in the water had time to remove the harness the animal had kicked out with its hind legs and caught a man full in the stomach. As he foundered, his crew mates came to his aid, forgetting about the horse in their efforts to keep the man from sinking under. In the chaos another man was kicked in the side and the situation began to look desperate.

"When you get ashore," I said to the others, "mount up and ride. I'll catch up."

"But..." Delsi began.

"Do it," I ordered, heedless of her rank. "The kalkar await the sunset and you three must get away. I'm not important to your cause. I'll be alright."

Without waiting for an answer or a protest, I dove into the water and struck out for the melee in progress.

Coming up in front of the frightened horse, I took hold of her bridle and calmed her. I worked quickly to release the harness and pointed the animal toward shore. When I was sure the mare was swimming strongly, I turned back to help the injured men to the ladder.

As I watched them climb, I glanced upward to the watchers on deck. Atwin was there, staring out to shore where my companions were already preparing to ride and the punt was returning for me. As I scanned the crowd on deck I saw the revealer behind Atwin's right shoulder. For a moment, my gaze locked with that of the Artisan and I was drawn in again by the magnetic pull of those eyes.

I felt the revealer's gentle probing in my mind and blocked it automatically. Surprised fascination flickered in his eyes and was quickly snuffed, replaced by the placid mask of the trained revealer. With great reluctance I broke eye contact, snapping the mental link with a pang of regret.

I turned away, swimming out to meet the little boat. I took the offered hand and climbed aboard. As the boat started once more toward shore, I looked back to those on deck. Atwin stood still, watching the shore. The revealer watched me, his face masking the barest flicker of... admiration? I longed to feel again the intimate contact of his mind, but his mental shield was tightly closed.

Wistfully, I turned my gaze frontward and watched as the sun slowly sank behind the cliff. The kalkar stood in a row waiting for the setting sun, and I sent out a tentative mental search, trying to catch the moment they awoke.

As the boat ran up onto the beach, the frozen figures on the cliff top came to life, the departure of the sun signalling their awakening. For a brief moment my thoughts touched the group mind of the kalkar, and I pulled away with a gasp at the raw terror I found there.

Without bothering to saddle Cheena, I threw a blanket

over her back and slung the saddle and the remaining packs from the boat onto the pack horse, tying them quickly and securely. One of the sailors offered another blanket and I wrapped it about myself and mounted with his help.

I nodded thanks to the crewmen in the punt, and glanced once more toward the handsome ship. Alarmed shouts from on deck reminded me of the danger, and a warning voice caressed my mind.

'You'd best make haste.'

Suppressing a shiver of more than just cold, I digged in with my heels and spurred my horse. The kalkar were gathering on the sand, attempting to block my passage. I had caught their attention with my intruding thought, and now they were focused solely on me.

Well, I thought, at least Netta and her family would get away. I pointed Cheena straight at them, the pack horse following close behind, connected to us by a rope I held wrapped about my wrist. One kalkar clutched at my wet skirts as I passed. Its hot fingers brushed the skin of my ankle and I was pulled again into that group mind. A tangle of individual thoughts were overpowered and subdued by one command: *Catch!*

I heard a guttural grunt of surprise, and glanced back to see the thing that had touched me staring, bewildered, at the steaming blob on the ground and the stump where its hand had been a moment before. I shouted defiance into that collective consciousness and as one they flinched.

We broke through the line, almost bowling them over. The kalkar fell back to avoid touching my clothing, filled with the water that was so very dangerous for them. I galloped away totally unharassed, watched in fear by the kalkar and amazement by those on the ship.

FOUR

I caught up to the others sometime around midnight, when they had stopped to rest the horses. As I rode up to their little circle they all stood and gathered about, anxious questions in their eyes. Delsi forestalled them.

"You must be cold. You have been riding damp all this time."

"I'm alright. I've been colder." I dismounted and wrapped the blanket more tightly about myself. Netta wordlessly removed the other blanket from Cheena's back and put that over me too. Then she unloaded the packs, took the two horses, and began to rub them down. I sat on the ground and huddled up in the blankets for warmth.

"What did you do back there?" asked Ordel. "We have had no sign of kalkar all evening."

"Truly?" I asked, staring up at him. "That's strange."

"You must have given them a good scare."

"No, not really. One of them melted its hand trying to grab at my wet clothes, but I don't think that was enough to scare them off."

"Then where are they?" asked Delsi.

"I have no idea."

"They know where we are," said Netta from beside the horses. "And they know where we are going. Do they really need to chase us all the way?"

"You think they may have gone on ahead?" asked Delsi.

"It is possible," said Ordel. "They may try a repeat of Sar

Sor when we get closer to Shirall."

I thought for a moment, then looked to Delsi. "Your amulet gives no sign?" I asked, and she shook her head. "Then I suggest we light a fire and have something to eat. I need to dry out properly before I catch a chill."

Several days later, after a quiet trip and no sign of the kalkar, we approached Shirall City. Early in the afternoon, we rode slowly through the outskirts, avoiding the crowded inner city and marketplace. Already we had noticed strange looks and curiosity in the people we passed, and a faster pace would have drawn even more attention.

Delsi rode with her hood over her eyes and her head bowed to avoid possible recognition. A crowd began to gather as we dismounted outside a well frequented inn. As we entered, the elderly proprietor bustled out from behind the counter, mumbling under his breath as he came toward us.

"Well, Sir," he addressed Ordel. "State your business."

Ordel glanced at his wife, surprised at the gruff tone. "We wish to enquire about hiring a messenger."

"Well, you might," said the man, looking about. "But that all depends on who the message is from, and where it's going."

"Why is that?"

"Well, Sir we're a trifle wary of strangers in these parts." He looked about himself again and dropped his voice to a whisper. "The evil ones are about, you see, and you can never be sure of strangers in town."

Delsi put a hand on her husband's arm and stepped forward. "I know of the troubles, Algernon," she said.

Her voice, though soft, carried to others in the room and a hush fell over the crowd as all faces turned toward us. The old man remembered that voice, and stared at the

Queen in awe.

"You can trust me. I am no stranger here." She reached up with one hand and pushed back the hood. Algernon gasped and excited chatter filled the room.

The old innkeeper began to kneel with a murmured "My Queen!"

"Not now, Algernon," she said quietly. "We need to talk."

Algernon quickly rose. "Of course, Your Majesty. Follow me." He bowed and backed out of the room.

We sat in the back room of the inn, which was small and sparsely furnished but comfortable. Delsi sat, as did Netta and myself, but Ordel stood behind his wife, his protective hands resting on her shoulders. Algernon stood before his queen, listening with face intent.

"Algernon, I need to re-establish my connections in the city. You are hereby reactivated. I want it to be made known that I have returned. Due to those troubles that concern you so, I cannot myself go about openly."

"Of course, Your Majesty."

"This," she indicated the Princess, "is Netta, my daughter. Make it known that she is here also and have her description distributed so that she will be known when it is time for her to meet the public."

"It shall be done, Your Majesty."

"I am giving you authority to conduct any business necessary to reopen communications between the city and the palace. You are to act at your own discretion in my name." The Queen glanced about. "Algernon, have you any wax?"

"Of course, Your Majesty." He called softly through another doorway and a nervous young boy entered. "This is my grandson, Your Majesty. He can be trusted. His name is Eusta."

"Hello, Eusta."

The little boy bowed awkwardly and blushed.

"Would you find me some wax?" Algernon said.

The boy grinned, nodded and ran from the room. He returned in a few minutes with a small lump of used candle wax. Delsi moved toward the fireplace and held the wax near the warmth to soften it, then worked the soft mass into a roughly circular shape, and drew out her amulet from beneath her cloak. She pressed the gold into the wax, making an impression. The Queen handed this mirror image of her protective medallion to the old innkeeper.

Algernon turned to the boy. "Take this and put it in my locked box. Here is the key. Go straight there and come straight back with the key."

"Yes, Sir," said the boy, turning to bow again to the Queen.

The Queen smiled. "A nice child, Algernon. He will go far." The old man beamed with pride. "Now," said the Queen, "we will have some refreshments before continuing on to the palace." She smiled again and Algernon jumped to do his queen's bidding.

All was quiet as we left the inn, but I could not shake a feeling of unease. I saw Delsi hesitate. The worried queen spoke to her husband, and he drew us all into a tighter group and urged us to make haste. We made our way through the city and up the long hill which led to the ruined palace, breaking into a gallop. A glance at the Queen's face showed a pain greater than ever before, and though it was still not dusk I knew that something was terribly wrong.

Approaching the palace we saw why the kalkar had not bothered us before. Here they stood, a whole pack of them, clustered in our path and sizzling in the afternoon light. They stood among the ruins of the old palace, and a concentrated group blocked most of the road leading up to the gate.

With difficulty we were able to pick a path through them. I glanced behind and saw several black cloaked riders in pursuit. I shouted a warning, and in one last burst of speed we approached the gate. Waiting right in front of the gate were three kalkar, preventing our passage. As the riders at our rear picked their way up the hill toward us, Ordel grabbed his flask and hesitated, unsure where to do the most damage.

"Under its hood, Sir," I said.

He splashed the water up under the hood into the creature's face, then emptied the rest of the contents inside the hood to run down the neck of the middle kalkar. In a cloud of steam the creature melted and bubbled, its fire quenched and its flesh eaten away by the water. Ordel threw his cloak over the steaming blob that remained and we picked our way over, rushing to the gate.

"Halt, strangers." A sentry planted himself behind the gate, his spear pointed through the bars at us threateningly.

"Let us pass, guard," Ordel ordered. "We have no time to waste, if you notice what is following."

"Who are you?" asked the suspicious guard, glancing at the riders swiftly approaching and ignoring our agitation. "Why are you seeking refuge here?"

"Hurry man, let us through," said Ordel anxiously. "If you love your queen let us pass."

"What has the Queen to do with this? She's far away, in hiding."

"Not any more," Ordel said, "you are looking at her." Delsi drew out the amulet and waved it in front of the sentry's nose. "Now let us pass," said Ordel furiously.

The sentry gasped and hastened to open the gate, but too late. As we slipped through, I heard a twang and something whistled past my ear. With a cry, Delsi crumpled in her saddle.

Ordel jumped from his horse in time to catch her before she fell to the ground. We raced across the yard and into the decrepit old building, carrying Delsi's limp form with us. We left the horses in the entrance hall of a once great palace now open to the sky and followed the repentant guard down a long, steep flight of stairs into the caverns beneath the palace.

Finally, we entered the grand audience hall far below the ground and with a cry the Princess Regent rushed to Ordel's side, calling anxiously for physicians.

Ordel paced the corridor while the medic worked on Delsi behind closed doors. Occasionally, he would stop outside the door and listen, frustrated at not knowing what was going on inside. Netta sat despondently on the floor, back against the wall, legs pulled up out of the way of her father's pacing. The Princess insisted that I stay with her, so I cannot say what went on in the sick-room.

Finally, the medic emerged and signalled Ordel to enter. Netta sprang to her feet to follow. Inside the room, the medic spoke to Ordel in a hushed voice.

"All is well. She will recover." Ordel sighed with relief. "You must realise," the medic continued, "that my lady is extremely lucky. It's unusual to find an arrow that isn't laced with a deadly poison. I've found none, and as you can see she's sleeping well."

"We thank you for your vigilance, Sir Medic. I am sure that your skill alone has saved my wife and for that I am eternally grateful."

"She'll sleep for some hours. I suggest you try to do the same."

Ordel shook his head and the medic nodded.

"Call me if there is any change," he said and left the room.

"I think you girls should get some sleep," said Ordel. "I see no reason for us all to stay."

"No, I want to stay," said Netta.

Ordel shook his head.

"But..." Netta protested.

"Sleep. You are exhausted," he said in a tone which brooked no argument.

I returned to the Queen's chamber early the next morning. Netta was asleep in a chair. She must have returned some time during the night. Opposite the girl, Ordel was kneeling by his wife's side. He did not even look up when I entered. Netta woke with a start and looked about, rubbing at her neck. There was a noise from the bed. Delsi was regaining consciousness. Her eyes flickered and slowly opened. The Queen looked at her husband and whispered his name.

"Yes love," he said, stroking her hair. "I am here."

Delsi looked about and reached a hand out to her daughter.

"Angel...?"

Netta rushed to the bedside and took her mother's hand in both of her own.

"Yes, Mother."

As the little family talked quietly together I moved to the door, ready to slip away, but Ordel called me back.

"Do you think you could find Averil?" he asked.

"Yes, of course," I said.

"Would you let her know that Delsi is recovering?" he said quietly. "Take Netta with you."

"But..." Netta began to protest.

"Go, angel," said Delsi weakly. "Your father and I need to talk."

*

We found the Princess Regent in a small drawing room off the main audience chamber, deep in conversation with a stranger in a revealer's cloak, a flash of red at the hem. The cloak disguised his form and the hood kept his face hidden, but I recognised him immediately with an involuntary shiver.

Briefly, I wondered what had happened to his travelling companion, but I forgot almost instantly in the thrill of meeting the revealer again, feeling an irrational rush of pleasure. Averil paused and looked up as we entered.

"I am truly sorry that we could not have met in pleasanter times, Netta," she said with a smile. "But nevertheless I am very happy to have you home at last, my dear. How is my sister?"

"She is recovering well, Aunt. The bolt was not poisoned."

"I am relieved to know that." Then the Regent looked at me.

"Oh, I'm sorry, Aunt," said Netta. "This is Miyam."

"Hello Miyam. You are most welcome."

"Thank you, Your Highness."

"We do not stand on ceremony here. Call me Averil."

"Thank you, Averil."

"This is Evelar," Averil said motioning to the man. "He is a skilled revealer and loyal to our cause."

The revealer raised his head to show his face under the red lined hood of his cloak. He nodded but said nothing. Netta returned the nod.

I glanced at his name badge, remembering the meaning of the secret characters and reading it easily. Sand. I chose not to use the name, storing it away for future reference. I might just need the leverage it would offer one day.

"Sir Artisan," I said instead, bowing just a little.

He blinked, showing his surprise that I should know his

rank. His eyes captured mine, and I instinctively blocked the mental probe he sent out. I cocked my head, daring him to try again, and I sensed that he was curious enough to consider it.

He had no knowledge of my past. So far as he knew I should not have known the rank designated by his red-bordered cloak. I should not have been able to sense his probes, let alone block them so easily. Most importantly, I should not have known about the secret powers of the trained revealer. As Averil continued speaking, his piercing gaze held me in thrall, powerless to look away.

"My daughter will be here shortly," said Averil. "If you are willing, she will show you around the palace and introduce you to the more important members of the household staff."

"Thank you, Aunt. I would like that."

"Kandina has been eagerly awaiting your arrival, Netta. She is only sixteen, but I see no reason why you should not strike up a friendship." The Regent smiled. "She is forever reminding us that her birthday is fast approaching."

A light tap on the heavy wooden door heralded the young princess, who greeted Netta profusely.

"Oh cousin, I am so glad that you are finally here!" she cried. "You cannot believe how lonely I get sometimes. I hope you are going to like it here, Netta. Come. When mother is organizing business it is best to stay out of her way. Let me show you around."

At the door, Netta turned back.

"Are you coming, Mym?" she asked.

"Ah... I'll catch up," I replied vaguely.

When the two princesses had left Averil looked at me inquiringly, and the revealer finally released my gaze. I shook myself free of his compelling mental grip.

"I hope you don't mind, Averil," I said, "but there is something you should know about the attack on Delsi."

"Oh? Go on."

"I didn't want to worry Netta with this, but I think there's a greater threat than we originally anticipated."

"In what way?"

"When Delsi was shot, it wasn't yet dusk. The sun was still visible on the horizon."

Averil drew in a breath. "Not dark? Are you sure?"

The revealer watched, eyes boring into me as he tried to read my thoughts, sending me slightly off balance.

"I noticed it when it became clear that Delsi's amulet was burning her," I continued. "I suspected that something was going to happen."

"Did you voice your suspicion?" asked Delsi.

"We all knew something was wrong. We could see that the kalkar had gathered at the gate, but they were still dormant. It was still light. We thought we had enough time."

"So..." Averil mused. "The kalkar have found a way to move about before dark."

"It was not the kalkar," I said quietly. "The attackers were mounted."

"On horses?" asked Averil, surprised.

"They had to have been human, which means..."

"... that the kalkar are enlisting human aid," the revealer said, his voice low and quiet, a hint of an exotic accent sending a delicious shiver up my spine.

"Yes," I continued breathlessly, "but I think there's more to it than that. There's something else we noticed on the journey here."

"What was that?" Averil asked.

"There were kalkar both behind and ahead of us."

"Your point being?" asked Averil.

"When we left Martose the kalkar had just discovered Delsi's location. They blockaded the cottage, but we escaped during the day. The only way the news could have passed us was if they sent a delegation ahead before morning on the night they made the discovery. But until now I would have said that was impossible."

"Why?"

"Because," Evelar broke in with that voice made of silk, "the kalkar work in packs and they don't separate for any reason."

"Which means that the kalkar must have found some other way of communicating," I finished.

"I still do not follow..."

"They failed to catch us before we set sail from Sar Let..." I said.

Evelar nodded. "But they were already waiting in position at Sar Sor," he said.

"Therefore," I continued, "there must have been a messenger on an earlier ship. And since the kalkar themselves cannot set foot on a ship without burning it to a crisp..."

"That messenger must have been human," said Averil in dawning comprehension.

I shook my head in confusion. I had been carried away by the ease with which the revealer had taken over my thoughts and the conversation had not gone the way I intended.

"I thought so too," I said.

"What do you mean?" asked Averil.

"I saw something on the voyage that confused me at the time... I think I saw a flying kalkar, tracking us."

"Flying?" said Averil. "I have not heard of that. Are you sure that is what you saw?"

"No, Your Highness," I said uncertainly. "Right now, I'm not sure of anything at all."

FIVE

I found Netta with her cousin in a small private garden. In this underground palace, the construction of such gardens must have been expensive and arduous.

I could see cunningly concealed pipes running down the walls, channelling heated water under the floor. Light from the surface was refracted down through slanted tunnels lined with mirrors and sealed off with strong iron bars. Soil had been carted down and plants propagated with care. The high roofed cavern was converted into a tropical rainforest. The effect was pleasant, despite the absence of sky.

The two princesses were sitting together under a large tree, heads together, chatting and giggling like old friends. As I approached Netta smiled and called me closer.

"Kandi, this is my very dear friend Miyam."

Kandi looked me up and down and turned back to Netta dismissively. I took a moment to examine her, now that we were not in the distracting presence of a certain revealer.

My first impression was of a self important teenager, ready with the look of disdain and a privileged chip on her shoulder. This girl had never interacted with anyone lower than her own station, and she had no idea about the real world outside her small household.

She was talking incessantly, giving Netta no chance to get a word in.

"Anyway, Netta," she was saying. "I was hoping you would come with me later to watch the changing of the guard. It is a most satisfying thing to see. Of course I would never approach any of them, they are only soldiers after all, but they do keep themselves fit. I like to watch and wonder what it would be like to single one out, you know, give them the chance to flirt with a princess!"

Netta looked a bit shocked at that.

"Oh do not look so scandalised, Netta," she admonished. "Have you not dallied with a boy before? If not then it is high time you did!"

"Well, I..."

"Of course you have, you lived on a farm did you not? Tell me, what was it like? I bet those farm boys are just as fit as my soldiers. I love a boy with good shoulders, you know, muscles from all that hard work!"

"Kandi, I do not think..."

"Oh, Netta, do not be such a prude! I have nothing better to do around here than watch the boys, honestly, you act like I am out there snagging them left right and centre... Well I would be if they were not so low and sweaty!"

"Kandi!"

Kandi giggled, then turned serious and leaned in closer. "Let me tell you a secret. I may look, but I would never touch. There is only one man for me and he is not here right now."

"Oh?"

"I am a princess, Netta, after all. Only a prince for me, you know. He comes here quite a lot, though and one day I will corner him and give him a flirting he will never forget! He will not know what hit him!"

Netta gasped.

"Netta, will you stop gasping at everything I say? You might pretend you never mingled with commoners, but you let your diction slip sometimes, you know. Surely you have some boy you would like to catch?"

Netta shook her head.

"Oh, come on, cousin. You are so beautiful, surely you have them running after you everywhere you go."

"No, I do not!"

"Pity, with your life on a farm you could have had all sorts of adventures and told me all about them. What a waste. What about you, Miyam?" she rounded on me, sitting beside Netta trying to be invisible. "You have the look of a commoner, so you must have met lots of boys."

"That's really none of your business," I said, trying not to take offence.

"You are not a princess, you do not have to wait for the right prince to come along. You could have anyone you wanted and nobody would care. Sometimes I wish I could have that kind of freedom. Are you seriously trying to tell me that you have never had a boyfriend?"

I sighed. "Well there was someone once, a long time ago, but I had to leave."

"You never told me that!" said Netta.

"It was when my mother was alive, before I came to live with my father. I was very young, about your age, Kandi, maybe a bit younger. But then my mother died and everything changed."

"Is that it?" said Kandi. "Is there no one else?"

I shrugged, ducking my head to hide my blush.

"Oh, there is!" Kandi giggled. "I can see it, you like someone! Come along, confess it."

"I'm sure I don't know what you mean," I said.

Netta and her cousin quickly became fast friends. Every day Kandi dragged her along on some harebrained scheme, either to watch boys or eavesdrop on some meeting, or play some trick on an unsuspecting servant.

At first, somewhat reluctantly, I was drawn into the

excitement along with them. The two princesses were infectious in their exuberance, and I had an ulterior motive in tagging along. I wanted to avoid the revealer, although a part of me feared he might think I was as scatterbrained as them. But in the end I could not pretend to enjoy their silliness.

"Come on, Mym," said Netta as I held back.

"No, I think I might stay here this time," I said.

Netta shrugged and they hurried off. I settled down on the grass and sighed with relief, closing my eyes as I lay back. I really wasn't interested in such mischief and it felt much nicer to be quiet for a while.

"I'm glad you did that," said a quiet voice with a ghost of an accent. I opened my eyes to see Evelar standing over me. "May I join you?"

I sat up with a nod and he settled beside me, sending a quiver through my soul.

"I've been hoping you would let them go," he said.

I sighed. "I had hoped to keep them out of trouble, but I'm past all that silliness. I hate to think I'm giving up on my friend."

"She won't mind. They need each other right now, but she'll come back."

I felt acutely uncomfortable. He kept his distance but I found myself wishing he were a little closer. Yet I knew that if I spent too much time in his company I may find myself drawn into something I could not control.

"Why did you stick with them so long?" he said then. "You're smarter than that."

"You know why," I replied with a heavy heart.

"We need to stop avoiding each other," he murmured.

"I know," I sighed. "But not yet. I'm not ready for that."

"No," he said with a smile.

I was torn between protecting myself and letting him in.

I desperately wanted to give in to him, not just for myself, but to tell him what I knew of the kalkar, and the longer I waited the harder it would get.

As the days passed, Kandi did settle down a little. Her compulsive chatter calmed and eventually we were able to have a reasonable conversation. One afternoon we were again in the garden when Kandi finally remembered our eventful arrival, and the fact that Delsi had been injured.

"She is recovering," said Netta when asked.

"But Cousin, was it terribly awful? I cannot imagine being chased like that. It must be dreadful knowing that someone is out to get you."

Netta shuddered.

"Why do you think the kalkar hate you so much?"

"I know not," said Netta. "It has something to do with what happened years ago, when we had to go into exile."

"Yes and when the palace was ruined and we had to come down here," Kandi said. "Sometimes I wish we could live up there in the old palace. It must have been so grand."

"It's filled with kalkar now, my father says," said Netta. "He will not let me go up there. I miss the sun," she sighed.

"I wish I could see them," said Kandi. "I hear Mother talk about them, but I have never seen one."

"You really don't want to see them," Netta replied. "They're evil. Terrifying. Sometimes I cannot get them out of my head. I keep seeing them, either blocking us or chasing us. I don't think I will ever forget."

"You know what? I do want to see them, just to find out what all the fuss is about!"

Netta shook her head. "No, Kandi, it's too horrible. I never want to see them again."

"Come along," said Kandi eagerly. She grabbed Netta's hand and dragged her to her feet.

"But I'm not supposed to go up there!"

"Oh, Netta, where is your sense of adventure? Besides, I know where we can see without actually going outside."

Reluctantly, Netta allowed herself to be pulled along and I trailed behind, curious. I was slowly learning my way about the underground palace, thanks in part to Kandi's rather scatterbrained company, but this was different. She led us up the long tunnel toward the gate at the surface, but before she reached the gate she turned right and disappeared through a hidden doorway.

Following, I found we were on a long steep stair heading up above the ground inside the thick wall of the palace. At the top a barred doorway let out on to the battlements and a spiral stair continued up into the tower.

Climbing higher, Kandi eventually pushed open the door at the top and led us into a round room. The windows were barred, but the glass was long gone and the room was open to the elements, though secure and protected by a solid roof.

Kandi hurried to a window, standing on her toes, hands clutching the bars and straining to see into the courtyard below. Netta held back, but I moved forward to stand next to the younger princess. She looked at me in awe then stared back down at the creatures standing dormant in the sunlight.

"They really are awful, are they not?" she said in a hushed voice.

I shrugged. "They're different."

"I am glad they were not chasing me. I think I might have collapsed in terror. What have they got wrapped about them?"

"I'm not sure. It's skin and it protects them from the rain. I suspect it might be wings."

"They have destroyed the grass and the trees," she said

sadly. "Why did they have to do that?"

"They don't have a choice. They can't help how they are. They burn everything they touch."

"How gruesome!" she exclaimed. "What would happen if I touched one? Would I burn too?"

"Probably."

Kandi shivered. "How very dreadful."

Delsi recovered well from the arrow wound and soon she was calling her family and advisors together for a meeting.

"I would like a banquet to be prepared so that Netta can be presented to the leaders of Sharné," she began. "It is time for Netta to be officially named as heir."

Netta looked nervous at that but her mother hushed her.

"It is traditional at this time to pass on the legacy of the Queens of Shirall, the guardianship of the Queen's Amulet," Delsi explained to her daughter. "You are of age, there is no reason to delay."

"But I'm not..."

"This is a momentous occasion," said her father proudly. "It requires a suitably momentous event. The banquet will be part ceremony, part celebration."

Averil nodded in agreement. "The other royal houses are due to come to Shirall soon for the Conference of Kings. It can be planned to coincide with their arrival."

"Conference?" I asked.

"The Kings are gathering mainly to discuss the looming kalkar threat, although it coincides with a regularly scheduled round of peaceful meetings," Averil explained.

Delsi nodded. "Netta's banquet should be held in the presence of the Kings, since she will be taking part in the council and will need to be introduced to them anyway." She turned to her daughter. "And you, young lady, will moderate your language. You have been speaking like a peasant!"

The palace was thrown into a flurry of activity, and ultimately into bedlam and utter chaos. Kandi dragged the Princess along with her in her excited preparation for the eagerly anticipated event.

Together they bombarded the kitchen staff with suggestions of food and they drove their respective parents to distraction with their opinions regarding the guest list. It was a whirlwind introduction to the lighter side of palace life and a crash course in court politics.

Finally, they hounded the seamstresses to create new gowns. I hung back, watching as the girls picked out fabrics, wondered over design drawings and stood expectantly for measuring. When they were done, the head seamstress motioned to me. I shook my head, but she would not be refused.

"Don't think I've forgotten you, my dear," the woman said. She looked me up and down and shook her head, clicking her tongue in chagrin.

"That just won't do," she said archly.

I looked down at myself. What was wrong with my usual tunic and hose with long boots? It was comfortable and I could move freely. But I was not to be spared the indignity of being prodded and poked by an army of seamstresses determined to fit me into a new gown.

The head seamstress watched as her assistants brought several bolts of material in different colours. There was a nice green I could live with, or maybe the red, but she rejected them all. She looked at me appraisingly.

"For you, my dear," she mused, rummaging at the back of a shelf and pulling out a wrapped bundle. "I think this will do nicely."

She opened the parcel to reveal a length of polished silk, pristine white. I shook my head in horror.

"Please, anything but white!" I groaned.

The head seamstress smiled as she held the fabric up against my body. "Oh, my dear, with that dark hair and tanned skin, this will be just perfect."

SIX

Ordel paced and Delsi sat wrapped in a shawl by the fire.
I had been called to Averil's drawing room to find an anxious
group gathered. Averil, as usual, was in conversation with
the revealer, but she looked up as I entered.

"Have you seen Netta this morning?" Averil said.

"Not that I recall, why?"

"She seems to be missing."

"Missing?"

"Nobody has seen her since last night and she was gone
when her maid went to wake her this morning."

"Ah," I said. I closed my eyes and carefully searched
with my mind for Netta's life force. There was no sign of
danger and I ended the search, acutely aware of Evelar's
eyes boring into the back of my head. I blocked another of
his mental probes and turned back to Averil.

"I don't think we need worry as yet," I said.

"What do you mean?"

"Just that I know Netta and I don't think she is in any
danger." I could not tell Averil how I knew. The arts of the
mind were the secret of a select few and Averil would not
have been able to grasp what I had done. But the revealer
did.

"Where is she?" he asked.

"She's riding," I replied with a shrug.

"Riding?" asked Averil.

"Yes. Netta is headstrong and sometimes she doesn't

think things through. She likes her freedom, she is a lover of nature and she finds solace in a peaceful ride. She has been cloistered here for two weeks now, led on by Kandina's exuberance, worried about her mother. She's had to adjust and frankly I'm surprised that she lasted as long as she did. She isn't used to palace life. Remember that she has spent most of her life on a farm."

"But it is dangerous out there!" Ordel exploded. "There are kalkar everywhere. I thought she knew better. I told her not to go up there."

"I'm sure she's fine, Sir. Kalkar can't hurt her in the day time."

"No," he assented. "But people can. Just look at what happened to Delsi."

"What should we do?" said Averil.

"Wait. She'll be back before breakfast."

"And if she is not?"

"Then we'll know that she's not out riding."

"That is not very comforting," said Ordel wryly.

"Sorry," I said. "If it will make you feel better, I'll ride out and see if I can find her."

"Let me arrange an escort," said the Regent.

"Thank you, Averil," I said, "but that won't be necessary."

"You cannot go alone, it is too dangerous," she said.

"I can look after myself."

"At least let Evelar accompany you," Averil said, determined to offer protection. I could find no reason to refuse, apart from my own trepidation at being alone in his powerful presence.

"Alright," I said in resignation and I let him follow me out to the stables. I need not have worried, though. Now that he was occupied in finding Netta, his shield was tightly in place and his compelling personality was hidden behind the mask of the revealer at work.

"Do you know where she's gone?" asked the revealer.

"Of course," I said. "I know exactly where she's gone."

"Somehow, I knew you were going to say that," he said.

I swung up onto my horse and kicked in with my heels, galloping out of the yard, with the revealer close behind. Once we had left the town, I slowed Cheena to a walk. As we rode I noticed the kalkar were still gathered about, even this far from the palace.

Even after two weeks their numbers had barely diminished, though they had made no attempt to infiltrate the underground palace. It was as if they had settled into some kind of holding pattern. Having failed to stop the return of the royal family to their home, they now sat waiting for the next round.

I shivered, thinking about what they might be doing during their active night cycle. What did they do out here while we were all asleep?

The revealer walked his horse up beside me and I looked sideways at him, feeling once again that piercing gaze. This was the first time we had actually had the opportunity to talk together completely removed from the constant interruptions of the palace and I have to admit that I was more than a little curious.

"Can I ask you something?" I said.

"Ask away."

"Is it my imagination, or are you rather young for an artisan?"

He shrugged. "I'm the youngest ever." It was a statement. No boast, no pride, just fact. Holding his eyes, I tried to see into his mind, but he was still shielding fiercely. Something was there though, under the surface, threatening to break through, something he did not want me to see. Something he was... afraid to let me see, I realised with a shock.

"Now it's my turn," he said, breaking my concentration.

"Ask away," I said, deliberately echoing him.

"You seem to know an awful lot for a layperson."

"I wondered how long it would take you to ask that question," I said with a chuckle. "I was taught by... my mother."

"Is your mother a member of the College, then?"

"She was," I said quietly.

"She's no longer active?"

"You could say that. She's dead."

I spurred my horse away from him, but as I moved off he sent a wave of sympathy to wash over me, bringing a lump to my throat. Even after five years I still missed her, more so even than my more recently lost father, and Evelar's concern was overpowering.

Not wanting to break that intimate contact I dismounted and stood at the side of the road staring out over the scorched fields. I heard his boots on the gravel as he came up behind me, his physical closeness bringing a shiver, and his thoughts unshielded now.

I realised then what I had sensed from him before, and I remembered I had felt the same back in the palace garden. He was struggling with himself, wanting to show me his feelings but afraid to let them out in case they took over, undermining his professional edge. He wasn't used to being out of control and he didn't know where this attraction might take us. At the same time he was acutely aware that this might be our only chance to find out.

I took a steadying breath and turned to face him, finding him close behind, eyes ready to catch mine, smouldering with unexpressed longing. My heart was racing, my breath shallow, my confidence rattled. I yearned for him to take me in his arms.

But the clattering sound of approaching hoof beats shattered the moment. He stiffened as his mental shield snapped back up, then he turned and swung fluidly up on to his horse.

I stifled a sob, struggling to regain composure as I mounted my own horse and we rode out to meet the approaching rider. Netta came galloping up and slid to a halt in front of me.

"He knows who I am!" she cried in a panic.

"What?" I said vaguely.

"He knows who I am!"

"Who?"

"Atwin."

"Yes, I know."

"You know? How can you know?"

"I suspect he knew almost as soon as we met him."

"What? How?"

"I'm assuming Evelar told him. Remember, they were travelling together."

Netta looked from me to the revealer. "Is that true?" she asked suspiciously. Evelar merely nodded once.

"Perhaps you'd better tell me what happened," I said.

Riding away from the town to avoid notice, the Princess let her mount set its own pace. The horse enjoyed the freedom as much as she and her caution ebbed despite the presence of kalkar on the roadside. The girl passed out of the grain fields and the graze meadows and further.

Totally engrossed in her exploration, the girl forgot to watch for strangers and she cried out as her horse pulled to a sudden stop, jarring her as she fought to remain mounted. The girl raised her head to see why they had stopped.

"Please do not be angry, Dayna," he said. "This was the only way I could stop you."

"Why did you want to stop me?" she asked in apprehension.

"Who would not?" The young man hesitated. "Look. I wanted to talk to you about Shirall."

"Shirall?" she said, disconcerted.

"Of course," he said. "You are staying there surely you have seen the Queen?"

She nodded uncertainly.

"I have heard only rumours," he continued. "They say she has proclaimed an heiress."

"That is true."

Atwin dismounted then, offering a hand to the Princess. She hesitated and with reluctance allowed him to help her dismount. They began to walk, Atwin asking questions of the Princess, first about the Queen, then her daughter.

"I have heard she is very beautiful."

"The Queen? Yes she is."

"I know the Queen is. I remember her from my early childhood. I was only eight or nine when she left, but I remember that she took her daughter with her. Now they say that they have both returned."

"Yes, they have."

"How can they be sure that she is the same girl?"

"Of course she is," Netta snapped, forgetting herself. "I mean... the resemblance is obvious," she finished lamely.

"So they say," he said, watching her intently. "They also say that she rivals her mother in beauty."

"Oh?"

"Surely you have seen her. Do you agree?"

"I..." she let it trail off, trying to find a fitting answer. "I... cannot say."

"Cannot say? You have seen them together."

"I'm... I am no great judge..."

"Tell me who you think has the greater beauty."

"Whom I think? I think the Queen has the greater beauty."

The Princess hoped he would not press the matter and he did not, but he continued walking with her, making polite conversation. The girl grew anxious, wanting to escape and worried that she would be missed. She excused herself as she remounted.

"Let me escort you," he said, also remounting.

"You will have to keep pace with me," she said and spurred her horse.

After the initial surprise, the young man spurred his own mount. They were almost in Shirall when he caught the flowing tail of her mount, which reared in response. He hastily let go, but the girl showed expert control, calming her mount with ease. She then turned toward him and she was laughing.

"I love to run like that," she said. "Thank you." The Princess then assured him that she would travel home alone and turned away.

"One more thing, Dayna," he called.

"Yes?"

"I have received word of the banquet to be held at the palace next week. Will I see you there?"

"Of course," she said. "I cannot miss it." With that she spun her horse and was gone.

It was late, but I could not sleep. After following the Princesses around all week to avoid facing my feelings for the revealer, I just could not switch off my mind. The remembered sound of the girls' giggling kept interfering with my meditation routine, letting in other more disturbing thoughts. I just had to get them out of my head. I needed air.

Pulling on my cloak over my night clothes I slipped out of my room and made my way in the dark toward the gate house. From there I climbed the stairs, feeling my way with a hand on the rough stone wall, and reached the tower room.

The night was crisp, and I pulled the cloak tighter about myself, but I sucked the cool air deep into my lungs, letting out a long slow breath. Moonlight slanted through the barred windows, casting long shadows across the tower room.

I moved across to a window and looked down. The Kings had begun to arrive over the past few days, each bringing a small military escort. I could see the many fires of the visiting soldiers, dotted amongst the tent city that had sprung up in the courtyard inside the main gate.

The kalkar had been cleared from the inner courtyard, but they were still clustered in force outside the defensive wall. There they were, milling around, the enemy pack. I didn't dare reach out to see into their mind, for fear of discovery. If I kept quiet they would never know I was there.

My thoughts kept turning to the kalkar I had seen flying, and the group mind I had encountered twice during our panicked journey. The revealer had to know. I could not tell Averil, she knew nothing of that side of College training.

In the peace of the night, the room was silent. I heard no sound, and the light did not change, but I felt him enter. I turned and there he stood, watching me. He came closer and stood beside me at the window, staring with me at the force gathered outside the wall.

Even without touching, I could feel it. The air between us was electric, and I had to force myself to stand there calmly without turning and fleeing down the stairs. This was just too much and I had to break it.

"Have you ever looked at one close up?" I blurted.

I felt his surprise at my evasive question. "No," he said.

"Well I have," I said. "They're so... alien, so different. Not human at all."

"What are you trying to say?"

"Their minds are alien too," I said in a small voice.

He cocked his head, but made no attempt to read my mind, content to let me take my time.

"What have you been up to?" he said.

"Nothing yet," I replied. "Not really."

"So what's bothering you?"

I took a deep breath and began. "When I told Averil about the flying kalkar I said I wasn't sure. That wasn't exactly true. I didn't think I could explain all this to her. Not without letting out the secrets of the College…"

He sighed. "You let me worry about that. Now tell me what you saw."

I faced him, finally meeting his eyes. "I touched its mind, Evelar. I heard its thoughts! And it's haunted me ever since." I shivered.

He reached out to me, but seemed to think better of it and dropped his hand. "What did you find there?"

"The creature's own mind was buried, linked to all its fellows. The pack shared one surface mind, united by a common purpose, while their individual thoughts were completely hidden. Read one, you read them all."

He let out a slow breath. "It makes sense," he said. "We know they travel in packs, so why shouldn't they be connected in some way. But is it by design, or instinct, or choice?"

"I would say all three," I replied. "There was a definite sense of many conscious minds joined together, but they were enslaved by the common purpose." I shivered at the idea of losing my mind and being controlled like that.

"What should we do with this?" he asked.

"There's more," I said. "While I was in contact, I wondered why they didn't attack the ship. They answered. There was an overwhelming sense of fear, from every individual, fed through the common link. Fear of the water."

He grasped the implication at once. "You think we can find out more in the same way?"

I turned away with a shuddering breath. "It would mean opening up, giving in to this..."

He was at my back then, hands on my waist, sending shivers sparking up and down my body.

"Would that be so bad?" he murmured.

My breath caught, my heart thundered. Almost, I gave in, leaning back into the warmth he gave.

He pressed in close and whispered in my ear. "Soon..." Then he was gone, the night air cold on my back.

SEVEN

The Master of Ceremonies stood before the great double doors into the banquet hall. I had to slip past him somehow, to avoid the formal introduction at the head of the stairs. The last thing I wanted was to be the focus of all those eyes as I descended the stairs into the hall.

I felt distinctly uncomfortable in my pristine white gown with its elaborate lacing and voluminous petticoats. In desperation I had slipped out of the palace and into town where I had searched the market until I finally found a diaphanous dark blue silk stole, which I now wore about my shoulders in a dramatic statement against the white.

I looked at the crowd gathered waiting to be admitted and took a bold step. I wrapped myself in a shield of normality and reached into the collected minds of those about me, ordering them not to notice me. Then I slipped past the Master of Ceremonies and down the stairs. Only when I had reached the bottom and melted into the crowd did I release the spell.

"Very smoothly done," said a low voice at my ear. "Better even than my solution, I do believe." He stood close behind and my stomach turned a somersault.

"How did you get past him?" I asked the revealer, a trifle breathlessly.

"I simply switched everybody off for the few seconds it took for me to descend the stairs," he replied, promptly demonstrating by enclosing us both within his shield.

"I prefer a more subtle approach," I said over the tap dance going on in my chest.

"It works admirably well," he said. "Might I compliment you on your attire?"

"I can barely move."

Almost hesitantly, his hands brushed my shoulders. "This incredible stole can hardly have been the idea of that stuffy head seamstress."

"I detest white," I said, by way of explanation. "It's far too visible."

"I couldn't agree more," he murmured. "But it does flatter you and the blue is quite stunning."

"Thank you." I took a deep breath and pulled away, turning to look at him. "I see that you didn't entirely escape her either."

He glanced ruefully down at his clothing. Beneath the red-bordered midnight blue cloak, which he had somehow managed to retain, he wore a blue tunic and trousers instead of his customary black. The hood which normally covered his head was down, the red sash which normally held it in place was tied about his bare head and his long black hair hung luxuriantly about his shoulders. His face was open and expressive, letting me see the man behind those eyes.

"We all have to make these little sacrifices," he said with a shrug.

"What is it about these functions that dissolves people's minds?" I said, attempting to lighten the mood. "Do you realise we just wasted several minutes talking about clothes?"

"Sickening, isn't it?"

"I just remembered why I so dislike these affairs."

"Just go with it," he said, moving in close again. "Enjoy yourself. Pretend you're a normal person for one night."

"I will if you will," I challenged.

He held my gaze, lingering for a long, tantalizing moment. Then he sighed and shook his head, his mental shield suddenly blocking me out and his habitual mask back in place. "Sorry, I need to keep my wits tonight. I have work to do."

"Can I help?" I asked then, feeling suddenly shy and uncertain. "I mean, you're working solo, without the usual assistant. It can't be easy."

"I can manage," he murmured.

"Ladies and gentlemen, your attention please. The royal party is about to descend."

The crowd hushed and looked up at the head of the stairs as the members of the royal party were introduced one by one.

"Averil. The Princess Regent." Averil descended, smiling, in a lovely sea green gown, and made her way to the royal table.

"The Princess Kandina." Radiant in blue, the girl descended, moving just a little faster than ceremony demanded, and followed quickly after her mother.

There was a pause and in a ringing voice the Master of Ceremonies continued. "Her Royal Majesty, Queen Delsi and Prince Ordel, the Royal Consort."

The pair stood at the head of the stairs as the entire crowd roared in thunderous applause. They began to descend with slow graceful steps. The crowd parted for them as they made their way to the royal table.

There was an even longer pause and the crowd hushed. In a voice filled with wonder, the Master of Ceremonies spoke again. "Her Royal Highness, Heiress to the Throne of Shirall, next Keeper of the Queen's Amulet, Princess Nettayna."

As Netta appeared and stood regally at the head of the stairs, the silence was immense, every eye in the room turned up to gaze on her flawless face. She was resplendent in violet satin, perfectly matching her eyes, her glorious hair piled high and cascading down her back.

Then, as she began to descend, the applause was deafening. The ovation continued as she moved through the crowd and took her place at the royal table. As the noise gradually subsided, Evelar and I made our way to the royal table to greet our hosts.

"My dear Miyam," said Averil. "You look lovely."

"Thank you, Averil."

"You have a great beauty, my dear. You should show it off more."

I had no answer for that.

'She's right, you know,' said a certain revealer's voice in my mind.

As the Master of Ceremonies called once more for attention, Evelar and I dissolved back into the crowd. One by one, the visiting kings were announced, each following hard upon the last. I envisioned them all clustered outside the hall impatient to enter, and was glad that I had slipped in unnoticed.

"From Nella Fillenga, Derrek, King of the Fillens," said the announcer as that outspoken king entered.

He made his way to the royal table, where he greeted first the Queen, then her daughter, then Averil and then he went to his place at the table.

"From Zelona, King Lenent."

Lenent was a forthright man who greeted the royal party with blunt courtesy. He seemed a little suspicious of Netta's sudden appearance, but he said nothing, giving her a cursory bow and turning to Averil, placing a kiss on her hand before moving to his seat.

"King Erris of Mytar."

A quiet man who spoke little but seemed friendly enough.

"Umbro, King of Yerterma."

Umbro entered nervously, but held himself well in front of the crowd. He was softly spoken and very polite.

"Tarnel, King of Tellemot."

He was a very intelligent man in his mid thirties and he greeted the royal party with a certain delight.

"For King Gerard, Atwin, Crown Prince of Drasmil."

At this last name, Netta lifted her eyes in surprise and I turned to Evelar, who merely smiled. Atwin bowed to the Queen, turned to Netta and bowed, face giving no indication of recognition. Then he greeted Averil and moved to his place at the table.

Evelar led me to a place he had reserved for us to one side near the royal table. It had the advantage of being inconspicuous while offering a good view of the hall, and he sat like a coiled spring, outwardly relaxed but ready to move at a moment's notice. When the shuffle for tables was over and the noise had subsided Delsi rose to speak.

"Friends," she said. "I am sure that you are aware of the current political climate. The time approaches when kalkar must once again be driven from our cities. As these events unfold, I have returned to begin again the task that has been delayed for so many years. I have brought with me my daughter, who is now of an age to accept her title. As some of you may know, it is customary at this time to pass on the legacy which began with the granddaughter of Rexa. I wear about my neck Leena, the amulet that once was hers. It is now time to pass it on, into my daughter's keeping."

As Netta rose to stand beside her mother, the amulet

about the Queen's neck began to glow with a strange white aura. The light engulfed the Queen and within the glow she lifted the chain over her head and held it toward her daughter.

The glow grew to encompass them both and Delsi lifted the chain over her daughter's head until it lay about the neck of its new keeper. When Delsi removed her hands the aura slowly dissipated from about her, but Netta remained bathed in white light for a moment longer.

Eventually the glow subsided until only the amulet itself still shone whitely. The residue of the light remained about Netta's throat throughout the night.

A sumptuous meal was served. Tables groaned with six kinds of meat, huge platters of roast vegetables, salads and sauces. Accompanying the meal were red and white wines, beer and mead. For a time the only sound was of people eating and talking between mouthfuls.

When the main course was winding down, the plates were stacked and taken away and the dessert course was brought out. There were fruits and cream, huge cakes, chocolate sauce in a giant fountain and various biscuits and pastries. The guests somehow fit it all in even after the enormous meal that preceded it.

Finally the meal was over and it was time for the festivities. All but the royal table were moved back to clear the floor for the dancing to begin. As Atwin stood and moved toward where the Princess sat, Evelar also stood.

"I have to hear what they say," he said, moving off.

I followed. "Why?" I asked.

"This is the main reason I'm here," he said. "I have to make sure those two get together."

"What? You're matchmaking?" I asked in surprise. "Since when has that been the job of the College?"

"I have no time to explain right now."

We made our way through the crowd to the general vicinity of the royal table and found a spot behind the Princess where we could hear without being seen.

"Well," said Atwin to the Princess. "This explains a lot."

"What explains what?" she asked pleasantly.

"All this," and he gestured at the room and everything in it, "explains you."

"Oh," she said.

"I knew you were no farm girl."

"Oh but I am," she said. "I lived on a small farm from the age of six," she explained. "The only life I knew was farming."

"But that does not fit," he said, sitting on the table in front of her. "Your whole manner is regal, not rustic."

She laughed at the unusual expression, drawing curious looks from those about. "That is very poetic," she said.

"You say you spent twelve years on a farm and yet your skin is smooth and your hair is finer than any here."

"I know, it's confusing but true," she said. "My parents told me nothing about this until only a few weeks ago."

"Then why do you not look like a farm girl?"

"That is the confusing part," she admitted. "Mother was very careful to see that I was educated. She took great pains to keep me 'regal' as you say."

"And you never questioned her actions?"

"Oh I questioned, but she never gave me any answers. Just dressed me in skirts and chastised me for speaking like a commoner."

"So when you learned the truth all was explained."

"Yes," she said. There was a long pause before she spoke again. "I'm... I am afraid I was very rude to you," she said.

"Yes," he answered, "but I was just as bad." She smiled, reassured. "Shall we dance?" he asked.

"Well, that's a relief," said Evelar.

"What's going on?" I asked.

"It's vital that those two form a bond."

"Now wait a minute!" I said, worried. "Netta's my friend. I won't have her played like this. I think you'd better tell me what this is all about."

"When the first princess of a new generation is born," he said, "the Queen's Amulet makes a choice from all eligible boy children throughout Sharné. When it has found a suitable child it tells the Queen that the choice has been made. Within the next five to ten years, when the boy reaches his tenth year, he receives an irresistible call to travel, alone and unaided, to Shirall. When he arrives, the amulet tells the Queen that this is the boy. The boy then becomes a ward of the state and is raised with the Princess.

"When Atwin first came to Shirall, the Queen was not present. She had already fled. Averil communicated with her sister, telling her that she thought the boy had come, but without the amulet to identify him they could not be sure.

"Because the Princess was not present in Shirall and because Atwin was a prince in his own right, it was decided that he should remain resident at Drasmil. Averil and Delsi are concerned that because the two were not raised together there will be no bond to build upon. It looks like they need not have worried."

"Does Kandina know any of this?"

"I doubt it, why?"

"I think we have a problem."

"What do you mean?"

I indicated to where Kandina was sitting, a frown on her face, staring at the couple on the dance floor. "Did you notice her watching Atwin while he was talking with Netta?" I said. "She can't take her eyes off him."

"Your point being?"

"She's in love with him."

He frowned. "Are you sure?"

"Of course I'm sure. How often does he visit?"

"The call to visit was always strong. Due to his father's madness, he felt more at home in Shirall than in Drasmil. Because his father was too deranged to train the boy himself, Atwin was cultivated for kingship by Averil. After all, by law he is the ward of Shirall, though he's still heir to Drasmil. Averil became like the mother he lost and he visits often."

"In that case, Kandina has had ample opportunity to bond with him herself. Hopefully she's reading more into it than is really there. She may not win his heart, but she'll try."

"But she's a child."

"She's sixteen years old. A crush is a very serious thing to a girl that age. She'll do everything in her power to come between them."

"Then I think we have a problem."

"Didn't I just say that?"

When the Regent Averil approached us some time later in the evening, Evelar and I had been so busy keeping Kandina occupied, finding partners for her to keep her mind off Atwin and Netta, that I had lost track of the time.

"My dear Miyam," she said. "I have not seen you dance tonight."

"No," I said. Usually the dancing was the only thing which made these affairs bearable for me, but I had become engrossed in helping the revealer in his work. We had settled into an unconscious rapport, completely at ease in each other's company, and any prospective partners had been quickly shooed away.

"Well," said Evelar, "I think we should rectify that, don't you?" He offered me his arm, an enticing gleam in his eyes. Thankfully, I saw Kandina being led up the stairs by her maid, having reached her curfew, and I allowed him to lead me on to the dance floor.

It was late and many of the guests had tired of dancing. People sat chatting and watching those still on the floor, and there was plenty of room. To my surprise, Evelar spun me into the starting position for one of the ritual dances of the College. A little surprised by his choice, I hesitated and looked a question at him. He raised an eyebrow provocatively in challenge. We had caught the attention of the spectators now and, in trepidation, I executed the first move.

As the dance progressed I relaxed a little, and almost unconsciously slipped into the rhythm of it. We fell easily into a natural harmony, an almost instinctive union of body and soul, and the bright glamorous world around us seemed to disappear. Our minds joined in an intimate meld as our shields dropped and we let each other in.

The complexity of the dance came easily, its moves seductive and intensely sensual. We moved together as one, our flesh crackling with erotic charge, sparking and shivering each time we touched. We completed the last move, ending facing each other, standing very close but not touching.

I was breathless and a little unsteady, drowning in those dark eyes. The observers burst into applause bringing the world crashing in on us once more. Evelar brushed past me and strode brusquely from the floor, leaving me standing there alone.

I looked around at the milling crowd, feeling awkward and more than a little mortified that we had allowed our growing attraction to become so public. After some hesitation I followed after him, coming up slowly behind him in the shadows and placing a hand tentatively on his arm.

He jumped at my touch, and as I stood there he looked sideways at me. I could see that he was shaken and a little surprised at himself.

"Why the Qarama?" I asked carefully, naming the dance.

"Why not?" he said.

"If there had been even one other Art member here to witness it, we would be married now."

"Yes," he said, seeming unsteady. "Would you have minded terribly?"

For a moment I could not speak, falling into his unshielded and enthralling gaze, unable to pull away. "No," I said in a daze. "Not at all..."

He reached out with a trembling hand to tenderly touch my face and then carefully pulled me close. "You do realise, I'm breaking my cardinal rule here," he said in a husky whisper.

"Oh?" I whispered. "And what's that?"

"Never get involved while on a case."

"Well, if my mother hadn't gotten 'involved' while on a case," I said, "I wouldn't be here."

"Interesting point," he murmured, bending to kiss me at last.

* * *

"Ah... I think we'll leave it at that, shall we," said Miyam, cheeks red.

"What?" said the Maestro.

"Oh, nothing," said Miyam, blushing even more.

"It was our wedding night, Sir," murmured Sand from the shadows. "Do you really need to hear the details?"

"Oh!" said the Maestro. "No, I suppose not. Please continue, my dear."

* * *

EIGHT

Late the next morning, we wrapped ourselves in a facade, carefully hiding our hearts from the world, and went our separate ways. Evelar went in search of Averil, who would be organizing the first round of preliminary meetings with the assembled kings. I found Delsi in the garden, instructing her daughter in the use of the amulet.

"You must promise me one thing," she said. "This is most important, for it will save your life. You must never take the amulet off. Once the amulet is removed the enemy will instantly know your exact position and you will no longer be protected from harm."

"I will remember," said Netta gravely. "Mother? What's wrong?"

Delsi was looking down in bewilderment at her feet. Suddenly she grabbed at an overhanging branch, her face stricken. Ordel leaped up from where he had been sitting quietly watching the instruction and caught his wife in his arms as her legs seemed to give way beneath her.

"Delsi, what is it?" he asked anxiously.

"My feet," Delsi cried. "I cannot feel my feet!"

The Queen clutched at her husband as he led her to a seat, leaning on him with all her weight. Ordel removed her light shoes and sat back to examine her feet. At first glance there seemed to be nothing amiss, but on closer inspection the skin seemed too pale, and was cold and clammy to the touch. Delsi was quiet, but there were tears of anguish rolling down her face.

"Ordel, I am afraid," she said in a whisper.

"And I," he replied.

"Please take me to my room."

Ordel nodded, lifted her light form and carried her out of the garden. As Netta followed her father and the Queen, I made my way quickly to Averil's audience chambers, where the Regent summoned the medic.

After a close examination, the medic turned to us in consternation. "I'll tell you now that I have no idea what this could be. I can only say that it must have something to do with that arrow. I can find no trace of poison and there's no illness in her blood. Whatever it is, it's nothing I've ever seen before."

"Are you sure this is something physical?" I asked and the medic looked at me. "I mean... Perhaps the arrow was charmed in some way."

"You may be right," the medic agreed. "But such things are not within my own sphere of knowledge. There's nothing I can do to combat such an illness."

Ordel exchanged worried looks with his wife and daughter. "Then what shall we do?" he asked.

In Delsi's chamber, Ordel paced while Netta knelt by her mother's bedside, arms about her mother's torso and head on her chest. Averil sat in a chair next to the bed and I stood by the door, Evelar a silent strength beside me.

Ordel mumbled as he paced. "We need to find out what is causing this. There must be someone who can help!"

Averil shrugged helplessly. "I know not."

Ordel stopped in front of the revealer. "Can you not do something?" he accused. "You revealers have plenty of mind tricks, surely you can break a charm like this!"

I gasped. I had no idea how Ordel knew about the mind powers, but Evelar just shrugged it off.

"I'm sorry, My Lord," Evelar sighed. "A charm is very different to the mental tools we use. It's just not part of our training."

"Perhaps it should be," said Ordel petulantly.

"Is there no one you could consult?" I suggested, trying to ease the tension. "Surely there is some healer or wise woman who has knowledge of charms."

"You mean some sort of witch doctor?" said Ordel.

"If you want to call it that," I said. "Certainly someone unconventional, someone who knows the old ways?"

Ordel nodded then, calming a little. "I will go down into the city and talk to Algernon. He will know if there is someone who can help."

He glanced toward his wife, then spoke to Averil. "Look after her while I am gone."

Averil nodded as he hurried from the room. When her father had gone, Netta raised her tear-filled eyes to look at her aunt.

"Why are they doing this to us?" she said brokenly. "What have we done?"

"Oh, my dear," said Averil. "Why do you think it has anything to do with you? All royal houses are under threat."

"No, Aunt, they are not!" Netta cried. "No other house was chased into exile. No other house has been hounded and hunted like us. No other house is forced to hide under ground! What do they want with us?"

Averil shook her head. "I know not, my dear."

"It feels like the whole world is after us," Netta sobbed. "First it was the kalkar, then those people who shot Mother, whoever they were, and now this! I just wish somebody could tell me why they are doing this!"

As I watched Netta break down I felt dreadful. I knew

there was something I could do, but I could not say anything. How could I betray the revealers by suggesting their mind powers could find the answers? Evelar would never forgive me.

His profession relied on secrecy. If anyone knew what the revealers could do they could never fulfil their contracted duties effectively. It wasn't my place to tell. Yet I had to do something. My friend was in pain and needed answers.

I felt such guilt that I could not remain in that room.As I slipped out I felt a questioning thought from Evelar, and made a cryptic reply. *'We need to talk.'*

I vaguely heard Evelar excusing himself, and then he was beside me as I moved quickly down the corridor. He caught my hand in his.

"What's troubling you, my love?" he said.

My breath caught in my throat. How could I ask this amazing man to betray the secrets of the College? I was completely unworthy of him. I directed my gaze forward and pulled him along with me, heading up the steps toward the entrance passage, through the barred door onto the battlements, and out into the sunlight.

The scorched fields outside the main gate were filled with kalkar, many more than the last time I had been up there. They stood all around, dormant, radiating heat, the grass at their feet burnt and blackened. I stood looking out at them, preparing myself for what I was about to do.

He waited in silence, his mind wrapping me in concern. I drew in a difficult breath. He took my arm, and turned me to face him. Holding me by the shoulders he compelled me to meet his eyes.

"What's this all about?" he murmured.

I let him read my worry that when he knew what I thought he must do it would drive him from me. He smiled and took me in his arms.

"Nothing could do that, my love," he said. "Now what is it you need to tell me?"

"I was thinking about Netta, how she needs answers. Maybe we could get them for her, you and me. But..." I bit my lip, afraid to say it.

"Go on," he said gently.

"If we do this it might mean giving away College secrets," I blurted. "You would have to admit what you can do, or they won't accept it."

He chuckled. "Is that all? It wouldn't be the first time!"

Laughter was the last thing I had expected.

"But that's not what's really bothering you, is it?" he said.

"I just... I didn't want you to think I was...crossing some line, or meddling... interfering in your work..." I trailed off as my fear of alienating him stopped my voice.

A wave of reassurance washed over me as he smiled, a twinkle of laughter in his voice.

"I think it's a brilliant idea!" he said proudly.

We had no chance to put our plan into action. That afternoon we gathered again in Delsi's chamber. Ordel stood by the bedside, pensive and anxious as he explained what he had learned.

"Algernon says there is a man who may know what we need, but he has not been seen in years."

"Where is he?" said Netta with a catch in her voice.

"Nobody knows. He is something of a hermit, so he almost never appears in town. He lives out in the wilds alone, hunting and grazing for food."

"What makes you think he can help?" said Averil.

"Because before he went solo he was a well known herbalist in the town. Everybody went to him for medicines and other less conventional remedies."

"Do you think we can find him? Did Algernon give you any clues?"

Ordel shook his head. "Algernon cannot even say if he is alive or dead. He was old even before he went out on his own."

"Oh, Father, it sounds hopeless!" Netta sobbed.

Ordel smiled. "Worry not, my sweet, we will find him. I will leave as soon as I may."

"No, Father, do not go! Let someone else do it!" Netta cried.

"Now, Netta..."

"I mean it, Father. It would be too dangerous. We are the ones they are after; we should stay here."

"I think she may be right," said Delsi. "It is us they want to stop. I cannot have you putting yourself in harm's way."

"Then who?" he said in frustration.

"The revealer can go," said Averil then. "Would you agree, Evelar?"

"Of course, Your Highness. I will leave within the hour."

'Not without me, you won't,' I said silently.

'I didn't want to speak for you, my love,' he replied.

"I'd like to volunteer, Your Highness," I said aloud.

Less than an hour later, we were riding out of the palace, the prospect of days alone together bringing a warm glow and a smile to my face despite the reason for it. I glanced across at Evelar riding beside me and saw that he was smiling too. His eyes caught mine and I felt his happiness wash over me. I ducked my head in embarrassment and he chuckled.

'Behave yourself, we have a mission,' I admonished, silently because I could not trust myself to speak.

'Do I look worried?'

'Sir Artisan, you are on duty!'

'So?'

I tried to hide the giggles that came bubbling up to escape in spite of all my efforts to stop them. I had no right to be so happy, not while the Queen lay ill and possibly dying with my friend grieving at her side.

"You have every right, my love," he said then. "You care too much about everyone else and you forget to take care of yourself."

"Look who's talking, Mister Keep-This-Revealer-Face-On-So-Nobody-Can-Get-In!"

"You got in..."

I laughed. "I guess I did at that!"

"You ripped off the mask and broke it into tiny pieces. I had no choice."

I was giggling again, damn it. *'Be serious! We have a job to do.'*

"The way I look at it," he said seriously. "We have a difficult search ahead of us that could take an indeterminate number of days. I intend to spend as much time as I can making you giggle like those silly princesses do!"

I shook my head. "I already feel guilty enough. I can't stop thinking about Netta's face when Delsi fell ill again. I owe it to my friend to find help."

"That's not the only reason you wanted to come with me."

The smile had come back. I just could not stay serious and no amount of ducking my head could hide it. *'I've only just found you. I'm not letting you out of my sight!'*

'I should think not.'

I giggled until I was breathless, then saw his broad smile and giggled some more.

We reached the farm lands outside of town well before night fall. The kalkar were still dotted about, but they were more spread out. It was strange to see them singly or in pairs or threes, when they should be in packs.

Passing a lonely farm house, I was reminded of the life Netta had left behind. I saw two boys, making mischief despite the enemy presence. They ran across the road in front of us, each carrying a bucket of water. We stopped to watch as they approached a lone kalkar, quietly sizzling at the roadside.

The creature appeared oblivious to the boys as they teased it. Curious, I opened my mind to listen. They took handfuls of water and drizzled it over the creature's shoulders, laughing as it steamed and dried on the protective skin membrane. They plucked blades of grass from the road and touched it to the creature's flesh, gasping and pulling their hands away as the grass caught fire, almost burning them.

One boy lifted his bucket and tipped the entire contents over the kalkar's head. Most of it ran off harmlessly, but some found its way inside the protective layer and the flesh began to bubble and melt. I heard the creature's pain as a low moan in my head.

The boys stared in horror and stepped back, but then they grew brave again. One boy found a large stick and used it to pull back the skin at the front to expose the delicate mottled flesh underneath, while the other hefted the second bucket and threw the water at the creature's defenceless form. My head exploded with pain as the poor thing screamed silently in its agony.

The kalkar's body steamed and melted, dissolving into a formless mass of bubbling flesh. The boys used their sticks to poke at the mess, exclaiming in disgust and laughing at what they had done. Then they ran off to find more mischief.

I stared at the remains, tears streaming down my face. I glanced across to Evelar and saw by his grim face that he too had heard that awful scream.

"Come, let's get away from here," he said softly.

I nodded and kicked my horse to follow. We rode at a gentle canter, with no aim but to get as far from the dreadful scene as we could before sundown. I rode in a daze, staring ahead, trying to shut out the memory.

We spoke little, our happiness of earlier subdued and our easy companionship overshadowed by what we had seen. Finally, Evelar led me off the road and through the trees until we came to a small clearing by a little stream.

"Let's stop here tonight," he said, dismounting.

He quickly went about gathering wood for a fire. Blindly I watched him work at setting up camp, but I could not move, could not even climb down off my horse. When he realised that I still sat there, he was at my side in an instant.

"What is it, my love?"

I looked down at him, vision blurred by tears as he reached up to help me dismount. Then I was in his arms, sobbing into his shoulder. I felt his alarm and then his soothing thoughts calmed me as he led me to the fire.

"I'm sorry, I'm just being silly," I said.

"No," he said. "You're anything but silly. You're wonderful."

I smiled through my tears.

"I should have realised it had effected you so," he said then.

"I have no idea why," I replied. "I've seen it before."

"Maybe, but you've never felt it."

"Did you hear? That scream!"

"Yes, but I blocked it."

"I wish I hadn't tried to listen."

"You couldn't have known how it would be. It's never a good idea to listen to death."

"They can feel when they're asleep," I cried. "I never

dreamed..."

"I suspect it only felt once it was injured. The outer skin stopped the water at first."

"Yes, but... that scream was almost human!"

He pulled me into his embrace, murmuring soft words of comfort.

NINE

We sat together watching the fire and spent the night in each other's arms. I awoke to the delicious aroma of rabbit roasting over the fire. The sun was already high and Evelar sat nearby, polishing his sword.

'Good morning, my love,' he said in my mind. *'I hope you're hungry.'*

I sat up with a grateful smile. "How long have you been awake?"

"Since first light. I rarely sleep later, even if the night was eventful," he said dryly.

I giggled in spite of myself and felt my face grow hot. "That's more like it," he smiled.

"You should have woken me," I said, trying to remind myself of the seriousness of our mission. "We need to get on with the search."

He put down his sword and lifted his eyes to capture mine. "I've been thinking about that," he said. "I thought we might stay here for a while."

I cocked my head. "What do you mean stay here? You know how important this is!"

"Just hear me out. We both know we could find the hermit in moments if we just sat down together and *looked.*"

"Yes, and Delsi needs him as soon as possible."

"I know, but as far as they know we could be searching for days. We should take advantage of that."

I stared at him. "How can you say that? I thought you

took your profession more seriously!"

"I do." He stood and came to me, pulling me up and into his arms. "But you're forgetting something. We performed the dance of marriage. I take that seriously too, and if we had done it in the College in front of the Maestro we would now be officially off duty for a week."

"I'm not forgetting anything. But we don't have that luxury."

He pulled away. "Are you saying you don't want to stop for a while and just be together?"

My heart melted. "Of course I do. But I can't forget what we're supposed to be doing either. How could I look Netta in the face and tell her honestly that we searched as quickly and as carefully as possible if we did this?"

He sighed, dropping his arms. "You're right, my love. So we *look* for him now, find him today or tomorrow and head back to Shirall."

I bit my lip and nodded, not trusting myself to speak over the lump in my throat. Going back was the last thing I wanted to do, to be condemned to ignoring each other in the day time and meeting only at night, when all we wanted to do was be together to explore each other...

Reading my thoughts, he pulled me back into his embrace. "So let's stay here," he said.

I nodded, completely overwhelmed. I felt awful for abandoning our mission, I felt guilty for wanting to, and I felt dreadful for being so happy about it. But in his kiss all was forgotten.

After three days, it was almost accidental when we did find the hermit. In the end it was the singing that finally gave him away. We had made a mental search and knew his general location, but we had delayed as long as we dared before setting out to find him. It was conscience that eventually made us strike camp.

As we rode slowly through the woods, I could hear a croaky old voice raised in song. I could not understand the words and I suspect that it was only gibberish, but he sounded decidedly pleased with himself. I sighed, disappointed that our extended tryst was at an end.

We followed the sound and soon broke into a clearing, where we found an old man sitting by a small fire, merrily feeding sticks into the flames. The smoke was thin but fragrant, smelling slightly of moss. I noticed a rosy glow in the old man's cheeks, which suggested that he was slightly intoxicated. He looked up as we dismounted and grinned, gap-toothed at us.

"Found old Percival at last, then?" he said with a chuckle. "Percival's help you need."

"Yes..." I began.

"Come," he said. "Sit. Breathe the jundo sticks."

"We come not for ourselves," said Evelar.

"Sit," he repeated. "Forget trouble for now."

We exchanged a look and Evelar shrugged his shoulders. We sat together by the fire, opposite the old man to avoid smelling his unwashed body. The old man threw more of his precious jundo sticks on the fire and cackled to himself. The fragrance of the jundo was soothing and I found myself relaxing into the calm of the evening. With difficulty, I pulled myself out of the reverie.

"Sir, we need you to come with us to Shirall," I said.

"Hush," he replied. "Queen can wait."

"How did you..."

"Hush," he said again. "Watch the flames, breathe the jundo."

I looked to Evelar for help, but he merely smiled and shook his head slightly. I looked into the flames and felt their hypnotic influence. I tore my eyes away.

"Fight it not," the old man said.

"Relax, my love," Evelar whispered to me.

"But..."

"He's searching for a vision in the flames."

"Be at ease," said the old man. "All is well."

I sighed in resignation and gave in to the flames and the jundo sticks. I leaned back into Evelar's arms and felt myself begin to drift...

I stood at the shore watching the waves roll in. The sky was grey and I was alone. The world spun and lifted me to dizzying heights. I flew over the sea and into darkness. A great collection of shadows filled the world and there was terrible suffering and tormentuous flame. In no time all was black and burning and I was alone again. Nothing was left and in nothing I battled for sanity. I shuddered at the emptiness within. Again I rose high, through endless cloud, to rest in a white fog. There was a sense of everlasting peace and overwhelming love. Then, of a sudden, all was blue. And I was myself...

I awoke slowly and languorously, lulled by the gentle rise and fall of my pillow under my head. I heard someone moving about and raised my head from where it rested on Evelar's chest to look around. As I did so, my revealer opened his eyes. Together we sat up and the happy old man tottered over to us, carrying a steaming cup.

"Drink, my dears. Help you wake."

As we shared the drink I described my vision. At the mention of blue, Evelar looked surprised. When I had finished I asked what he had seen.

"Nothingness at first," he replied. "Emptiness, sucking me into its cavernous depths. Then a multitude of colour saved me from the nothing and in a great arching rainbow flowed into me. The greatness of the colours filled me with terrible power but as the rainbow tide grew rough I foundered as if in the surf. As my body was tossed in the waves, so my mind was thrown into turmoil. Then the colours dissipated, dissolving and leaving me hollow. When the white light came and bore me up I thought I must have died. All thought was gone, and silence ruled. And then all was blue."

"Future you see," said the old hermit. "Fate fulfilled."

Evelar and I exchanged a bewildered look.

"Jundo dreaming filled with riddles. Meaning comes in time," the old man continued. "Now we move. See your queen."

We rode at a walk back toward Shirall and the ailing queen. The hermit rode a tired old gelding, scruffy and unkempt, its stubborn lethargy slowing our pace. The poor horse smelled almost as bad as the wizened old man and our own mounts flicked their ears and snorted whenever it came near.

The closer we got to the town, the more kalkar sizzled by the roadside. They were no longer standing in singles and small groups but rather in large packs, clustered on and near the road. Their numbers had almost doubled in the short time we had been away.

Approaching the palace, we realised there was no way through.

"What now?" I whispered.

Evelar shrugged and shook his head. "I suppose we could find some water and melt our way through."

I moaned at the memory of pain and shook my head in denial. Now that I knew the horrible suffering that would cause I had no desire to repeat it. Evelar sent a reassuring thought, smiling gently at my distress.

"There may be another way," he mused.

He dismounted, approaching the nearest kalkar. I could feel him gathering energy for something, but what? He took a deep breath and reached out a hand to touch the creature on the head. I hissed a warning, worried that he might burn himself.

'Don't worry, my love,' he said in my head.

He placed the hand palm down on the top of the creature's head. I heard the crackle of burning and steam rose upward from his hand, while at the same moment I felt the rush of power. His hand glowed and smoked as he sucked the heat right out of the kalkar.

I groaned at the pain I felt from him, but he continued until the creature was cold, then gave a little push and it toppled over dead. He kicked it out of the way and moved on to the next one. Three more were dispatched in the same way, but each required more power from my revealer and I could hear his breath growing heavier with the effort.

I dismounted and led the horses, treading carefully along the narrow path he was making, the hermit following behind chuckling to himself. Evelar radiated heat and pain and my worry made me snap at the old man.

"What's so funny?"

"Percival want be revealer, when young," said the hermit. "Marvellous!"

I glared at him and moved up to Evelar's side as he finished off another kalkar, panting as if he had been running for miles. Before he could reach out to the next, I caught his arm and he looked at me, eyes glowing red.

"You need to stop," I whispered. "There's too many!"

He shook his head, looking up the hill at the long line of kalkar blocking the road to the palace. The thick scrub to either side of the road was burnt by the gathered packs which stood in and around the trees as well as on the road.

"We have to keep going," he said. "We must get through before nightfall."

I took his hand, turned it over to see the skin red and blistering. I touched his face to feel the heat radiating from him, like a fever. But I knew he was right. If we were caught here when night fell we were all dead.

"Show me how," I said. He opened his mouth to protest but I stopped him with fingers to his lips. "Don't argue. This is something you can't do on your own."

"Alright, my love," he nodded. "Watch and *listen*."

I did as asked, watched and *listened* as he cooled the next and I moved on to another. I reached out my hand, readying myself for the pain and determined to get this right.

I was not prepared for the sheer effort it would take, but I persisted and finally pushed it over with satisfaction. Together we continued our long slow progress up the hill to the palace. It took hours but finally, as the sun dipped low in the west, we arrived exhausted and gasping at the gate.

"Guard!" Evelar called, voice a mere croak. He peered through the bars and the guard timidly appeared from the guardroom.

"Who goes there?"

"We bring the hermit for the Queen."

The guard looked us up and down, noting our dishevelled state and staring at the long path we had made up the hill.

"Well?" said Evelar pointedly.

"Ah... of course, Sir," said the guard, hurrying to open the gate.

We made our way through the assembled armies in the courtyard, who stared at us as we passed and exclaimed at the smell of the bedraggled old man who trailed behind.

A disused fountain stood in the centre of the courtyard. The pipes no longer flowed, but the pond at its base still held water, cleaned and made fresh for the soldiers' use. Stumbling in our weariness and gasping with the heat that still ravaged our bodies, we struggled toward it.

Plunging our arms up the the elbows in the cool water we sighed as the heat seeped out and into the pond. As our flesh cooled the water began to steam and bubble and when we removed our hands we felt refreshed and calm while the pond boiled.

Without delay, we stabled the horses and led the hermit down below, heading straight to Delsi's chamber. As I reached up to knock, Evelar pulled me aside, taking me in his arms.

"Before we go in," he whispered and kissed me while the hermit chuckled at us.

When he pulled away, the revealer face was back, mental shield up and mask in place. He gave me a nod and I gathered my own defences and tapped on the door, opening it without waiting for a reply.

Ordel rose explosively from his chair as we entered.

"Miyam, Evelar," he exclaimed. "Thank the gods!"

We took in the scene. It had hardly changed, but for two extra people. Netta was on her knees by the bed and beside her, back against the bedside and knees drawn up, sat Prince Atwin.

Averil sat in her chair by her sister's bed and her daughter Kandi sat petulant and looking bored on the chaise in the corner.

Netta looked up at her father's shout. "Mym!" she cried and jumped up to grab me in a hug.

Beside us, Atwin had also risen to his feet to grasp Evelar's hand. "Glad you are back," he said.

"You're still here," said Evelar.

Atwin shrugged. "I wanted to stay until help arrived."

"He has been at Netta's side the whole time," said Averil with a pleased smile. "Did you find him?"

Evelar gave a curt nod and turned to look for the old man. "Percival?"

The hermit poked his head around the door frame and with hesitant steps sidled into the room.

"Come," said Averil with a smile.

He shuffled across to the bedside, wasting no time on words. Delsi's condition had deteriorated. With the increasing coldness of her limbs the Queen had grown more anxious. The paralysis had spread up her legs, mysteriously freezing the flesh into immobility.

The hermit Percival gave one cursory glance toward the Queen and seemed immediately to determine the cause. He lightly touched the clammy skin of her ankle and his satisfied expression gave mute evidence that his thought was confirmed.

He turned to explain his theory. "There is... aura... polluted. Until now had... protection... now gone."

"Show him the amulet, angel," said Delsi.

Netta took it out from under her clothing.

The hermit drew in his breath. "This is she," he said, meaning the amulet. "Knew her as part of you," he said to Delsi. "Now you be separate, her guard of you be gone."

The man leaned forward to study the amulet more closely and Netta flared her nostrils as she smelled him. For a moment the hermit's eyes clouded over and his expression became totally blank.

After several tense, intent minutes he shook himself from the trance. "This calls herself Leena," he said in a voice hushed in awed reverence. "In past long gone knew she another, name of Naali. He lives, but hidden. She and he rejoined must be. Only then Lady be healed."

A horrified silence descended on us. Finally, Ordel

turned to his wife and spoke to her softly.

"We will find Naali," he said with hasty conviction, "and we will bring him back to you."

"Be warned," the hermit said quietly. "In time past Naali live in Chambers of Exalted, known by you as Sacred Halls. Disturbed now, moved from there. Find him you must."

TEN

The next morning we took a break from the vigil at Delsi's bedside, leaving Ordel to spend time alone with his ailing wife. Averil sat with Netta in her audience chamber coaching her in preparation for the meetings she would now be attending in her mother's place. Evelar stood silent by the door and I sat by Netta, her hand grasping mine in mute evidence of her continuing worry.

"My Lady, I am sorry to disturb you," Atwin said to Averil as he strode into the chamber. He nodded to Netta and me.

"Nonsense, you are always welcome," said Averil.

"I merely came to bid you both goodbye," he said. "For the moment."

"Oh?" said Averil.

"I must return home, for my father will insist on being present at the conference," he said, smiling ruefully. "I have delayed too long and I will never hear the end of it if he realises how much he has already missed. I must bring him while we are still in preliminary talks, before the main conference begins. He is very stubborn about these things."

The Princess Regent sighed regretfully. "I suppose we have to put up with him," she said in resignation. "I hope you will accompany him?"

"My hope is the same."

"Is he likely to refuse your attendance?"

"With my father it is hard to say. I never quite know how he will react to my suggestions. No doubt he will fight me every step of the way."

"Oh dear," said Averil in dismay. "Is he still accusing you of treason every time you make a decision?"

"Of course," he said, with only the briefest hint of pain in his tone. "I work around him as well as I am able but I am used to it now," he said bitterly. "I think there should be no doubt of my presence here."

"I am glad of that," the Regent said. "Forgive me if I am blunt, Atwin, but your father is now totally incapable of making a rational decision. We need you here."

"Thank you for your confidence in me, Averil."

"It is well deserved," she replied. "I only wish you could take Evelar with you, just to be sure."

My head snapped up, a silent *'No, no, no,'* escaping me as our eyes met across the room.

"I would welcome that," said Atwin, turning to him. "What do you say, my friend?"

"I..." Evelar hesitated.

'Please no,' I whispered into his mind.

Averil held up a hand. "I am sorry, dear Atwin it was an idle wish."

I breathed a sigh of relief. Netta gave me a puzzled look. "What is wrong, Mym?" she whispered.

"Nothing now," I replied without explaining further.

"Unfortunately," Averil continued. "I cannot let him go this time. I need him to help me keep these kings in line, even if they know not that he watches in secret."

"Of course, Your Highness," said the Prince.

"I will hold the talks as long as I can. The Kings will understand. Travel safely, Atwin and return soon."

"I will, My Lady," he said, bowing. "Princess," he bowed to Netta, then turned and strode from the room.

"What was that all about?" asked Netta when he was gone.

"It is very sad," Averil replied. "I know it sounds horrid, but every sovereign in the council will be glad when King Gerard is no more," she said with vehemence.

"Why?"

"Some years ago, Gerard was captured by the kalkar. He managed to escape, but they did something to his mind and he has never been the same since." Averil sighed sadly. "He was once a great leader and a brilliant tactician, but soon after his capture his wife was killed by poison. His mind broke completely and he actually blamed Atwin for the outrage.

"The Prince was only ten years of age. He ran away." She hesitated. "Few people know that he actually came here. We sheltered him in his grief until he was ready to return. When he did, his father denounced him publicly, and only the emergency intervention of the council prevented him from proclaiming another heir.

"Gerard has declined rapidly and he is now quite insane. For the past ten years Atwin has performed the duties of king in his father's name. Unfortunately, Gerard thinks he is a usurper and refuses to abdicate. He is totally unfit to rule, but we can do nothing to help young Atwin's cause."

She sighed once again. "The Prince hides his pain well, but we all know it is there. All we can do is offer our wholehearted support and admiration, for he is as brilliant as once his father was. The waiting is hard for all, but we must endure."

Later that day, Netta and Kandi were talking in the garden as I sat quietly to one side, observing. Evelar was working, listening in on Averil's discussions with the assembled kings, and I missed his presence.

I was not important enough in the hierarchy of Averil's advisors to be invited to attend such meetings, and Netta had decided to forgo them to spend time with Kandi, who was too young.

"It is high time you decided to come to the garden, Netta," Kandi was saying. "I was beginning to think you were avoiding me."

"Why would you say that, Kandi? You know what has been happening."

"I know you are worried about your mother, but honestly Netta, you have been positively aloof."

"Kandi, what are you talking about?"

"Nothing," she grumbled.

"Kandi, what have I done?"

"Ignoring me and monopolising Atwin, anyone would think you did not want me around!"

"That is untrue, Kandi."

Kandi grumbled, but smiled. "So, what shall we do today?"

"You tell me," said Netta. "Your choice."

Kandi clapped her hands mischievously. "Oh good! Come on, I have something planned."

As they hurried from the garden I heard a familiar voice in my head. *'Stay there, I'm on my way.'*

"Mym?" Netta called, seeing me hang back.

"You go," I said. "I like the quiet here."

Moments after they left, Evelar was there in the garden and I rushed into his waiting arms. When he eventually released me from a passionate embrace I looked about nervously.

"Someone might come," I whispered.

"So?"

He had me giggling again at that. "Why are you here? Are the meetings over for the day?"

"No, but I need to talk to you."

"What's wrong?" I asked, worried at the serious tone in

his voice.

"I need to follow Atwin," he began and I shook my head, opening my mouth to protest. But he shushed me and tapped his head. "In here," he said, by way of explanation.

"Oh," I said with relief. "Why?"

"As Averil said, it's vital that Atwin attends the conference. But there's a chance his father will resist and I need to be there in my mind to nudge him the right way if needed."

"I can help," I began, but he shook his head.

"This will be easier my way. I'm sorry, my love. I'm afraid I might be a bit distant for a while and I wanted you to know why."

I gave a sad smile. "I understand."

"Just think of it as work. I should be fine at night," he said suggestively, and I giggled again.

So he sat himself down in a secluded corner of the garden to concentrate on his long distance psychic surveillance. I had no intention of letting him go off without me, so I settled down nearby and carefully reached out to him with my mind.

Though he insisted that he did not need assistance, his mission seemed to be taking a sinister turn, and I suspected he would need me soon in spite of his confidence. I had to be careful or he would feel my presence, but his mind was already far away. I hooked on to his consciousness and listened.

The young man strode purposefully down the corridor. Lamps illuminated the narrow passage periodically, revealing the concern in his eyes. Calib was heartily sick of trying to reason with the ailing king, whose ridiculous accusations left him fuming with anger.

These regular visits were tedious enough without having to put up with the old man's continuous complaints about his 'disloyal' brother. Calib approached the door to his father's study in apprehension.

The guard on duty snapped to attention as the Prince came, saluting smartly. Calib hesitated before opening the door. He squared his shoulders, took a deep breath and reached resolutely for the door handle.

When the Prince entered, his father was sitting in his favourite chair by the window, a glass of something potent in his hand. Calib politely cleared his throat to gain the old man's attention.

"Come in, Cal," he said, turning to face him.

The Prince went to his father and knelt at his feet. He had learned long ago that this was the best way to placate his father, but he always resented it.

"Rise, my son," said the King. "Your loyalty gladdens my heart."

"You sent for me, Father?"

"Yes. Where is your brother?" He spat the word, his voice full of contempt.

"I received word today that he is in Shirall, Sire."

"What pressing business calls him there?" asked the King rudely.

"Sire," said Calib, hesitating. "The Queen has returned." The Prince stepped back, anticipating his father's fury.

"What?" the King of Drasmil exclaimed. "Did he then leave without seeing fit to consult me?" he asked in anger.

"You had one of your fits, Father," the Prince tried to explain. "You have been delirious for several weeks."

"Do not lie to me, Calib," the old king said furiously. "Has your brother managed to steal you away from me as well as the rest of my household?" He rose quickly and went to the window.

"Forgive me, Father. My words were not necessary."

"You are forgiven, My Son." The King returned to his seat and took a long swig from his glass. "Still, I seem to have lost track somewhere," he said in confusion. "What have I been doing?"

"I just told you, father, you have been delirious."

"Ah yes, so you did." His anger flared anew. "I suppose your treacherous brother drugged my wine again!"

"Father, that is not at all fair!" the Prince retorted.

"Do not talk back to me, Calib," the King shouted.

"I am sorry father," he said mildly. "I spoke hastily."

"It is of no moment."

'Have you heard enough, Mym?' said Evelar's voice in my head. I abruptly pulled out of the mental link I had made and looked about myself nervously. I felt guilty for my breech of etiquette, feeling even worse for the carefully masked touch of hurt in his tone. But how could I help him if I did not know what was going on?

The cloaked rider entered the clearing at a trot and skidded to a stop. He dismounted in a fluid movement and his horse moved to the stream to drink, obviously familiar with the spot. Calib stood slowly from where he had been sitting by the stream, one hand resting on the hilt of his sword.

Hearing the slight sounds, the rider spun and then froze. The cloaked man seemed to relax as he faced the Prince. Calmly he reached up and pushed the hood back, revealing his face. Calib's eyes opened wide as they locked with those of his brother. Then he grinned delightedly and in two steps was grasping Atwin's hand in a warm greeting.

"How is father?" asked Atwin.

"The same as always," Calib answered. "The delirium

has passed."

"I suppose that means another tongue lashing for me."

"Probably."

"Tell me, Cal, does he still dote on you?"

"Unbearably."

"They tell me you are the only person he will listen to now. What is it like?"

"What do you mean?" Calib asked.

"What is it like to talk and have him listen?"

"He really does not listen all that often, 'Win. Only when it suits him."

"At least he does listen sometimes," said Atwin bitterly.

"It is hell, brother," Calib burst out. "All he ever thinks about is your supposed 'disloyalty' and whenever I speak out to defend you he turns on me. Then it only takes one word from me and he is back to being the 'good-old-loving-father'." His voice dripped sarcasm. "I put up with his moods for at least two hours every time he summons me and I never know how often that will be. It is getting so I feel I am about to crack, myself."

"Please do not say that, Cal."

"It is true. He thinks he has me twisted around his little finger and all the while I am hiding my true feelings from him just to keep it that way. If that is not madness, I know not what is."

"That is good sense, brother, not madness. If I had been smart enough to do that I would probably be wearing the crown by now. It surprises me that you are not."

"I refused it."

"What?"

"He has offered several times to proclaim me and I have refused. Another offer is about due."

"Why do you not take it?"

"Atwin, please!" he said in anguish. "The crown belongs

to you in every possible way and I have no right to take it from you. There is not a person alive who could convince me otherwise."

Atwin clasped his brother's shoulder in unspoken gratitude. "Shall we face the demon together?" he said, and quickly mounted. Calib grinned and followed suit.

"What do you think you're doing?"

I jumped and turned in surprise. Somehow Evelar had managed to seek me out even in the grip of his surveillance, without me realizing that he had felt me in his mind, nor that he was coming to find me.

"I'm listening. What does it look like I'm doing?"

He said nothing, watching me with arms folded in front of himself and a painful, betrayed look on his face.

"Relax, Sand," I said and he jumped at my unexpected use of his Art name. "I'm no spy."

He frowned then and I suddenly realised what my meddling must look like, and how much it was hurting him. I stood to face him.

"Don't you trust me?" I said and my voice caught on my words.

He softened then and came closer. "Of course I do," he said. "But..." he sighed painfully. "Should I?" he whispered.

I could not speak around the lump in my throat and blinked back the sudden tears. He groaned and pulled me roughly to him.

"I'm sorry, I shouldn't have said that," he said, stroking my hair.

I laughed through the tears. "You're not regretting 'getting involved' are you?"

He lifted my chin with one forefinger, forcing me to meet his eyes.

"Never," he whispered.

*

The brothers waited patiently as their father stood at the window. They could see the tenseness in the muscles of his shoulders and back, and his temper was almost palpable. Finally, the old man spun around to face them. His face was contorted with rage, and his eyes burned with hatred as he looked at Atwin.

"So you finally decide that I am sane enough for your company?"

Atwin exchanged a bewildered look with his brother. "Father..." he began.

"Do not call me that!" the old king screamed. "Your latest actions convince me even more that you are unworthy of that privilege."

"How have I angered you?"

"Do not insult me with your protestations of innocence. You take advantage of my illness to leave Drasmil without consulting me. You have been off who knows where and only now do I find that you have been gone for almost three months."

"I was called to the north on pressing business."

"Nonsense," he said scornfully. "Why would they send for you and see fit not to consult me?"

"Father, you have been ill. I could not wait for you to recover."

"Of course I have been ill. I do not doubt you had something to do with it," he accused. "What was so urgent?"

"Kalkar are on the move. I was called for advice."

"So you had to poison me to stop me from keeping you here?"

"That is untrue, Father," Calib burst out. "And it is unfair of you to accuse your son!"

"You keep out of this, Calib," the King said coldly. "What brings you crawling back?" he snapped to Atwin.

"Father, I came to escort you to the conference."

"Ah, yes. When do the meetings start?"

"Within a week."

"Fine. I will go to Shirall. Calib will come with me." He looked at Atwin in contempt. "You will stay here."

"But..."

"No buts. Calib comes with me. You stay here."

"But Father, I must be allowed to go!"

"Must?" the King screamed in rage. "You are too impudent for your own good. Calib will accompany me and you will stay here."

"Yes, Father," said Atwin in suppressed anger.

"Father, do you really think that is wise?" said Calib.

Atwin spun to stare incredulously at his brother as he continued.

"After all, he is already gaining too much influence here."

"Calib, what are you saying?" Atwin asked his brother in anguish. The younger prince ignored him.

"Would you leave him here alone and unguarded, where he can further consolidate his own position?"

Atwin stared at his brother in dawning horror. "Cal, no..." His voice was choked.

The King looked from one to the other and began to laugh. "Why Cal, you make me proud," he said in delight. "I had not looked at it that way. I thought I had lost you, my son, but I see that you are as loyal as ever. What shall we do with him?"

"We could lock him in a dungeon," said Calib with a wicked smile that struck Atwin's heart with grief.

"No..." Atwin whispered and the King laughed.

"No," said the King, turning back to the window.

As Atwin began to hang his head in sorrow, Calib caught his brother's arm in a firm grip. He said nothing, but he gave his brother a broad grin and a wink that spoke volumes.

"If I lock him up," said the King, "he will be free minutes after my back is turned." He spun around to face Calib. "If he is as popular as you say?"

Calib nodded in agreement.

"I think I will have to watch him myself. I will not leave a serpent behind to poison my realm against me!" He looked at Calib. "I am sorry, my son, but you will have to stay here and watch things."

"Yes, Sire," the younger prince said.

The old king returned to gazing out the window, turning his back on Atwin. He spoke over his shoulder to Calib. "Get him out of here, son, and do not let him out of your sight until we leave. Make sure he is ready in two hours."

"Yes, Father," Calib said.

The brothers turned as one and left their father's study. They strode side by side down the corridor under the watchful eyes of the guard. Once they had turned the corner and were out of hearing range Atwin caught his brother in a rough embrace.

"Cal, I thought I had lost you," he said shakily. "Never do that to me again."

"I am sorry, but it had to be done and I had no time to warn you. Besides, it was your reaction that convinced him."

"Brother, you are a wonder," he said in admiration.

"Sometimes, Brother, it is best to advocate his prejudice in order to gain that which you desire."

"Your wisdom does you credit."

"It stems from experience. Come, we must get you ready."

'Are you sure you're not a spy?' asked Evelar in my

mind.

'*Don't you trust me?*' I said, a little guilty.

He chuckled. '*Since you're going to keep listening in anyway, you may as well come and join me.*'

'*I thought you'd never ask!*'

And that was that.

ELEVEN

"But Mother, why not?"

Netta and I trailed along behind, not really wanting to be drawn into the argument.

"Kandina," Averil said, and by the use of her full name Kandi should have known that she was going too far. "You know very well that you are too young to witness the council in action. When you are older and more experienced in these matters you will be able to attend."

"But the next conference is not for another three years!"

"By then you should be ready."

"I do not want to wait until then. I will be seventeen in two months."

"And you will not be of age for another two years."

"Netta, you think I am old enough do you not?"

Averil raised a hand imperiously. "Netta knows that one must be able to control one's mind before she displays it to others. Be a little more mature, Kandi and a little less jealous."

Kandi looked an appeal at her cousin.

"I am sorry Kandi, but your mother is right."

"You may wait for us in my garden, if you like," said the Regent.

"Come along, Kandi," I said, leading her away, while Netta and Averil moved on to the council chambers.

"I never get to do anything!" Kandi pouted.

When we were out of sight of the others, Kandi tore her

arm from my grip and raced ahead. When she reached the end of the corridor she turned, not right toward her mother's garden, but left toward her own quarters. I breathed a sigh of relief and, released of my burden, went in search of a place from which to listen in on the conference.

When I encountered Evelar, closeted and listening, the conference was already under way.

"What have I missed?" I asked.

"Not a lot," he replied, no longer surprised at my ability to appear in all of his secret places. I settled down beside him to listen.

"Kalkar activity has increased tenfold in the last two months," Tarnel, the King of Tellemot, was saying. "I suspect that this phenomenon is in direct relation to our proximity to Shirall, since the dark ones seem to be concentrating here."

"But why are they so interested in us? Chasing us from our home, making us hide down here. What is it about Shirall that so interests them?" asked Netta.

"We know not, Your Highness," said Atwin.

"It may be that we need to investigate this further," suggested Tarnel. "If this is a precursor to invasion, we need to know."

"You are probably right," said Averil. "Lenent, have you seen any evidence of kalkar in Zelona?" she asked.

"We have encountered what look like kalkar sites," he answered. "And several villages claim to have been attacked by what the people call 'dark robed people with burning eyes who come at night.' That sounds very like kalkar to me."

"Prince Atwin," said Derrek, the King of the Fillens. "Have you, in your recent travels, discovered anything concerning kalkar and their movements?"

There was a pause before Atwin replied. "I travelled along the trade route as far as the Dragon foothills and I noticed several abandoned sites. I think Lenent will know what I mean when I say that they 'felt' like kalkar."

"It is not something you can miss," the King of Zelona agreed. "The atmosphere is horrible for days after. It is as if the very ground has been fried by the evil that has been there."

"There is a smell too, dark and smoky," said Atwin. "It clings to everything."

"We certainly need to find out what is going on," said Averil. "Have you any suggestions, Your Highness?"

"I carry with me ancient maps from our library in Drasmil," Atwin replied. "They show accurately the position of past kalkar incursions in our lands. These we will compare with those held in the library here and if our study is profitable we can pin-point the most likely places of any future occupation," he said.

"Good," nodded Averil. "I will see what other avenues I can utilise."

"Any knowledge is helpful," said Netta. "But I would like to know more about the people who attacked the Queen, my mother."

"A good question," said Averil. "We know they were not kalkar, so we appear to be facing hostility on two fronts. Do we have any information regarding a possible human invasion?"

"I returned from the north about six weeks ago..." Atwin began.

"North?" Lenent interrupted.

There was a pause. "I was in Eeasto," he said.

"What business had you with the revealers?" asked Lenent in suspicion. "They never let outsiders into their precious College!"

"Hush, Len," Averil said. "Continue, Atwin before the fit passes," said Averil.

"Yes, quickly," said Tarnel. "Before he wakes up."

I looked a question at Evelar in the darkness of our hole.

"King Gerard is in one of his trances," he whispered. Then he stood up and was gone, the slight movement of the curtain which separated us from the conference room the only evidence of his passage.

"Speed is essential, Atwin," said Evelar.

"Who are you?" asked Lenent suspiciously.

"My lords," Averil said. "This is Evelar, a high ranking revealer, and he is here at my request."

"The Prince was with us at Eeasto at our invitation," the revealer said simply. "Tell them quickly, my friend," he said.

Atwin hurried to explain. "I was meeting with the College healers, searching for a solution to my father's... illness."

"I see," said Lenent with an embarrassed cough.

"But while I was there," Atwin hurried on. "I also consulted their library for information on previous invasion events, both kalkar and human."

"What possessed you to do that?" said Tarnel.

"I noticed several small towns along the foothills that had suffered attacks. I wanted to see if it was indicative of a trend or something new. It pays to be prepared."

Derrek nodded. "The Chedd River Path is becoming increasingly hazardous. Attacks by the mountain people have doubled in the past few months. I think that they may be under the influence of some other force, since until now they have been relatively friendly."

"In any case, I think this is strong proof of the urgency of our situation," Atwin continued. "I have placed guard posts at strategic points along the trail. The villages in the surrounding areas have been alerted and they have prepared signal fires and runners. If anything occurs we will know it."

"We must secure that route," Derrek said urgently. "If trade is severed between our two countries everyone else will be adversely affected.

"This, then is where we must concentrate our efforts," Averil said. "Has anyone else any information which may help?"

"Umbro and I have both encountered trouble from The Heights, as well as from the Dragon Mountains," said Erris, the King of Mytar. "Recently we joined forces to combat the problem. We have increased surveillance, of course and have created signal points. If any village sees one of our fires they know to be ready. But the incidents are as yet few."

"The mountain people are increasing in strength," said Umbro, the softly spoken King of Yerterma. "Perhaps there is a connection between our troubles and that in the west."

"That is not possible," said Lenent. "There is a lot of very rugged terrain between the east and the west. There is no way the two could be connected."

"Excuse me," said Umbro, "but my country is separated from Mytar by seemingly impassable mountains, yet Erris and I are in constant contact. We can expect no less of the mountain tribes."

"Gentlemen," said Netta. "The tribes have lived in mountainous country for many generations and they are very resourceful. We are all too concerned with our individual problems to notice the similarities which are so obvious. Could it not be that the kalkar are using the mountain people to weaken our borders in preparation for a coming attack?"

There was a long pause and I envisioned the Kings looking sheepishly at each other.

Finally, Atwin spoke. "Your Highness, I think that may be true. If we do nothing, all our lands will suffer. However, if we join together we may just be able to repel this danger before it gains hold. Perhaps it is time to discuss the alliance."

"Be silent, traitor!" Gerard suddenly burst out. He must have awoken unnoticed from his trance. "Who are you to speak for my kingdom? You seek to undermine my authority and take charge of my affairs! Only I will speak for Drasmil."

"Be calm, Sire," said Averil. "He is your son, Atwin."

"This is not my son," he spat. "The boy who was he was lost to me years ago. Now I suffer the plots of a snake who seeks my throne!"

"Father, please," Atwin entreated. "Our land is ravaged by bandits and you speak of traitors where there are none."

"See the feigned solicitude of the faithless serpent! Will you sit idly by while he endeavours to injure my person?"

"Why must we listen to the ravings of a madman?" Derrek exclaimed.

"I see I am not welcome here," said Atwin. "I will leave you to your plans. This is no place for a family quarrel."

"Atwin, sit down," said Averil.

"Your Majesty," said Tarnel. "Do not be more of a fool than you need to be."

"Fool?" said Gerard in a strangled voice. "How dare you..."

As the mad king's voice died in an astonished grunt, I noticed a blue glow coming under the curtain into my little hole.

"Your Highness, sit down," said Netta. "Your Majesty, your sanity fails you and you forget where you are." The silence as she paused was almost audible. "None will speak of treason unproven in this conference. We are on the brink of a conflict more severe than anything that has occurred in almost twenty years." Her voice as she continued was filled with a deep emotion. "My mother lies in her chamber consumed by an illness that cannot be explained, and we sit here bickering like children!"

She took a deep breath, regaining control of her voice, and continued. "Let me suggest that we close this meeting. Let us all think on what has occurred and turn our minds to the common aim. We will return on the morrow to discuss our ideas and prepare a strategy."

There was a great scraping of chairs as the assembled monarchs all rose to bow to the Princess. Unable to resist, I peeked through the curtain. The blue nimbus which originated from the amulet about her neck shone about the Princess.

As she moved toward the door, she extended one arm to Atwin and the other to Evelar. They fell in beside her and the blue light expanded to engulf all three, proclaiming her complete trust in these two who had faced suspicion, before it faded into nothing.

Averil rose silently and followed them out of the room, leaving the stunned monarchs staring after them in awed amazement. I carefully let the curtain fall back into place and slipped out of the spy-hole.

Standing in the tower room, thinking about what Netta had said, I stared down at the dormant kalkar outside the wall and wondered. I was convinced that I could find the answers if I just reached into that disturbing collective consciousness and asked.

"You might get that chance," said a familiar voice behind me.

I spun in surprise as Evelar came to me and took my hands, his happiness washing over me and bringing that compulsive thrill bubbling up from deep inside.

"Why are you here? I thought you would be back at the conference!"

He chuckled. "I thought you would be looking for me there. What are you doing up here?"

"I asked first!"

"I've been given a new assignment, so I'm excused."

"Oh?"

"Averil has asked me to find out what I can about the kalkar threat, and why they seem so selective in their occupation."

"Oh! So you think we should try it then?"

"I can't think of a better place to start."

"Well let's go then!" I exclaimed. "Oh, but... dormant or active? Which would be better?"

"No time like the present," he replied. "It's probably safer in daylight. We know they're able to feel, so hopefully they'll be conscious enough to answer."

"I wonder if they dream?"

"Let's find out."

We looked down at the pack gathered below and he slipped his arms about my waist from behind. I felt a rush of excitement for what we were about to do. This was the first time we had attempted a full mind link, completely different to the simple mind reading and eavesdropping I had experienced so far. I would have to give in and immerse myself in his mind, allowing him to get right inside my head.

I was finally ready. I closed my eyes and opened my mind, all shields down, and waited in anticipation. When it came it was so easy. His mind slipped gently into mine and we were melded utterly, one thought away from total fusion. For a moment we hung there in blissful union, savouring the most intimate of joinings, nothing hidden and everything sacred.

I felt his pleasure within me and his thought filled me.

'I'd almost forgotten how wonderful this can be. I've been working alone for so long.'

His mind picked me up and took me with him, down to where the enemy waited, and focused in on one random creature. Hovering at the edge of its mind we peeked inside at the alien consciousness sleeping just beneath the surface. Its dreadful dreams took us into a world of fire and fear.

There it was underneath, that group mind joining it to all its fellows even in the deep sleep of dormancy. We sent a careful thought into that mind, a simple question to start: *why are you here?*

The thought went swirling and bouncing from mind to mind within the collective, returning with the same answer each time it hit: *stop her...*

Stop her? Who did they mean? We sent a new question: *who do you want to stop?*

Again it went whirling away, the answer bouncing back over and over: *the one who kills...*

Another cryptic reply, but where to go from here? It was going to take forever at this rate. Maybe a more pointed question: *who is she who kills?*

It came back, this time a multitude of thoughts all with the same meaning, bouncing around in our head, hammering our mind with pain: *she comes; she kills; she takes life; she rips away; she is death...*

We reeled from the onslaught, but recovering we sent a commanding thought: *who?*

And the answer came in one reverberating wave from every voice in the collective all at once, a long drawn out sigh of anguish: *Leeeeennaaaaa!!!*

With that shocking thought we were cruelly ejected from that great collective mind and sent crashing back into ourselves, our own meld shattered too. My knees gave way under my own weight and the sudden cold loneliness of my single separate mind left me shivering and fighting to stay conscious. An incredible grief struck me dumb. We sat huddled together on the floor, stunned and racked with pain.

TWELVE

My eyes hurt, so I kept them shut. The soft pillow felt like rock under my head. I have no idea how I made it to my room, I must have passed out and been carried there. I tried to lift my head but groaned in agony and gave up.

"Stay still, my love."

A gentle hand was stroking my brow and the pain eased somewhat. I forced my eyes open and tried to focus in the dim firelight.

"I'm sorry," he whispered. "It's not supposed to be ended like that." I felt his concern and guilt wash over my bruised mind. "I should have been ready. I shouldn't have let it happen."

"It's not your fault!" I said, struggling to rise, but a wave of dizziness hit me and I sank back down.

"Don't rush. I'm so sorry, my love," he said then. "I should never have gone against my professional judgement. You're untrained and there's a reason why the College keeps it secret. You could have been seriously damaged."

"Stop it!" I felt mortified. "I'll be fine!"

"I got carried away and it won't happen again."

I opened my mouth to protest but he silenced me with a shake of the head. "Someone's coming," he said. In a flash he was gone, dissolving into the shadows as I heard a knock at the door.

"Come," I called.

The door opened slowly and Netta entered. Seeing me

lying in bed, she rushed to my side.

"Mym, are you ill?"

I smiled. "Just a headache, I'll be fine."

"When you were not at breakfast I was worried. Do you want me to send for the physician?"

"No, Netta, it's nothing. I just need to rest."

She gave a dubious nod. "I have to head in to the conference soon, I just wanted to see what had happened to you. Is there anything you need?"

I shook my head and winced at the sudden pain. "Could you ask Kandi to come later? I need her to take me to the library, I want to see what I can find out about Naali for you."

"There is plenty of time for that, Mym. You rest your poor head." She patted my arm. "See you later."

I hurried to follow Kandi as she fairly ran down the corridor. The girl was still unhappy about being excluded from the conference, and her attitude toward me was less than respectful. She had been distinctly put out when I asked her to show me the way to the palace library.

Reaching a nondescript door at the end of a long corridor lit by too few lanterns, Kandi paused to let me catch up. Then, without word or ceremony, she opened the door and gestured for me to enter.

The unmistakable smell of musty parchment hit me as I stepped past her and found myself in a cavernous room filled with row upon row of books. The rough rock walls were hung with old tapestries, in front of which were set huge freestanding bookcases eight shelves high, lining the walls.

More bookcases radiated out toward the centre of the room, where a large circular couch surrounded a round hearth and a huge round iron stove with a thick flue reaching up into the darkness of the cavern roof.

"They have to keep the fire lit day and night," said Kandi in a hushed voice. "To keep the books dry."

"Do you often come here?"

"Yes, before Netta came I was here every day," she shrugged. "I had nothing better to do."

"It's amazing!" I whispered, looking about in awe. All those books! How was I ever going to find what I needed? "Is there a librarian?"

"There is an old man who tends the library. He keeps the fire going and wanders about straightening shelves and reading. I believe he has a room somewhere where he lives and one of the servants brings him food. I have heard that he never leaves here. Even when the palace was up above ground, before it was moved down here, he never left the library."

"Where will I find him?"

"He will find you," she said as she headed off to find a book. A few minutes later, while I was still gazing about wondering where to look first, she reappeared and flopped down on the couch to read.

Feeling a gentle psychic pull, I drifted to the left, slipping into the aisle between two book cases, scanning the shelves without really knowing what I was looking for. There waiting for me was Evelar, a frown knitting his brow as he came close, a hand at my waist.

"You should not be here," he whispered. "You should be sleeping."

I smiled at his concern. "I told you I'm fine. I need to do this, for Netta."

Our research progressed slowly, frustratingly so. The legend of Naali was simply not documented. As for the so-called 'sacred halls', nowhere was there even the slightest reference to such a place. It seemed that with the loss of Naali all knowledge of his existence faded away. The farther back we took the search, the less extant material of any sort could we find.

Finally, buried within a later copy of a chronicle some eight hundred years old, I found a cryptic reference to Rexa's quest. From this meagre beginning I managed to chase up a few more fragments, but the clues they offered were dubious at best. At last we had found all we could and presented our findings to the council. For the first time, I was admitted into the chamber to report to the assembled kings.

"The most I can tell you," Evelar said to the gathering, "is that Rexa himself already had possession of the Queen's Amulet, which he gave to his granddaughter."

"At some point," I said, "another appeared which was kept by the King. This must have been Naali."

"Somehow it was lost," Evelar continued. "The sources are vague, but from a certain point all references to the King's amulet dry up."

"Also, and I think this is important, from the moment Naali disappeared from history there has not been a king in Shirall." I finished.

"So the amulet itself confers kingship, when paired with Leena," mused Tarnel.

"Yes, Your Majesty," I replied. "I think Leena is the one who rules, since she was the first."

"This alone accounts for the fact that Naali has simply dropped out of the record," said Evelar.

"If he was the ruler, history would have followed him," I concluded.

"How do we find him again?" asked Lenent.

Evelar shrugged. "The hermit spoke of the 'Sacred Halls,' or the 'Chambers of the Exalted,' but there is no reference anywhere to either name."

"So we have reached a dead end?" asked Netta quietly.

"So I fear," I replied.

"Perhaps not," said Averil.

"What do you mean?" asked Atwin.

"You said that the record simply stops mentioning Naali," said Averil.

"Yes," I replied.

"It is possible, then, that Naali simply vanished from human sight, so to speak."

"That would seem a logical conclusion," said Evelar.

"Then we are not going to find him with human eyes."

"What do you suggest?" Atwin asked.

"We have our greatest ally right here," said Averil, looking at her niece. "We have Leena."

Ordel had carried his wife to the garden, where she sat with her back against a tree. Delsi believed that the search would be more effective when cast amongst nature.

"What must I do?" asked Netta nervously.

"First you must relax," said Delsi. "Now, I want you to sit with your legs crossed and your arms rested in your lap." Netta sat as requested. "Close your eyes and clear your mind. Now, reach out with your mind to the awareness in the amulet. Now ask the spirit your question: where do we find Naali?"

As we watched, the amulet began to glow, and the aura grew to encase Netta in its light. Then it faded and with a sigh Netta opened her eyes.

"She does not know." Netta said, head bowed.

"Then we will ask something else," said Delsi.

Netta closed her eyes again.

"Ask her: where are the Sacred Halls?"

Again the amulet began to glow. This time, as it grew

to encase the girl, the white glow changed to blue. Netta remained long in trance. Then, of a sudden, her eyes snapped open and the glow flared brightly before dissipating. Netta jumped to her feet.

"The Nursery!" she cried.

"Follow me," said Averil.

As we all raced to follow, Delsi called out to her husband to stay behind with her. Netta and I raced after Averil. Suddenly, Netta cried out again.

"No, not this way," she said. "I mean the old nursery, upstairs."

"Upstairs?" asked Averil, bewildered.

"Yes, in the old palace above ground."

"But there is nothing there. We brought it all down here twelve years ago."

"There is something on the wall."

The door creaked as I pushed it open. The dust was thick on the floor. As we entered, our eyes were drawn instantly to the faded mural on the far wall. It was a map, beautifully detailed with writing, a story, superimposed over it. Above, in elaborate lettering, were the words 'The Song of Rexa.' I hung back as Netta and the Regent moved closer and reached out to my revealer with my mind.

'What is it?' I heard his voice in my head.

'I think you'd better come up here. Bring some parchment and something to draw with.' I broke the link and joined my companions.

"I had forgotten this even existed," said Averil.

Back in the conference room, we quietly discussed our discovery with the assembled monarchs. Even Ordel had left Delsi's side to join us, eager to help in the planning. The drawing had taken some considerable time, as the accuracy of the map was quite astounding. The text was equally intriguing.

"Look here," Averil said. "According to this, Rexa actually created Naali himself, from his magic ring and other pieces of gold. Then he sealed his own spirit within, just as he had sealed his wife's spirit in Leena."

"But it still does not tell us where to find Naali," said Atwin.

"No," I replied. "It only says that Naali was lost."

"Then we are still at a dead end," said Netta.

"Not at all," Evelar said. "The map shows the exact location of the Sacred Halls; here, high in the western Dragon Mountains."

I pointed out the spot. "The hermit told us we should start there. Once we get there we should be able to pick up the trail."

"Should?" said Ordel. "I like not the uncertainty of all this. We cannot even be sure the location is correct."

"I admit we will be taking a great risk if we chase this up," I said slowly, "but it is the best clue we have."

The next day the council met again to discuss the coming mission to find Naali. Once again I was excluded, so I squeezed in next to Evelar in his hidden spot to listen.

"Netta will have to go, of course," said Averil.

"Is that a good idea?" said Ordel in a worried tone.

"She wears Leena now," Averil explained. "Only she can trace Naali. Without her we will never find the amulet."

"Who else?"

"Atwin also must go," she said.

"What?" Gerard interrupted.

"He is the one destined to carry Naali and he must be present when they find him."

"I will not allow it," said the mad king angrily. "You

cannot trust the life of your queen to a traitor!"

"The matter is not open for debate, Your Majesty," said Averil sternly. "Now, are there any further suggestions?"

"Your Highness," said Tarnel. "I believe we should send the revealer also."

"Oh?"

"The revealers are known for their uncanny ability to sniff out information. If the Princess cannot find Naali, then perhaps he could."

"A wise precaution," Averil said. Then she raised her voice slightly. "Evelar?" My revealer slipped out from our place behind the curtain. "Are you willing to undertake such a task?"

"Of course, Your Highness," he said.

'Not without me, you're not!' I admonished silently.

'Hush, my love,' he replied. *'I won't let that happen.'*

"I would like to go too," said Ordel in a quiet voice.

"No," said Averil.

"I must, to keep Netta safe."

"Ordel, no, Netta can look after herself and she has the Queen's Amulet to protect her."

"I want to help."

"You can help much more here. Delsi needs you. She needs your strength. Please."

"Then I will stay."

"If I may, Your Highness," Evelar said. "I suggest we take Miyam along. I think she could be of use to us."

"I trust your judgment, Evelar and she has proven herself helpful so far, but would she be willing to go?"

"I believe so. Shall we ask her?"

"Of course," said Averil. "I will ring for someone to fetch her here."

"That won't be necessary, Your Highness," said Evelar. "Why don't you step out here for a moment, Mym?" he called out to me.

In chagrin, I slipped out from behind the curtain, to the astonishment of all the assembled monarchs.

Lenent actually rose in anger from his chair. "What is this?"

"Who else have you hidden behind there?" said Derrek, slightly shaken.

"No other, I assure you," said Evelar.

"How much have you heard?" asked Lenent with a frown.

I shrugged. "Enough," I said.

"Miyam has a habit of eavesdropping," said Evelar.

'You wouldn't want me to get rusty, would you?' I teased.

"Miyam," said Averil, "would you be willing to take part in this mission?"

"Of course, Your Highness," I said, almost unconsciously mimicking Evelar.

"Excuse me," said Umbro, "but can we trust this girl?"

"Remember we would not have learned as much as we have without her," said Averil.

"I trust her," said Ordel. "I have known her for many years."

"Surely you realise that familiarity does not always guarantee loyalty?" said Lenent.

"My Lords," said Evelar. "Be calm. I'm satisfied that she's not a spy."

"How can you be sure?" Tarnel asked.

"You would doubt a revealer's word?" said Evelar in a dangerous tone.

Under that calm gaze, Tarnel shrank into his chair. "Sorry," he said in the voice of a mouse.

THIRTEEN

We planned to set off at first light, following after King Gerard and his military escort on our way towards the mountains and hopefully our first clue. We would travel a while with the King as he headed home to Drasmil, until our paths diverged. But first we had to make a path through the gathered kalkar.

Just before dawn, the soldiers formed ranks in the courtyard outside the tunnel, the first rank squashed in together in the passage behind the gate as the horde settled into position outside the wall awaiting the sun.

We stood in the tower watching the milling enemy as they moved to blockade the main gate. Netta stood clutching the Queen's Amulet in her fingers with a confused expression.

"Is Leena burning?" I whispered.

She shook her head. "No. Mother said she would burn, but I feel nothing. I do not understand!"

The sky lightened to grey and the movement below slowed. Then finally, a shaft of light flashed out low on the horizon and as one the kalkar froze with a crackling, sparking clap of sound.

Instantly, the gate swung inwards and the first soldiers used their swords to lift the protective membrane, and others dumped bucket loads of water on the foremost of the enemy, melting them into the ground.

With an ache in my soul I shut my mind to the silent screams as the tears flowed. I promised myself I would never forget the pain this assault caused the poor creatures as they died.

As the soldiers slowly pushed out of the gate, we descended from the tower and followed behind the mad king in his litter. After what seemed an eternity, passing through the second gate and down the hill, melting kalkar all the way, the column reached the road and bypassed the town, heading west.

The road was easier now, the way clear of enemy, though they still stood clustered along the roadside. We picked up the pace, the soldiers almost jogging in their eagerness to put the beleaguered queendom of Shirall behind them.

Four days out of Shirall, the column which had accompanied King Gerard broke off and headed toward Drasmil. As we watched them depart, two soldiers turned back at the King's order and came up to Atwin.

"I'm sorry, Your Highness," said one soldier with a hesitant smile. "But the King has ordered us to take you into custody."

Atwin stiffened. "He cannot be serious!"

"I'm afraid so, Your Highness."

"He knows how important this is!"

"Yes, My Lord," said the second soldier apologetically.

"I do not suppose you could ah... let me escape... so to speak?"

"Do you realise what he would do to us, Your Highness?"

"I thought as much," Atwin said, disheartened. "You could come with us," he suggested.

"And leave my family to fall prey to the King's anger? I think not, My Lord," said the first soldier. "Forgive me, Your Highness, but I must insist."

"Of course, Captain Sildez. But I will not forget."

"You must realise that I have no choice."

"Yes, Sildez," said Atwin quietly. He spurred his horse in the direction of the retreating column. The two soldiers looked shame-faced at each other and followed.

Netta and I exchanged a worried look as Evelar watched the retreating soldiers.

"They cannot do this," cried Netta. "What are we going to do?"

"We're all in this together, Netta," I said.

Evelar looked at me and I nodded in perfect agreement with his unspoken thought. Then my revealer raised his voice and called out to Atwin.

"Wait, Your Highness," he said and Atwin turned. "We'll come with you."

By mutual consent, we followed after them, while Atwin waited gratefully.

"Thank you, my friend," he said when we reached him.

Then we set out, the four of us together after Gerard's escort, with the two soldiers trailing hesitantly behind.

At the palace in Drasmil we were escorted to a small room, where we were told to await admittance into the King's presence. Atwin paced, his anger barely controlled, while Netta and I sat together on a hard bench seat. Netta was trembling and I slipped a reassuring arm about her shoulders.

Netta was sobbing. "It's not fair!" she cried. "We were finally getting somewhere!"

"It won't be for long," I tried to reassure her.

"Oh, Mym, I cannot take this anymore. This whole mess has been one delay after another. Since Mother got sick it seems all we have done is sit around and talk. We were finally doing something!"

I looked to where Evelar stood, deep in thought.

'I hope you have a plan to get us out of this,' I sent.

'I'll think of something.'

"What are we going to do?" the Princess wailed. "We need to get moving!"

Atwin stopped his pacing at that. "I promise, we will be out of here very soon, Your Highness," he said gently.

She raised her head and her eyes flashed. "My name is Netta!" she exclaimed.

He blinked in surprise. "Of course... Netta," he said. "I was just being polite."

"Well, I'm a person not a 'highness'. This is hard enough without that!"

He raised his hands in front of himself in submission. "I apologise, Netta, I meant no offense."

She sat staring at him with tears rolling down her face. "I'm so sick of sitting around. I wish people would stop skirting around what needs to be done and just let us get on with doing it!"

The Prince looked to Evelar and then back to Netta and me, his confusion evident. "What do you want me to say? I promise I will sort this out! I can deal with my father."

"Every moment sees my mother slip further into darkness and nobody seems to care. I cannot take any more of this!"

"I care," he said softly. "I promise you, we will be back on the road before you know it."

She let out a sob and in a sudden movement she threw herself toward him. He took an involuntary step back as she thudded into him, her arms clutched about his waist, sobbing into his chest.

For a moment he stood there, arms outstretched as he stared at us in consternation. I laughed in spite of myself at his expression, a study in confusion. Evelar's mask had slipped and with a chuckle he gave the Prince a wink.

Then Atwin very gently and tentatively allowed his arms

to close about her, murmuring words of comfort.

Just over an hour later, a guard conducted us to the audience chamber, where the King waited, flanked by two burly soldiers acting as bodyguards. He was dressed in full regalia, his battered crown lop-sided on his head.

"The prisoners, Your Majesty," said the guard, who then bowed and backed out of the room, closing the doors firmly after himself.

The King looked at us in some surprise. "I did not intend to have you all brought here," he said. "It is only the snake I wish to detain."

"Begging your pardon, Your Majesty," said Evelar. "But we felt it was our duty to respectfully remind you that in arresting Prince Atwin you are going against the express wishes of the Conference of Kings."

"We are not at the conference now," said Gerard in contempt. "We are in Drasmil, where my word is law. Here I do not recognise the requests of the conference. You others are free to go, but the snake does not leave these walls."

"As you wish, Your Majesty," said Evelar, and Netta looked at him in concern.

"But in all due respect," he continued. "Let me point out that in holding him here you jeopardise this mission. Atwin is needed to carry the King's amulet back to Shirall. The burden is not mine to bear. Without him, our mission will have failed before it has even begun. If our mission fails, Delsi will die."

His voice was calm and his tone conversational, but his emphasis was clear.

"And," said Evelar then in a voice that cracked like a whip. "If the Queen of Shirall dies because you are too arrogant to obey the decisions of the conference, the blame for her death will fall squarely on your shoulders and you will be guilty of high treason. The crown you so jealously guard will be taken from you and Atwin will rule in name as well as fact!"

The King sat in stunned amazement as Evelar continued, once more speaking in that deadly calm voice. "As a representative of the conference it is within my power to order you to release Prince Atwin. It would go better for you if I did not have to."

Gerard stared at the revealer. He tried to speak, but choked on his words. Then his eyes glazed over and he slumped forward in his chair.

Atwin jumped forward to catch the King before he slipped from his chair and the crown clattered as it fell to the floor. Evelar bent to pick it up.

Evelar spoke quietly to one of the soldiers, who left the room hurriedly. He locked eyes briefly with Atwin, and carefully replaced the crown on Gerard's head.

The door opened and two guards entered with a litter. With Evelar's help, Atwin gently laid his father in the litter, catching the crown as it slipped off again.

He held it in his hands only a moment longer than necessary before placing it once more on the King's head.

Atwin gazed at his father's limp form, anquish written across his face. Then he nodded to the guards, and they carried the King out of the audience chamber.

* * *

"Wait a minute," said the Maestro suddenly. "You yelled at a king?"

Sand shrugged. "It seemed like a good idea at the time."

"You sent him into a fit!"

"It achieved a purpose."

"But he's a king!"

"Well, we do have diplomatic immunity, don't we?" said Sand defensively.

"Yes, but he's a KING!"

"So?"

* * *

A servant entered, a little hesitant, and bowed to Atwin. "What is your bidding, My Lord?" he asked.

"See that my father is made comfortable," said Atwin. "Then have a meal prepared for us. We will be in my study."

"Yes, My Lord," said the servant, with more confidence.

"Oh and ask Calib to join us."

"Yes, My Lord." The servant bowed and rushed out.

"Come, my friends," said Atwin. "This place is a little too solemn for my liking."

Calib rushed into the study.

"Atwin, what are you doing here?"

"Our father had me arrested."

"He did what? Where is he now?"

"He had a fit. I suppose that means I am free to go."

"Then why are you still here?"

"I need you to do something for me. I need to know how many of our people have been touched by Father's prejudice. I need to know who my friends are. If I am not careful, this incident will cement my guilt in the minds of my enemies and that is the last thing I need."

"I think I can help you there," said a voice in the doorway. We all turned to see a revealer in the blue bordered cloak of a master. Evelar stepped forward and the Master bowed.

"Sir Artisan," he said and then he read the Art name badge at his neck. "Sand! I am honoured!"

"You are?" said Evelar uncertainly.

"Yes. You're famous, Sir. It's an honour to meet you."

"It is?"

"How should I address you, Sir?"

"I'm Evelar. How may I address you, Tong?"

"I'm Nashta, Sir."

"And how can you help us, Nashta?"

"I'm here in the employ of the King, Sir. Forgive me, Your Highness," he said to Atwin. "But I'm supposed to find evidence to expose you."

"And what have you found?" asked Atwin, a little cautiously.

"Nothing, My Lord. May I say, My Lord that in the light of today's events I'm glad. Your actions in the throne room completely exonerate you from guilt. Also," he said to Evelar, "it's well known that you're only called out for the most important cases and since you are working with the Prince he's obviously innocent."

"I am glad you feel that way," said Atwin.

"The court is full of sycophants who pay lip-service to the King, but behind closed doors most are loyal to you, Your Highness. Your enemies are few and even they are not solidly with the King. I think once they learn of how you respected the King's honour today they'll turn back to you."

"I hope you are right," said Atwin.

"Now that I know the King is wrong, I think I'll return to Eeasto and make my report to the Maestro."

"No, Nashta," said Evelar. "The King will only call for another member to take your place. I would prefer that we had someone here who knows the full story and not just the King's version."

"Of course, Sir. I had not looked at it that way."

"Where's your assistant, Nashta?"

"He's sleeping, Sir."

"Perhaps he should be kept ignorant of this."

"Why?"

"Nashta," said Evelar quietly. "I'm working without an assistant."

"Oh!" he said. "Top secret, then."

"Yes, Nashta. I would suggest that you honour it."

"Of course, Sir."

"Oh and Nashta, please stop that."

"Stop what, Sir?"

"Stop calling me Sir."

"But you're my superior, Sir."

"I'm no older than you, Nashta."

"But you're two ranks above me, Sir."

"So?"

Up on the battlements at Drasmil, Netta paced. I watched her in concern, but there was nothing I could say to calm her nerves.

"You know it's not safe to travel at night, Netta. We have to wait until morning."

"It was not a problem on the road here, Mym," she argued.

"I know, but we had the soldiers to protect us if anything happened."

"Once we leave here we will have no soldiers to protect us. What happens when we have to camp the first night out? Why not start now and travel while we can?"

"You know why not, Netta. If we wait until morning we can make a good start and pitch a secure camp before nightfall."

"I know. But it's hard waiting, Mym. I am sick of delays. Besides, there are no kalkar here."

"It's only a matter of time before they realise Leena has left Shirall. Then they will be after us."

"All the more reason why we should head off now!"

"You might get your wish," said a voice behind. Turning we saw Prince Atwin and my revealer.

"What's happened?" I asked.

"My father is waking up. I usually have longer than this.

We will have to get away before he realises what happened."

"Good," said Netta. "Time to go."

So we set off into the night. We travelled until dawn with no sign of kalkar, then continued through the day. That afternoon, we pitched camp by a stream to sleep as well as we could through the evening. Finally we were on our way.

FOURTEEN

As we rode through the rolling countryside of western Drasmil I could not shake a feeling of unease. Things had been too easy so far. Loathe to tempt fate, I chose not to mention the sense of foreboding as we rode ever nearer to the mountains, but I could tell that I was not alone in my concern.

Evelar rode far to the front, scouting the trail ahead. Netta rode quietly beside me, speaking little. Atwin rode to the rear, stopping often to glance about. Finally, the Prince rode up to us, looking worried.

"What is it?" asked Netta.

"I like this not."

"What do you mean?"

He glanced at the sky, noting the almost full moon. "We left Shirall almost two weeks ago," he said, "and in all that time there has been no sign of kalkar."

"I noticed that," said Evelar as he rejoined us. "It could be that the amulet is protecting us, but we shouldn't let it make us careless."

"One thing is certain," said Atwin. "It is making me nervous."

"Don't think about it," I said with a shudder. "We don't want to call them to us."

"Since when have you been superstitious?" asked Netta.

"I'm not," I replied. "I'm perfectly serious. We know the kalkar are skilled somewhat in mind power."

"They may just be able to read our minds," said Evelar, completing my sentence.

"And if so they could locate us by our thoughts," I concluded. "So it's safer not to think about it."

"We don't want to call them to us," said Evelar.

"I thought I said that."

'Just reiterating, my love,' he said mentally.

"What should we do?" asked Atwin.

"Just don't think about it," I said.

"Meanwhile," said Evelar, looking at the darkening sky, "it looks like we're in for a storm. I suggest we find shelter in Randok until it blows over."

The capital of the once all-powerful Randok Empire was a sorry pile of rubble. Of course, Randok was never really much of an empire. A pitiful city-state swelled by its own pride, Randok held on to its sprawling empire for less than a decade before collapsing under its own weight. As we rode through the desolate ruins I could not quite block the sense of sadness and broken spirit which permeated the place.

Evelar rode stiffly in his saddle, his face a grim mask. The amulet about Netta's neck glowed in an almost green light. As the rain beat down on our heads we disregarded our feelings of unease and searched for a building in which to shelter for the night.

The cottage we found was relatively intact, though the thatched roof was rotten and cold drafts whistled through the place. Where other, taller structures had fallen this squat little building had managed to stay erect. Silently, Atwin built a fire and we laid our cloaks out to dry.

When I awoke shivering, the fire had gone out and it was dark, and Netta and Atwin both slept nearby. I sent a mental query to my revealer where he stood on watch and a wave of welcome warmed me in the chill air.

'There's something I think you should see,' he said.

'What is it?' I asked.

'Come see, my love,' he murmured.

I found him staring out over the abandoned city, his cloak whipping madly in the gale. He held both my hands and pulled me in close, sheltering me from the cold wind. A gentle hand brushed the hair from my eyes and we gave in to the long awaited privacy of the moment.

Even in the rare abandonment of that intimate embrace I knew he was troubled. I could sense, rather than see, the direction of his gaze as he looked out over the ruins. A blue light glowed in the night, flickering and ethereal.

With a sigh of regret, Evelar took my hand and strode down into the ruins to investigate and I followed in trepidation. As we moved further into the city we could see shadowy figures moving about in the glow. From what I could see, we were witnessing an ancient battle between men and kalkar.

Evelar moved through them, knowing exactly who he was looking for. He stood squarely in front of one battling figure. The shade stood tall, his ghostly sword flashing as he felled his enemies. He was a mighty figure, wearing a silver crown. But what drew my eye was the amulet about his neck, its blue light mixing with the glow of the phantoms about us.

Suddenly, all but the figure of the King vanished.

"Who comest here to disturb the shade of King Morson of Shirall?"

"Forgive us, Your Majesty," said Evelar. "We seek the amulet you wear."

"The power of Naali is greater than the average mortal can bear. Seek not for him, lest he master thee in the end. The predestined King alone may wield the power without losing his mind and I sense that thou Art not he."

"You sense true. I am not the one, but we travel with he who is destined to bring Naali once more into the light."

"Ah. Then far must he seek. I succeeded, ere my mortal form faded from your world, in dragging that failing body as far as the tomb of the ancestors, the resting place of those who carried Naali before me. I am told thou callest it the Sacred Halls. A fitting name, for indeed it is a sacred place.

"There, with the last of my life, I gave up my burden. Naali was laid to rest. But the doings of thy world reacheth me even here and I have learned that gone is Naali from his eternal home. I regret that I cannot lead thy fledgling king to him. But I would know how thou didst summon my spirit from that place wherein I rest so contented? No mortal may call the dead from their sleep."

"It was not I, Your Majesty. But we travel also with she who carries Leena."

"Ah. Then Leena it was who called. The link between Naali and his mate transcendeth even death and calleth forth my spirit. I would see her ere I go."

Netta awoke with a start and sat up. She looked about and her eyes rested on the glowing form of the last king of Shirall. The ghost bent in front of her and Leena glowed blue in response. Transfixed, Netta reached out a hand to the ghost of Naali about the spirit's neck and the blue glow expanded to engulf her.

"Be thou at ease, my queen," said the shade of King Morson. "I bring the essence of Naali, that thee may know him. Thus may thee find him when all hope seems lost."

At that moment, Atwin stirred and rose from his blankets. He stood slowly, staring at the glowing phantom kneeling over the Princess. The ghostly king stood and faced him. The spirit looked long, then bowed in the profoundest respect. Then it disappeared.

*

As we rode, we considered our conversation with the shade of King Morson. He had answered a lot of questions. We knew now how Naali had disappeared and we hoped that the information would help when the time came to search for Naali's trail. The ghost's suggestion that Netta would know Naali now that she had seen his shade was sound and something told me that we would need that link.

"We also know that we are on the right track," I said.

"How do you mean?" asked Netta.

"The ghost told us that he took Naali to the sacred halls," said Evelar.

"And that Naali is gone from there," I added.

"Therefore, our first summation was right," said Evelar.

"Also," I continued, "if we were travelling in the wrong direction we would never have bumped into the ghost." I completed.

"Which means the map was right," said Evelar.

"I do not follow," said Atwin.

"The ghost said that he dragged his dying body to the sacred halls," I said.

"So we must be fairly close," said Evelar.

"Probably no further than a day or two of gentle travel into the mountains," I continued.

"Which we should reach within the hour," said Evelar, completing the thought. He stared at the looming mountains which dominated the landscape ahead, no longer merely sitting on the horizon.

"But how can we be sure that the mountains are the place to look?" asked Netta. "I mean, the King might have gone in any direction from Randok."

"I think not," said Evelar. "Look at this country."

"There is no other place it could be," I suggested.

"Atwin, you will agree," Evelar continued. "That any

ruin as important as the sacred halls could not have been forgotten..."

"If it was situated anywhere on these plains," I concluded.

"You are right, of course," said Atwin. "Nothing that important could be lost out here."

"Exactly," said Evelar. "Which means..."

"We're on the right track," I finished triumphantly.

"What is it with you two?" exclaimed Netta in frustration.

"What do you mean?" I asked.

"You keep finishing each other's sentences."

"We do?" we said together.

"Yes," she said. "If you were to string together everything you two just said it would sound like one person talking!"

"It would?" we said together.

"Yes!" she said with disgust. "You sound like an old married couple!"

Evelar and I looked at each other in bewilderment, and then we started to laugh as we shared a long conspiratorial moment.

"What's so funny?" Netta asked.

"Oh, nothing," I said between breaths.

"Well something is very amusing and you had better let me in on the joke!"

We stopped laughing and looked at each other, realizing what a relief it would be to let the secret out.

"Do you want to tell her, or shall I?" I said.

"You go ahead," he said with a gentle smile.

"Well? I'm waiting!" said Netta.

"Ah... actually..." I looked a question at Evelar and he raised an eyebrow. "Technically," I moved in closer to him but then turned to look at Netta. "We are married."

"What?"

"Technically we are married," said Evelar blandly, slipping an arm about my waist.

"I heard!"

"What do you mean, technically?" asked Atwin.

"Well..." I hedged. "It's not exactly official yet."

"Yet?" Netta cried.

"Perhaps you should explain," said Atwin carefully.

"The revealers live by ritual," I said. "We... I mean they... don't look at marriage the way others do. All it takes is a proper performance of the ritual in sight of witnesses."

"That sounds fairly standard to me," said Atwin.

"But the ritual serves as both the declaration of intent and the actual joining. The couple performs the ritual unannounced, without any celebrant, and is automatically married."

"We performed the ritual," said Evelar. "But there were no official witnesses."

"When?" asked Netta.

"At your banquet," I said. "We performed the ritual dance of marriage."

"That dance that caused such a stir?" she asked incredulously.

"Wait a minute," said Atwin. "There were plenty of witnesses there!"

"Not official ones," said Evelar.

"Who are the official witnesses?"

"Other members of the College of the Art," I said.

Netta shook her head in bewilderment. "I do not understand," she said. "You barely knew each other! Why would you do such a thing?"

Evelar shrugged. "We knew each other well enough to know it was right. Why wait?"

"But..." she sputtered. "How? When did you know? You were strangers!"

"Netta, please don't be angry," I said then. "We both knew from the moment we first laid eyes on each other, right back in southern Martose. We weren't strangers, really."

Atwin was chuckling under his breath. "My friend, you certainly keep your secrets well. For months you have given us the cool aloof revealer face, and the whole time you were in the grip of a secret romance! I am impressed!"

Netta was looking at me coldly. "I'm hurt," she said, pouting. "You got married and you didn't even tell me."

"It's not official," I said defensively.

"That makes no difference. In your mind you are married."

"I'm sorry," I said, looking to Evelar for support. "We didn't think it was important."

"Not important?"

"It's a private thing," said Evelar, pulling me closer and enclosing me protectively in both arms. "In the College we don't really talk about it because it only involves the couple. It's not anyone else's concern."

"But Mym is not from the College. She does not have to follow your rules!"

"My mother was a revealer," I said proudly. "I respect their ways."

"Oh," she said, and gave me a quizzical look. "I always wondered who your mother's 'people' were!"

FIFTEEN

We rode at a good pace through the morning, moving further into the mountains. The northern side of the Dragons offered a relatively easy climb, and we made good time. By afternoon we were through the highest pass. But the southern side was treacherous. Our pace slowed to a walk. At times we even had to dismount and lead the horses in single file.

Late in the afternoon we found ourselves on a dusty, ill-used road carved out of the solid rock of a towering cliff face. To the left was a sheer face, impossible to climb, to the right a deadly drop. More than aware of the vulnerability of our position, we hoped fervently that the kalkar would not catch us on this heart-stopping road when night fell.

As twilight darkened the sky we moved as quickly as we dared. Ahead, the path narrowed considerably, and we had to dismount and lead the horses. Atwin took the lead with Netta following, and myself and Evelar took the rear. As Atwin rounded yet another treacherous bend he halted suddenly.

A recent rock slide had almost covered the path, and we would have to pass dangerously close to the edge. Atwin led his sturdy horse, gingerly negotiating the narrow ledge. We all breathed a sigh of relief as he passed the slide and stood safe on the wider stretch of path at the other side. He turned, somewhat anxiously, to watch Netta's progress.

The girl's feet were confident and sure, but sadly her

mount's were not. The animal was not young and lacked the agility needed to safely traverse the distance. In addition, the horse shied away from the edge, scattering loose earth and rubble as it tried to climb higher.

Hearts in our mouths, we watched breathless. Netta was almost around the slide when the horse's scrabbling hooves loosened too much earth. The animal stumbled and, in trying to regain his balance, stepped backwards off the path.

The horse scrambled for a moment before dropping with a scream as his legs were broken. Netta's own scream echoed her mount's as she too was pulled over the edge.

Atwin had begun to run forward as the mount stumbled and now he made a desperate dive, barely managing to grab the girl's wrist as it disappeared over the side. As the rubble began to slide over the edge, Atwin searched about for something to hold on to. Then both were lost in the rubble.

When the landslide eased, Atwin could still be seen clutching a small but sturdy stump growing out of the cliff face. The Prince clambered laboriously to his feet and grabbed Netta's wrist in both hands, hauling her up. The girl caught at his wrist with her free hand and soon she was on her knees at the edge of the cliff. Then she was standing as Atwin held her closely to him and both stared down at the ground so far below.

With a shudder, Netta buried her face against his chest as she realised what had almost happened. Slowly, the two made their way to safety. I stared at the frighteningly narrow, rubble-strewn path. Our little group was separated and there was no other way around.

"You should probably go next," said Evelar in apprehension.

Terrified, I stared at him. He was right, but that did not make it any easier. I bit my lip and tore my eyes from his.

Then I started out across the narrow strip of rock. Though I moved with care, I could not prevent the rubble from slipping as I passed. I paused halfway, hearing an ominous rumbling from above.

I hurried on, reaching the other side as the rumble came again. Miraculously, there was no landslide and I turned to look at Evelar, alone with his stallion and my mare at the far side of the rubble.

'Why don't you whistle for Cheena,' he said in my mind. *'Lumen will follow.'*

He sent my horse ahead and I whistled. The mare pricked up her ears and started to come across, followed obediently by the stallion. She chose her footing gingerly, passing the slide confidently. College bred, intelligent and nimble, both horses traversed the distance easily. But from above I heard the rumbling again.

Then Evelar started to cross. I watched fearfully, listening to the ominous sounds and praying fervently for his safety. He was barely half-way across when the rumble grew to a roar. He broke into a run as the earth fell around him.

I screamed out to him both aloud and with my mind and sank to my knees in terror. There was an agonizing moment when all I could see was a cloud of dirt and rock... then he burst from the rubble and dove for the safety of the path, rolling and coming to his knees beside me, covered in dust.

"Hello," he said to me breathlessly.

He watched the landslide as it roared down the cliff face. Trembling, I slipped my arms about his waist and held tight, never wanting to experience such fear again. He wrapped me soothingly in his arms and kissed the top of my head.

"Atwin," he said quietly. "That landslide wasn't natural.

There's not enough loose earth in this whole range to cause something like that."

"You think we just walked into a trap?"

He turned to look at the trail ahead and gestured with a nod. "I'm certain of it."

I followed his gaze and gasped. Just around the next bend in the cliff we could see dark figures in single file, smoking in the late afternoon shadows, a long line of kalkar blocking the narrow path and snaking along the cliffside until it passed around a corner and was lost from view.

Netta's jaw dropped and she looked from the kalkar blocking our way to the landslide stopping our retreat and back to the kalkar again.

"But Leena is cold! I still feel nothing!"

"What now?" said Atwin.

Evelar stood, pulling me up with him, and dusted himself off. "We get down to business."

We made our way around the cliff face until we reached the first of the pack. Netta and I flattened ourselves against the side of the cliff so that Evelar could inch his way past. Before passing Atwin in the same way, my revealer gave him a stern warning.

"What you are about to see does not leave this company."

Atwin nodded, and allowed him to pass.

With a deep breath, Evelar reached out and touched his palm to the head of the leading kalkar. The smoke dissipated as the kalkar went cold and Evelar pushed it over the edge of the cliff to fall tumbling to the bottom far below.

"What did you just do?" said Atwin with an awed expression.

"I sucked the heat out of it," my revealer replied, proceeding to the next.

"But... how?"

Evelar hushed him with a raised hand. He continued

to freeze kalkar one after another, quickly settling into a rolling rhythm. Hand out, freeze, push, step forward, as we followed slowly behind. I could see him beginning to tire but he doggedly continued until he could barely lift his foot to take that next step forward and the hand he raised trembled.

I squeezed past Atwin and touched a hand to my revealer's arm. He looked at me with eyes blazing from the heat he had absorbed.

"It's my turn now," I said quietly and he nodded, letting me pass.

"Wait a minute," said Atwin. "You can do it too?"

I shrugged. "Evelar taught me," I replied, and set myself for the task at hand.

We continued in our slow progress as I cooled and pushed, over and over again. But there seemed no end to the line of kalkar, and the sun was setting. Panic lent speed to my efforts, but it also made me tire more quickly and I knew it was hopeless.

Then there was a touch on my arm. "Let me try," said Netta. "Leena says she knows what to do."

I was unsure, but I was too tired to argue so I let her pass, and bit my lip as I watched my friend. She reached out an arm, but instead of touching the head of the kalkar she held her hand palm outward facing toward it. About her neck, Leena began to glow blue.

Netta glowed brightly in the dimness of the setting sun and the blue nimbus travelled down her arm to arc across the small distance between the Princess and the kalkar. The blue flowed from the top of its head and down its body to its feet, freezing the flesh in a hiss of steam as it spread.

With both hands and an immensely satisfied expression, Netta pushed the frozen kalkar over the edge of the cliff and stood watching it fall. Then the last of the sunlight blinked out and, with a bright sparking charge and a crackle of sound that bounced across the cliff face as it echoed, the long line of kalkar came to life.

As one the line surged forward but Netta did not flinch. She rose up to her full height and stretched both hands in front. The blue glow consumed her as the freezing arc flickered its way along the line, jumping from one to the next. The closest kalkar wobbled with the violence of the charge, and each toppled of their own accord, falling soundlessly into the darkness.

Netta moved forward and sent another arc flying. As her confidence grew so did her power, and blue sparks filled the night sky like lightning, as bright as day. Then suddenly the kalkar were no more. The last of the line had turned and fled. Netta lowered her hands and the glow dissipated, leaving the night even darker than before.

The Princess turned to me, the amulet glowing softly, the angry light of before gone. She reached out her hands to take mine and the gentle glow spread to include me as it cooled the heat from my body and returned my flesh to normal. Then she did the same for Evelar.

We moved on into the night and finally came down off the ledge to find ourselves in a thick forest. The events on the trail had proven that we were not alone in these mountains, and we looked about anxiously as we rode. Sometime before midnight they silently closed in.

We stopped, seeing shadowy shapes in the trees ahead. We were surrounded, but they did not attack. At first there was no smell of burning earth, so they were not kalkar when we first noticed them. The kalkar came soon after, and Netta began to whimper in pain.

She slid from the stallion she shared with Atwin and sank to her knees. Before anyone could stop her, she ripped the amulet from her neck and threw it from her with a cry of fright. And then she vanished.

We stared at the spot where she had been. With a curse, Atwin jumped from his horse's back and rushed to the spot. He saw Leena lying in the dirt, glowing faintly. He bent with a grunt and picked her up and he too disappeared.

The kalkar dissolved into the trees and were gone, leaving behind only the shadowy human figures closing in. A group of tribesmen appeared from the shadows to surround us.

Evelar and I had no time to wonder what had happened. Evelar sent the horses galloping into the trees and hopefully to safety. As the tribesmen closed in we stood back to back awaiting the attack. When it came, the ferocity of it was frightening.

We fought hard to protect ourselves, but we were hopelessly outnumbered. At my back, I heard the grunts of pain as Evelar hacked with his sword at the enemies around him. Our one advantage was our skill at arms, for the tribesmen have no real military training. I felled two in the first few moments, and I know Evelar had finished a like number. But then I was beset by a warrior significantly more skilled than the others.

He was obviously the leader. I had tried to keep up with my training since leaving the College of the Art, but with only my knife and a short sword I could not hope to parry all of his lightning strokes. I cried out as pain shot up my arm and I dropped the sword.

I fought on, my right arm hanging limp at my side, but I knew I could not last. Involuntarily I sank to my knees, feeling a strange weakness and the leader moved in for the kill.

I heard Evelar spin, alerted by the sudden vulnerability at his back. I felt the wind of his thrust above my head as he ran the leader through. He savagely finished off the remainder, then dropped to my side.

"Mym?"

I felt strangely light-headed. I stared at the blood staining my hands and my clothes. How much of it was mine? I could not lift my right arm and the pain came in waves. Surprisingly lucid, I listened to the quiet, and heard a scraping from behind.

Without thinking, I grabbed the knife in my left hand, spun and threw. The knife pierced the tribesman in the throat and he fell down, his breath gurgling out as his lungs filled with blood. Then, my reserves drained, I collapsed into the dirt.

Vaguely, I could hear Evelar's startled gasp. He lifted me out of the dirt and cradled me in his arms. I caught snatches of his words as he mumbled under his breath.

"Don't do this, Mym... No...!"

I tried to drag myself out of the oblivion that threatened to claim me. He talked on... "I've done it again... Mist...! I've failed..."

I was drawn by that strangely familiar name, but couldn't make the connection. I was oblivious to the meaning of it.

"Don't go, Mym..." His voice was stricken. "Please, Mym... Don't leave me!"

I tried to shake my head, but could not. I tried to speak, but could not. I felt so weak that I could barely draw breath, but I had to ease his despair.

"I could... never..." I whispered with an effort... *'Leave you,'* I finished mentally.

"Mym?" I heard him say with relief. "Where are you hurt Mym? There's so much blood I can't tell."

I tried to speak but could not.

"Use your mind, Mym, it will be easier."

I formed the thought with difficulty and sent one word.

'*Arm...*'

I didn't even feel it as he lifted the injured arm and I barely heard his sharp intake of breath.

"Mym," he said quickly. "You've lost a lot of blood. You're going into shock. I need you to stay awake. Will you try?"

I clutched at the idea.

"What was that? You're not sending, Mym."

I gathered what little energy I had left. '*Try...*' I sent.

"That's my girl. Now, I need to make a tourniquet..."

I could not follow his words any more, but I clung to the sound of them as he explained what he was doing. I drifted in some nether land between life and death, oblivious to everything but my dear revealer's voice.

After an interminable time, Evelar lifted my head and ordered me to drink, forcing me to swallow some of the bitter liquid.

"Sleep now, my love," he said softly.

I did sleep, but it was a sleep disturbed by dreadful dreams.

I stood with my pack waiting for the night, watching the enemy approach. My thoughts were filled with fear, multiplied and amplified through the pack mind. The sun left and I could move again, but there was nowhere to go. In front of us the blue light shone, awful in its radiance, ready to kill. I wanted to run, to turn and flee, but the pack mind held me there.

Behind the light was a dark figure, rendered in silhouette by the freezing blue flame that came at us like death. The figure raised its hand and the cold flame came, jumping across the heads of my fellows, my family falling before me.

I shuddered in terror and shrank back in grief and pain, heedless of those behind in my overwhelming desire to escape. The collective could hold me no more and I fled and echoing in my mind from the group memory was the one thought, a feeling without words that said more than any words could. 'This is why she must be stopped.'

I remember nothing more until I woke huddled in the warmth of Evelar's arms as he sat with his back to a tree. I tried to raise my head, but I felt dreadfully weak and, with a groan, I gave up.

"Mym?"

"Hmm...?"

"Welcome back," he said gently.

"Hmm."

"How do you feel?"

"...tired."

"Are you hungry? I have some broth ready."

"Mmmm."

He laid me down and wrapped his cloak about me. Then he got up and went to the fire. By the time he came back I was shivering.

"Cold..." I whispered.

"Yes, I know. You've been like that for some time."

"Why?"

"Your blood is very thin right now. You are lucky to be alive."

He sat down and gathered me up again. Then he picked up a bowl from where he had placed it on the ground and I could smell the nourishing broth.

"This will warm you and give you strength," he said as he began to spoon-feed me.

I felt warmer already and the food did make me feel stronger, but soon I slept again.

I stood in a ring with my pack, looking at the human woman who stood cowering inside the circle. This was the one who carried 'her' and now we had captured her. The pack mind was enraptured by our success, glad to have separated the human from the dreadful Leena, but unsure what to do next. So we stood, the woman trapped, as day came.

We stood watching, helpless while the other human came with Leena in his grasp. The terrible light shone again and our mind erupted in pain as my fellows toppled and our circle was breached. Unable to do more than watch, the human woman escaped, joined once more with Leena the terrible.

The horror from the pack hit with shocking force. It was him, the one who will carry Naali! No, no, no, he must be stopped. We must not let Leena find him. If Leena finds Naali we are all dead! My grief and terror were overwhelming.

SIXTEEN

This time when I awoke I definitely felt better. I no longer felt so tired, though I was still terribly weak. I settled into a more comfortable position and Evelar closed his arms more tightly about me. I told him about my dreams.

"It makes sense," he mused. "You have been in contact with the kalkar mind. Now you're weakened you are channelling in your dreams."

I shivered. "It's dreadful."

"Think of it as a chance," he replied. "We wanted to learn more about them."

"What happened to the others?" I asked, suddenly remembering their abrupt disappearance.

"They are safe now," he said. "I received a communication from Netta a while ago."

"The horses?" I asked.

"I implanted an order in their minds to find our friends and bring them back here."

"Good," I said. Then I noticed the sling and bandage. "Your cloak!" I said in surprise. He had torn strips from the lining to bind my arm and to make the sling. "It's ruined!"

"It can be mended."

"But your cloak is your life!"

"No, you are my life! My cloak is merely a symbol of my profession. A cloak can be replaced. You can not."

"But..."

"It was necessary. You could have died and I couldn't

have borne that."

"I'll mend it."

"You'll mend yourself first."

I looked at the bandage and felt the injured arm with my left hand, wincing a little at the pain.

"How badly was I injured?"

"I had to stitch the length of your forearm."

"Will it heal properly?"

"I don't know."

We heard hoof beats approaching and Evelar reached for his sword, which was lying at his side on the ground. Then he relaxed. It was Atwin and Netta.

"What kept you?" said the revealer in false joviality.

"We ran into some old friends," said Atwin wryly.

"I know what you mean," said Evelar with a hollow laugh.

"Netta subdued them with her amulet." Atwin stopped and looked about. "What happened here?" he asked.

"If you remember, we were about to be set upon when you were whisked away," said Evelar.

The Prince looked around at the blood-stained earth and the tracks where Evelar had dragged the bodies into the bushes. Then he looked more closely at my white face.

"Are you hurt, Miyam?" he asked.

"I almost lost her..." said Evelar in a tortured voice.

Netta dismounted and came up to us, taking immediate control of the situation. "Let me look after her, while you boys go and bury those bodies," she said. "They are starting to smell."

Evelar and I sat staring at Netta. We had been alone with my injury for so long that we had settled into an intimate solitude and neither of us wanted to end it.

"Come along now," said Netta imperiously. "She won't fall apart while you are gone."

"I really need to get cleaned up anyway," I said with a sigh and he reluctantly helped me to sit up.

"Will you be alright?" he asked in concern.

"Of course she will," said Netta. "Now get moving."

Netta knelt beside me giving support as Evelar rose and headed after Atwin. My gaze followed his strong athletic form with an irrational pang of loss. Netta helped me remove my ruined tunic and hose and wrapped the revealer's cloak about me. Then she stoked up the fire and set a pot of water to boil. She took the clothes to the stream and began to scrub at the stains. She set them in a pot of cold water to soak and came back to the fire. Removing the hot water, she made a cup of tea and gave it to me. Then she used a rag and the rest of the water to wash the blood from my body. That done she returned to the stream, rinsed my clothes and wrung them out. She brought them back to the fire and spread them out to dry.

"What happened to you?" I asked as the Princess sat beside me. "Where did you disappear to?"

"The kalkar got me."

"How?"

"When I threw off Leena my position was revealed to them and they grabbed me."

"Delsi did warn you never to take the amulet off."

"Yes. But I had never felt the burning before. It surprised me."

"We've encountered kalkar before now, didn't it burn then?"

"No."

"Why not?"

"I have no idea. I think perhaps Leena was still getting used to me and had not yet learned how to warn me. But then after the cliff trail it was like she had tuned herself to me and the warning started working."

"So they got you. But Atwin followed you..."

"That was Leena. She knew I needed help. When he picked her up, she transported him to my position."

"Then he was captured too?"

"No. Leena is smart. She hid him in the bushes where he could wait until daylight. Then she helped him rescue me while the kalkar were dormant."

"What did she do?"

"I was totally surrounded by sizzling kalkar, with no way out. Leena froze some of them so that we could topple them and I could climb over. Then we had to find out where we were. That was when I tried to contact you. Evelar answered and Leena worked out our position in relation to you. And here we are."

"It all sounds a little too easy."

"Believe me, it was a lot harder than it sounds. Once night fell we were pursued relentlessly. We only managed to escape because Leena somehow hid us from them."

We looked up as Atwin and my revealer came out of the trees and I wondered what was wrong. They had not been gone long enough to bury the tribesmen. Atwin had a hand pressed to his side and Evelar was scolding him.

"You should have said something."

"It is nothing," said Atwin.

"Don't be a fool. You're hurt."

"I just twisted something, that is all."

Netta jumped up and went to them in concern. "What happened?" she asked.

"Our stoic friend here neglected to tell us that he was injured," said Evelar with disgust.

"It is nothing," said Atwin again.

"Somehow I doubt that," said Evelar.

They came over to the fire and Evelar ordered the Prince to remove his shirt. Atwin grunted as he tried to lift his shirt over his head and, with a curse, Evelar helped him.

"When did this happen?" asked the revealer.

"I think it was in the landslide."

"That was almost three days ago. You should be healing by now, if you only twisted something."

Evelar examined the Prince carefully and Atwin winced as he prodded gently.

"Just as I thought," said Evelar. "You have a cracked rib. You're lucky it didn't puncture a lung." He said it in a voice designed to shock and Atwin hung his head sheepishly.

"You've grown too good at hiding pain, my friend," said Evelar quietly.

Atwin refused to look at him.

"Come. I'll strap you up. Then we all have a few things to discuss."

Evelar came and knelt beside me. "I need some more lining," he murmured and proceeded to unwrap me.

"Evelar!" Netta cried, scandalised.

He looked at her. "What?"

She looked pointedly at my clothing draped by the fire. Evelar shrugged and continued what he was doing. Netta gave a strangled exclamation. Evelar looked at her again, bewildered. She was blushing furiously.

"Do you mind?" she said in a strangled tone. I coughed delicately, smiling behind my hand.

Atwin chuckled. "If it worries you, Netta," he said. "Do not look!"

She fumed in embarrassment. "It is you who should not be looking!" she exclaimed.

He shrugged. "It is nothing I have not seen before. Besides," he said, "you must admit she is rather attractive."

Netta gasped, shocked.

"Why thank you, Atwin," I said then. "I had no idea you felt that way!"

"How could you..." Netta spluttered.

"Relax, Highness," said Evelar then. "I'll make sure he sees nothing." He shot a pointed look at the Prince.

Atwin raised his hands in resignation and turned away.

"And what about you?" said Netta then.

Evelar looked at her in surprise. "What an interesting idea. My wife hiding from me the wonderful body I know she has?" he looked back at me suggestively. "That's rather erotic, actually!"

That surprised even me but, with a mischievous smile, I slowly opened one side of the cloak, holding the other about myself, revealing a flash of bare leg. Evelar groaned lustily, a twinkle in his eye.

"Oh!" Netta gasped, eyes flashing and hastily turning her back.

With a chuckle, Evelar ripped some more of the lining from his precious cloak and rewrapped me. He used it strap Atwin's ribs. Then, with the Prince dressed and made comfortable, Evelar sat wearily by the fire.

"What about those bodies?" asked Netta.

"I think we'll have to leave them," said Evelar. "We have no idea how long it will be before those kalkar who captured you catch up, so we should move out. Atwin's in no condition to dig graves and it would take too long for me to finish it on my own."

"I could help," said Netta.

"No, Your Highness. I need you to talk to Leena. With two people out of commission we could never survive another attack. We need protection."

Evelar ran a hand briefly over his eyes and I looked more closely at his haggard face.

"How long is it since you've slept?" I asked suddenly.

He thought for a moment. "Before the landslide," he said.

"You can't keep it up. Have you been absorbing all this time?"

He shrugged.

"You know how dangerous that is. It takes energy to absorb energy. Soon you will be unable to gather enough to cover your next attempt and your body will die."

"I still have some time yet."

"You need sleep as much as I do," I said.

"There's no time. When we're secure I'll sleep."

"Can I make a suggestion?" said Atwin.

"Go ahead."

"Why not stop talking and start riding? We have three horses between four people, so we will be slowed. Let us use the daylight to get away, rather than sitting here like sheep awaiting the wolf."

Evelar helped me up on to his stallion and swung up behind me, keeping one arm about my waist for support, while Netta took my Cheena. As we rode, Leena built a shadow about us. I could feel it pressing in on us, making us invisible.

I remember little of that day, since I dozed frequently, trusting Evelar's strength to keep me in the saddle. He rode stiffly behind me, quietly drawing in energy from the world around us. When we finally stopped, we found shelter in a small deserted cave at the base of a cliff. Netta used Leena to build a screen in front of the entrance to hide us, making the cave seem like just another piece of rock.

"Can she cover our brain activity too, so that the kalkar will be unable to trace us?" asked Evelar as he helped me down.

"She is already doing it."

"Good." Without waiting to eat, Evelar laid out his roll beside mine and we settled down together and went to sleep.

*

I remember no dreams that night, I awoke much stronger and was able to join the others at the fire just outside the cave for the morning meal. Before we set off again, Evelar removed the bandages from my arm to inspect it giving me the chance to see it for the first time, and I finally understood why my revealer had been so afraid for me.

It ran the length of the inside arm from the wrist to the elbow, a long jagged wound, stitched neatly. I winced as he prodded the stitches to ensure they were secure, and examined the wound.

"No sign of infection," he said with satisfaction.

He pulled out his knife, deftly rotating it in one hand to grasp it blade down, and with the point gently prodded my fingertips.

"Can you feel that?"

I shook my head, concerned now. The wound itself was painful, but my hand was like a dead weight. I could feel nothing.

"Can you move your fingers?"

I tried, but could not. It was as if the hand were no longer there. I shook my head again, the tears falling unheeded.

"What if I've lost feeling for good?" I whispered around the lump in my throat. "What will I do if it doesn't heal properly?"

He hushed me. "It could just be swelling and tissue trauma. As it heals we'll know more."

He carefully wrapped the arm again and replaced the makeshift sling.

Atwin and Netta had been striking camp and now they stood watching.

"We should get moving," said Atwin.

Evelar nodded and helped me stand. Netta came to me then and wrapped me in a hug, a wordless expression of her concern, and I smiled through my tears. Then Evelar helped me mount Lumen, swung up into the saddle behind me, and we resumed our journey in search of the mythical sacred halls.

SEVENTEEN

We dismounted with caution and approached the building on foot. From a distance the mound had seemed just another rise in the towering countryside, but on closer inspection we found an old but well preserved temple-type structure, half buried under the earth of centuries.

After an excited search of the perimeter, we located the open doorway of the ancient building. The stout wooden door was almost completely rotten, leaving only the bare iron framework, but it still hung miraculously by one intact hinge.

With reverence, we entered the structure, being careful not to disturb anything. We found ourselves on a mezzanine overlooking the main floor. We looked over the balcony and stopped, stunned. Faint beneath the dust, we could see a fabulous mosaic floor, a lovingly detailed picture of a palace ballroom filled with people.

We tore ourselves away from the enchanting sight and searched the building. The interior walls held many niches and cavities which were obviously designed to house statues and other relics, some of which still remained. After a thorough search we decided that the resting place of Naali was not on this floor.

"Perhaps he is downstairs," Atwin said with a shrug of his shoulders.

"Does anyone remember seeing a staircase?" I asked, looking about.

"Come to think of it..." Evelar scanned the Mezzanine walls. "No, I don't see one," he said, a trifle bemused.

This sparked another search, but there was simply no way down.

"Netta, what does Leena see?" I asked.

Netta closed her eyes and allowed the amulet to scan the room.

"This way," she said and led us around the corner of the balcony to the Eastern wall.

In the centre of the wall was another niche, larger than the others. The inside surface was covered with low relief carvings, vines and grapes and leaves, a simple but effective decoration. The Princess began to search the designs with her fingertips, pushing and prodding.

Her hand glowed blue, faintly but strongly, guided by Leena. A sudden soft click echoed in the silence of the hall and the inner panel slid quietly back to reveal a dark opening. Dank smelling and hung with cobwebs, a steep stone stair led down.

Treading with care we descended the ancient stairway. The lower chamber was a large open room. Here also there were niches in the walls, but from our vantage point at the head of the room our eyes were drawn almost unconsciously to the pattern of the mosaic.

From this level, the figures became less visible and we saw instead the spaces between. The clusters of revelling nobles were separated by wide areas of open floor which created a kind of anti-pictorial pathway, drawing the eye inexorably across the room to light on yet another niche in the wall.

Netta rushed across the room. Without hesitation, she again found the hidden latch and the wall slid open to reveal a small, darkened chamber and in the centre a pedestal with a shrine that could only be the resting place of Naali, the King's amulet.

Netta reached out and rested a hand where Naali had once hung, and the amulet about her neck began to glow. She stood for several moments, her hand engulfed in light, her eyes closed. Then she cried out in grief and sank to the floor, weeping.

"What did Leena find?" asked Atwin in concern.

"Nothing," she said. "He is gone. That is all she can see. She cannot get past the fact that he is gone."

We set up camp outside and sat dejectedly about the fire. We were at a loss. If Netta could not find the trail, we really were at a dead end. Quietly, Evelar stood and moved off into the darkness.

"Where are you going?" asked Atwin.

"There's something I need to do," he said and disappeared into the night.

"Excuse me," I said, getting up to follow.

"Of course," said Atwin with a wink.

I chose to ignore that.

I followed furtively as Evelar slipped back into the ancient building. I watched from the shadows as he approached the shrine where Naali had once rested and I gathered my energies for the search that my revealer was preparing. He placed his hands on the pedestal to either side of the shrine, closed his eyes and mumbled the ritual of meditation.

As he focused his mind on the ancient resting place of the amulet, beginning the probe, I opened up a mental channel and began to send my energy to him. Briefly, Evelar hesitated at the unexpected contact. Then he gave a mental shrug and accepted the channel, harnessing the extra power. I braced myself and secured the link. Together we began the search.

As Evelar probed with his mind, I supported with a steady slow-release stream of energy. I followed his mind as he grasped at the minute echoes within the rock. The shrine had been empty for a long time and we had difficulty breaking through the dust, but eventually Evelar found the echo of the amulet itself.

We followed the path of the amulet as it was lifted from the shrine and taken out of the building, where it crossed the mountains and joined a little stream. The stream soon joined a larger stream, which would eventually become the great River Nort. But at the joining between the stream and the Nort the trail veered to the east.

The path followed the line of the southern foothills of the Dragon Mountains, avoiding both the inhospitable mountain passes and the humid heat of the Wild Plain. At a point far to the south, the path veered again and actually crossed the Dragon Mountains. But at that point the distance was simply too great and it was useless to try to follow further.

To be honest, I was surprised that we reached even that far, and I was impressed by the power of Evelar's mind. Most would not have reached half that distance before losing the trail. Small wonder he was already an artisan. His power was phenomenal. But I pulled myself away from that thought.

For now we had to return to our bodies and that can be a lot harder than the search itself. Evelar carefully retraced the trail, drawing even more on the energy I willingly offered. We were both dangerously tired, riding on the edge of panic.

Finally, our minds came back into the sacred building and re-entered the shrine where we had started, climbing back up through the dust. Suddenly, I was inside my revealer's head and I carefully broke the contact. My mind came rushing back into my own head, and I sagged under the weight of my own body.

I had sensed, in that brief moment, Evelar's surprise at the extent of our search and I had learned that even he, despite his unusually great mental power, could not normally go nearly so far. It was not unusual for an especially powerful revealer to emerge but this was different. I was stunned at the power of the man and I felt there was something more to it.

I tried to remember where I had heard about this type of power, but the answer eluded me. I would have to think on this further. I looked up and Evelar straightened, turning to face me. I came out of the shadows and he began to walk slowly toward me.

At that moment, Atwin entered and came up behind me. I gave a start at the sudden presence as it broke the intimacy of the moment. Evelar hesitated and then continued at his slow pace.

"There you are," said Atwin. "What have you two been doing?"

"Searching for clues," said Evelar in a whisper.

"Are you alright?" asked Atwin.

"Yes, I'll be fine in a moment," Evelar croaked. "I need a jug of water and a stick of zestina about so long." He gestured listlessly with his hands a length of about a foot.

"Yes, of course. Right away," Atwin said. "In here?"

"Yes, if you don't mind," he rasped. "And make sure it's zestina."

Atwin hurried away. Evelar continued his slow progress and as I moved to meet him, my own steps faltered and I found myself on the floor, overcome with weakness.

I felt his worried thought and he redoubled his efforts to get to me. He sat before me in preparation for the ritual that would revive our depleted energies. Atwin returned with the

Ella Mortimer

jug and the zestina, and at Evelar's gesture placed them on the floor between us.

From under his cloak, Evelar drew out two yellow pills which he placed in the water. He used the stick to stir as the tablets slowly dissolved, turning the water a strange orange colour. Then he gave the stick to Atwin, who had been watching curiously.

"Take this. Do not touch the liquid. Put it in the centre of the fire and let it burn. The flames will turn green. Do not breathe the fumes and keep clear until the flames return to normal."

Atwin walked from the hall, the stick held gingerly away from his body. Evelar put both hands around the jug and I placed my hands over his. Together we lifted the jug and took turns drinking the sweet liquid until the jug was empty.

I felt its reviving properties working on my ravaged senses and soon I was able to think again. Then we put down the jug, joined hands and stood. Leaving the jug where it was, we moved toward the door. I felt drained and dizzy and he looked at me in concern as I leant heavily on his arm.

"You should be feeling better," he murmured.

"I am," I said.

He shook his head. "You shouldn't have done that. You're too depleted from your injury."

"I'm fine," I whispered, though I was not.

"Your mother taught you more than was strictly necessary," Evelar said then. "You know that the methods of the search are a trade secret."

"I know."

"It's such breaches of confidence which lead to illegal spies," he said.

"I know," I replied. "But I'm no spy. Besides, that's what

makes me so interesting!"

He laughed "You never cease to surprise me."

"Good. Then I'll never start to bore you."

Once outside we noted with surprise that the moon had risen. We had been gone for over an hour. Atwin and Netta looked up as we approached and tacitly ignored our joined hands. I admit that it was a welcome change to openly show our closeness, which felt too right to question or hide any more.

Netta smiled. "Come and eat," she said.

"What about the jug?" asked Atwin.

"Leave it," Evelar replied. "I'll fix it in the morning."

"That's an order," I said as an afterthought, very seriously.

I listened, swept along as my pack searched for the echo of Leena. She had been there a moment ago, the sound of her pain as she grieved for Naali a beacon in the group mind, leading us to her. But now she was quiet and finding her would be more difficult. Our best hope was to find her last location, the place in which she had communed with the stones that held the remembered presence of Naali. We flew in the direction of the echo, the one thought driving us forward. Find her, stop her, she must not find him!

It was about an hour before dawn and Atwin was shaking us awake. "Do not ask me how," he said as we sat up. "But they have found us. If we do not move right now we will all be dead before morning."

I went to wake Netta, finding her trembling and whimpering in her sleep. She shook her head, mumbling something in a fearful tone. The amulet about her neck burned hot, leaving a red welt where it touched her flesh.

I shook her awake and we hurriedly gathered our gear

together. It took only a few moments to strike camp, but by the time we were ready we could smell the heat of kalkar on the pre-dawn breeze.

We mounted up and fled, just in time. I could see the shadowy forms moving to surround our little camp and as they began to close in we burst out of their circle. The sky was a little less black. If we could just keep ahead of them a while longer we would be safe.

But it was not to be so simple. There was a sharp detonation and, with a scream, Atwin's horse collapsed under him. He managed to jump clear, but he was left defenceless to the mercy of the encircling horde.

Netta sprang into action, the blue glow of Leena engulfing the Princess as she shot bolts of cold flame at the enemy, spurring Cheena into the fray. We watched as Atwin caught the plucky mare and quickly mounted behind Netta. Then the Prince kicked and the horse surged away.

The kalkar fell back, shying away from the glow of Leena, as if afraid to get too close, allowing Netta and Atwin to break free of the pack and we sped ahead of them once more. The sky was definitely lighter now and there was a faint glow low on the horizon.

The kalkar began to fall behind as they felt the call of the dawn. There were no further explosions. Whatever that had been, the kalkar could no longer gather the energy to unleash another. Finally, the first ray of golden sunlight spread its benediction over the land, and the last sounds of pursuit faded to nothing.

We reined in and turned to look at the now motionless kalkar. Some had been caught mid run, their membranous cloaks draped about their skeletal green limbs, long clawed fingers splayed as they reached toward us.

"What was that thing?" asked Netta, voice hushed.

"A fireball," said Atwin, shaken.

"It's called a sunshot," said Evelar. "The kalkar's favourite weapon. They create it from the solar energy stored within their bodies, but it uses up a large part of their supply. See the one far to the rear?"

"Yes," said Atwin.

"That's the one that fired it. It used up its store of energy and could not keep up with its pack-mates."

"We should bury the horse," said Atwin.

"We really can't spare the time," said Evelar. "We have to get away."

"Still, I hate to leave him there. He has been a good friend."

"It's only a shell. The sunshot will have fried it from the inside out," said Evelar. "I'm sorry, my friend, but we have to go."

With reluctance, Atwin nodded. "I know," he said.

Morning broke crisp and clear and we emerged gratefully from our misadventures ready to face whatever the day offered, safe in the knowledge that kalkar could not follow us in the daylight hours.

"I sincerely hope we can travel without incident for a few days," said Atwin wearily. "How long do you think we can go before they find us again?"

"I don't know, my friend," said Evelar. "We've certainly taken a beating."

"Can Leena shield us as we ride?" asked Atwin.

Netta nodded. "She will try."

We descended from the mountains, passing through little pockets of rainforest. The air was cool and damp under the forest canopy, and green light fell over the path. The teeming wildlife gave a sharp contrast to the desolate cliff face. There were countless flying things, including a species of flitter bird and many breeds of finches, their myriad bright colours flashing past in the tree-tops and their song filling the air with sound. Any floor-dwellers, however, remained hidden in the ground-cover as we passed.

I felt uneasy and Evelar too appeared apprehensive as we rode. Netta and Atwin stayed close by. Something followed close to one side. I could not read its intentions. More, I could not locate its mind. But I knew it was following us, despite Leena's shield.

EIGHTEEN

We stopped for lunch in a small clearing, happy but subdued. As we talked, the Princess slowly drifted out of the conversation, until I noticed with shock that she had a blank look in her eyes as she stared off into the trees. Following her gaze, I saw something flash, like an animal moving through the trees. Suddenly, Netta rose and trotted into the forest.

Looking at each other in bewilderment, we got up to follow. After some few moments, we found the girl in a peaceful glen and we stopped, stunned by the beauty of the sight. The grass was green and cropped short. The shadows were broken by dappled sunlight and at one end a lovely waterfall formed a pool, feeding the small stream we had been following.

Netta stood by the pool, her hair released from its bun and flowing in golden ripples down her back. Standing facing her was a magnificent creature, built like a horse, but small and dainty. The animal had short fur of the most incredible colour, which shone even in the shadows, the purest of white. The mane and tail were long and silver. Because the grass was short, the hooves were visible and they shimmered with every colour of the rainbow. Its ears were pricked up in curiosity and from its forehead grew a single, multi-coloured, spiralled horn.

The fur over the creature's back seemed to change behind the shoulders, appearing to be what can only be described as feathers, soft and colourful. As if to confirm the thought, the animal looked at us and in one fluid movement the feathers burst open and outward to reveal beautiful, graceful and varicoloured wings.

Netta turned to look at us and her face was radiant. The mythical creature nudged at her back and the Princess turned back again. The animal bent a front leg and Netta climbed effortlessly onto its back. Then they raced past us in the direction of the camp. We hurried to follow.

When we found them, the creature had kicked dirt over the fire and they waited impatiently by the horses. Then, in a sudden startling movement, the creature spread its wings and leapt into the air, rising quickly above the tree-tops. It let out an excited whinny and turned to hover over us as we watched in astonishment.

"I think she wants you to follow," cried Netta in a voice that bubbled with excitement. Her face was flushed becomingly and at that moment her beauty and that of the mythical beast were one, radiant and breathtaking.

Prince Atwin was the first to recover as the pair flew away, jumping into the saddle and spurring Cheena to a gallop. We emerged from the forest at the top of a rise and looked out over the Wild Plain. Netta stood alone as the wondrous beast winged its way across the plain toward a distant cloud of dust.

We watched as the beast landed. After several moments it rose and returned, the dust cloud following behind. As they came closer, the approaching cloud became visible as a herd of wild horses, kicking up the dust as they galloped toward us.

The herd came to a halt some way out on the plain, the dust swirling about them. A magnificent black stallion separated itself from the herd and galloped on, his hooves thundering on the hard packed earth of the plain. The mythical beast landed beside Netta and watched. The stallion did not even slow his pace as he began to ascend the hill.

Worried that he would not stop, we backed hurriedly away. Lightning-fast, the mythical beast stepped between us and Atwin and prevented his retreat, nudging him forward with her nose. Atwin stood stock-still, watching the untamed animal approach, unable to back away. The stallion tore up the hill straight at the Prince.

Then he slid to a halt a foot from Atwin's nose and reared up onto his hind legs, pawing at the air in front of the Prince's face. Then he dropped back onto all fours, gave a snuffle and stood perfectly still, his eyes locked on Atwin's and his ears flicking forward and back.

Gingerly, Atwin reached forward with one hand and laid it on the horse's brow. The stallion nuzzled at his chest, curiously exploring the scent of a man. Suddenly, the stallion looked over Atwin's shoulder at us. Evelar dismounted and boldly walked forward. The wild horse looked at him and made a whiffling noise. A little surprised, Evelar looked at Atwin.

"Windfoot bids you welcome, Your Highness," he said.

"Ex...cuse me?" said Atwin, cocking his head to look at the revealer.

The horse made another series of... horsey sounds and Evelar spoke again.

"He says that Gliss has told him of your mission. He says 'the King of the herd recognises a king among men,' and he offers to bear you on his back for so long as your quest may continue."

I watched in amazement as Evelar calmly talked to a horse. Atwin stood dumbfounded.

"Who is Gliss?" he stammered.

"The one that Netta rides," Evelar replied patiently.

"What's your response?"

"I..." Atwin fumbled.

Evelar sighed tolerantly and laid a hand on the stallion's long neck. He concentrated for a moment.

"I told him that his proposal is greatly appreciated and that you would be more than honoured to accept whatever aid he may be willing to offer."

A strange idea began to form in my mind as I watched. How could he be talking to a horse? This was as impressive as the search for Naali had been. I still could not comprehend what I felt, the sense of something bigger about to happen, but I knew that some great event was in my revealer's future and something told me that these unusual powers were just the beginning. The horse nickered.

"He says you must prove that you are worthy. Control your fear and ignore your pain. You must jump onto his back."

Atwin looked at the revealer. Then he looked at the stallion. Evelar backed away and the stallion offered his back to the Prince. With a running leap, Atwin landed on the animal's back, suppressing a grunt as his broken rib was jarred. The stallion reared up and Atwin clung to his mane.

The great horse gave a loud cry and a young white stallion emerged from the herd to look up at his sire. Atwin dismounted and the stallion nuzzled at his chest companionably. Then the black horse left us and galloped to meet his white son.

"You have impressed him, Your Highness," said Evelar.

The black stallion spun on his hind legs and returned to us. He whinnied loudly to the new herd leader, who reared up and neighed mightily. Then the young stallion spun, as had his sire, and galloped back to the herd, leading them away in a cloud of dust.

The black horse trotted to stand beside a rock and offered his back to Atwin. The Prince mounted easily, using the rock as a platform. I walked up behind Evelar and touched him gently on the arm. He looked sideways at me.

"Have you ever done that before?" I asked.

"Done what, my love?"

"Spoken to a horse."

"I don't believe so."

"Has anyone else ever done that?"

He gave me a quizzical look. "Not that I recall, why?"

"Oh, nothing," I said. "I wondered if you had learnt it somewhere."

He shrugged. "I just knew how to do it. What are you getting at?"

"It just seems a little unusual, that's all."

When we stopped that evening, Evelar examined my wound again. It was healing well, the long scar knitted in a neat line, and my revealer decided it was time to remove the stitches. With the tip of his knife he carefully severed each stitch, pulling out the short pieces of thread that were left.

It was a long, slow process but when it was finished he inspected the scar for any weakness and seemed satisfied. Outwardly the arm looked well healed, the new scar pink and strong, but I still had no feeling in my fingers.

He turned his knife and handed it hilt first to me. "Can you grasp it?" he said.

I reached out to take the knife, but my fingers would not close about the handle. With my left hand I pushed the fingers closed about the knife, feeling tears of frustration welling up from deep in my gut.

Once my fist was secure about the hilt, Evelar slowly allowed its weight to rest in my hand, but my grip did not hold and he caught the tip of the knife between his fingertips before it fell. I sobbed as disappointment and fear overwhelmed me.

For several days we rode southeast along the foothills of the Dragon Mountains. Far to the right we could see the Wild Plain stretching for miles. To the left, the mountains rose towering to the sky. We rode in a peaceful ease, but it was difficult to keep down the nerves after our disastrous journey so far.

"Is Leena still shielding us?" said Atwin nervously.

Netta shook her head. "She says Gliss is protecting us now. Leena is looking for Naali."

"Is that a good idea?" said Evelar.

"What do you mean?" asked Atwin.

"The kalkar always find us after Leena has used her power," I replied.

Netta smiled. "Leena seems sure that Gliss can cover that too."

"Has she found anything yet?" asked Atwin.

Netta shook her head. "Not a sign," she sighed.

"Then we do not know if we are even going in the right direction!" said Atwin.

"Be assured, Your Highness," said Evelar. "Naali certainly came this way."

"How can you know that?"

"Because," I said wearily, "we mapped the trail from the sacred halls."

"You what?"

"Just a College trick," said Evelar. "The trail is quite clear."

Atwin appeared flustered at that. "You are certainly full of surprises on this journey. You revealers have so many secrets. What else have you not told me?"

Evelar shrugged. "We have to keep some things secret,

or we couldn't do our job effectively."

"You have been coming to Shirall for years. Whenever Averil called for a revealer it was you. I thought I knew you, but all the time you have been hiding this great power. You have shown me things on this trip I never dreamed you could do."

"Yes, it was unavoidable. But as I said before, it doesn't leave this company. You must not tell what you have seen."

"But why? My friend, you are amazing. Do you realise how powerful your order could be if everyone knew?"

"Everyone must not know."

"But you would have thousands flocking to learn!"

"So?"

I rode in a daze, noticing little and talking less. Our pace was slow. Neither Atwin nor I could handle any great speed. My Cheena seemed to sense my illness and moved carefully to help me stay seated. I held the reins loosely in my good hand, while the injured arm hung limp at my side. I remember very little of that time. I dozed often in the saddle, my weakness no less debilitating as the time wore on. And my dreams were vivid and terrifying.

I ran with my pack, the group mind spurring us on in its endless search. I could feel the echo of Leena, but it was muted as if seen through a fog. The crisp night air lent speed to the thought but every time the mind seemed about to home in on her location she slipped away like smoke. We could hear her as a faraway menacing presence, but something stopped us from finding her. The pack ran aimless, unable to even pinpoint a direction, and our path turned and twisted like a leaf on the wind.

The interminable journey wore on. At the end of yet

another week we finally reached the road which stretches straight as an arrow from the pass to Yerterma on our left to Nella Fillenga far to the south. Because it was as good a place as any, we decided to stop for lunch. I let my weariness overcome me, slumping forward in the saddle.

In an instant, Evelar had jumped down from Lumen's back and come to my side. I literally fell off my horse into his waiting arms. He carried me into the shade of the trees beside the road and laid me gently down.

My revealer was desperately worried. It emanated from him and some of that worry gripped at my own heart. As he made to release me, I clutched at him with my good hand. My right arm was now numb to the shoulder.

"What's wrong with me?" I whispered. "Why can't I shake this?"

He hung his head, refusing to meet my eyes.

"You know, don't you? This is something more than just loss of blood. I know what happens when a body decides it wants to die..."

Evelar looked up at me sharply. Then he looked away with a shuddering breath. Even through my weakness, I caught snatches of Evelar's concern when he looked at me.

"Evelar, I might be ill but I can see and I can think. Such a wound could not have occurred simply as a chance hit during a battle. It was deliberate."

He gave a curt nod, but still refused to explain. I was sure my revealer knew what was wrong with me and said nothing because he didn't want me to worry.

"Please. Do I have to pull it from your mind?"

He looked at me then, daring me to try. I gathered up my depleted energies and tried to send a mental probe. The link I formed was tenuous at best, but it was enough to hear Windfoot's comment.

'*Your mate is unwell?*' The great wild horse had walked

up behind Evelar unnoticed.

'*She has been injured,*' replied the revealer quietly.

'*Ah,*' said the horse. '*Will she recover?*'

'*I don't know. I would wish it so.*'

I could not hold the link any longer and I slipped out of his mind. My head throbbed and I almost lost consciousness.

"You shouldn't have tried, my love," Evelar murmured, stroking my hair.

"You knew I couldn't do it," I accused.

"You don't have enough energy."

"Then why did you goad me into trying?"

He sighed. "So long as you can still try, I can dare to hope."

"Is it really that bad?"

"The wound you received was part of a ritual style killing. It was calculated to kill through rapid blood loss. But it has a second, more deadly purpose, intended to cover the possibility that you actually managed to survive the wound itself. As the injury healed, the charm came into action."

"Is there no cure?"

"It is known only among the tribesmen of the mountains."

"But they're the ones who attacked us!" I said in despair.

"I noticed that," he said.

"Somebody is coming," said Atwin tensely.

Evelar tore his eyes from mine and I followed his gaze. Approaching from the north came two mounted figures wearing the midnight blue cloaks of the College of the Art. One wore the purple border of an adept, the other the green of a journeyer.

"I'll be back," said Evelar. Without looking again at me, he mounted and rode out to meet them. The Adept spurred her horse to a gallop and moved ahead of her companion. Evelar and the Adept dismounted then and continued on foot. When they met, they wrapped their arms about each

Ella Mortimer

other and held each other tight.

After some moments they separated and Evelar held both of her hands gently in his. They spoke for several moments, seemingly unaware of their audience. Then, Evelar planted a kiss on her cheek, they hugged again and she remounted and returned to her companion. As the strangers rode southward, Evelar returned to our little group.

NINETEEN

I hovered above the little group, tracking their progress. The pack was with me and my instinct told me this was the one. But even this close I could still not locate Leena. I could hear her, still calling for her mate, but I could not tell where the signal came from, nor where it was aiming. If it originated here, why could I not sense her? My mind should be screaming with her presence but she still shifted and slipped away.

I looked down at the travellers, trying to find her with my eyes. There was a male out front and another male to the rear. One of those was destined to carry Naali, but I could not tell which one, the something that hid their minds confusing even my sight. One of the others had to be carrying Leena. One rode a strange beast that froze my blood with fear. The other slumped in the saddle, barely conscious.

Completely befuddled by the trickery that hid their minds, I drifted away, searching along with the pack for a stronger signal. If only I could be sure, but the pack mind overruled my individual instinct, telling me that Leena had to be somewhere else. This was not the origin of her searching mental voice. The keening thought that sent shivers of terror through the mind of us came from elsewhere.

Netta and I rode side by side in one of my increasingly rare lucid moments.

"How can you be sure?" asked Netta worriedly. "Has he

told you who she was?"

"He doesn't need to," I replied.

"How can you say that?"

I sighed wearily. "I don't expect you to understand."

"He should at least have told you who she was."

"Why?" I said. "If he felt the need to explain himself, then I'd be worried."

"I do not want to see you get hurt, Mym."

"Why should I get hurt?"

Netta looked at me witheringly. I sighed. This argument had been going on for over a week, when I was awake. I would have to try to explain it to her. Again.

"I trust him. If I did not, what sort of relationship would we have?"

"Well I trust him not."

"He's a revealer, Netta," I said patiently. "They are the most trustworthy people in the world."

"How can you say that? They live by spying!"

"No!" I said vehemently. "Spying is a criminal offence, punishable by death according to College law."

Netta sighed. "I am worried for you, Mym."

"I'm touched, really, but there's no need. I know this man. I share his life, I share his mind and I share his bed..."

"Mym!" Netta cried out, shocked.

"He is my husband, Netta, after all."

"Not officially," said Netta, slightly panicked.

"As you so rightly pointed out, that makes no difference. We are married. If he had any doubts or lingering feelings for another he would never have tricked me into performing the ritual."

"He... tricked you?"

"Oh, did I forget to mention that?"

"Yes," she said dryly.

"Sorry. But surely you can see what that means?" I

looked up to where the revealer was riding some small way ahead of us. "I've never been so sure of anything in my whole life."

I could not find my pack. I felt no connection to the group mind and I was terrified at the loneliness within. I sat still, but somehow I moved. Something carried me and I wondered how that could be. I lifted my eyes to look about, trying to locate my pack mates, but all I could see were the humans.

Beside me rode the dreadful one, Leena the terrible, glowing and mocking me with her freezing mental gaze. I sat paralysed by terror, crying out in fear to my pack mates but hearing no reply.

I screamed in absolute anguish, struggling to get away from that unresponsive body. Somehow I broke free, seeing the human form I had just escaped slump forward in the saddle. I thrashed my way upward, kicking and flailing in my effort to get away, looking down in horror at the little group below. Reeling under the suffocating loneliness I flew in search of the great mind. Alone and anxious to find my pack I sailed away, calling loud and long in my despair.

An unknown number of days passed before I awoke from a coma. I was lying on a thin mattress in a large cavernous dwelling, blankets wrapped about me and a fire burning in the hearth pit by the entrance. Something inside me had changed. As I tried to sit up I found that my energy levels were really no better, but something was different.

My body was no longer dying. Though I was weary beyond belief, I felt good for the first time in over a month. I tried opening my mind. Within moments my tentative search reached Evelar. He must have been sitting just outside the cave, for he was at my side in a flash. His relief washed over me and I smiled.

"Where am I?" I asked as he sat beside me and took my hand.

"In the southern Dragon Mountains, in the home of Lord Netray, chief of the Elkwind tribe."

"Tribesmen?" I said in surprise. "Then I really am getting better?"

He grinned, something I had never seen him do before. "You most certainly are, my love."

"What made them agree to help us?"

"It seems there are two factions at work in the mountains. Apparently, many of the tribes have allied themselves with the kalkar, don't ask me why. The Elkwind are a rebel tribe, one of several, who resent the loss of freedom. Those tribes who are against the alliance have formed a pact and gone into hiding."

"Then how did you manage to find them?"

"They found us. We fell under attack and Netray brought his warriors to our rescue."

"And then they cured me?"

"In a manner of speaking. The cure has to be effected by someone close to the victim, so they told me what to do."

I raised my right hand and looked at it. I wiggled my fingers experimentally. "I can feel again!" I said happily.

"That was the core of the problem. Apparently the wound was only a doorway for the charm. In order to convince the whole body that it wants to die, the charm has to literally kill a small part and radiate from there."

"How did you fix it?"

"Basically, I had to switch off the charm. It had to be done at the cellular level in the wounded part itself."

"How?"

"It's a bit complicated. I had to enter your mind and then control it, so to speak. That's why it had to be someone close to you. For a time, I was you and you were me. I had to work with your own mind to control your body."

"I think it worked," I said rather joyfully. "I didn't want to die."

He kissed my hand. "I'm glad."

"My dear revealer," I said then. "What would you have done if I had died after all?"

"Don't speak of that," he said with a shiver. "You didn't and that's all that matters to me."

I reached up then, with my newly functional right arm and placed my hand at the back of his neck, lifting myself up. He wrapped his arm about my waist and lowered his head, meeting me half way...

Netta found us some moments later and caught our attention with an embarrassed little cough. We pulled apart and looked at her absently.

"Ah... should I come back later?" she said hesitantly.

"Of course not, Netta," I said, lowering myself back on to the mattress. "Don't be silly."

"Ah... I think maybe I should..."

"Not at all," said Evelar, signalling with his free hand for her to join us. He still had my hand captured in his. That seemed to embarrass the Princess, but we were not about to let that contact go.

Netta stayed a few moments, but kept her head bent and her eyes down. Before long she began to fidget, quietly uncomfortable. Then she stood up again.

"I... I had better tell Netray that you are awake," she said, looking steadfastly at her feet.

She ran from the cavern. Evelar and I looked at each other in bewilderment.

Over the next few days, as I slowly recuperated, we stayed with Netray and his people. Life there had a certain charmed simplicity that made us want to forget the troubles of the outside world.

During the day I would sit outside the chief's home under a canvas awning, Evelar constant at my side, and watch the gentle rhythm of the camp. Netta and Atwin would join us at times, either together or separately.

I took the opportunity to keep my promise to Evelar by mending his beloved artisan's cloak. It was a good way to rebuild strength and flexibility in my injured arm.

As the days passed, I began to notice something in Netta that had never struck me before. Sometimes I saw her talking and giggling with the maidens of the village, sharing in their chores and becoming almost one of them. But at other times I saw her nervously avoiding the attentions of the young men of the tribe, who flocked about her, mesmerised by her to-them-exotic beauty.

There was a shy, timid side to the Princess that I had never guessed at. Her confidence and her independence had somehow hidden it but now, when she was forced to associate with a bevy of suitors, her innocence began to shine through.

As the situation grew more difficult for her, Netta began to withdraw into herself. She began to avoid even Atwin in her growing inability to control the situation. But through it all, Atwin guarded her and watched over her, even when she did not know he was there.

"We're going to have to do something about that," said Evelar.

"Why?" I said. "She's so unaffected. Why burst her bubble?"

"She's too innocent. How are we ever going to get her and Atwin together?"

"I'm sure things will work out."

My revealer gave me a dubious look.

"Don't concern yourself too much, Dear," I said then. "I

have a feeling Naali will sort them out, when we finally find him."

"I hope you're right."

"Of course I am," I said with a smile.

At the end of a week, an urgent communication from Averil put an end to our stay. As I have said, life with Netray's people made you want to forget the outside world. So it was that I was awoken late one night by a hand on my shoulder and found Netta bending over me.

"Someone is trying to call us," she said quietly.

As my health had improved, Netray had given us the use of a spare cavern and so the four of us were able to gather in private to accept the call.

HOW GOES THE SEARCH? asked Averil anxiously.

THE TRAIL IS A LITTLE UNCERTAIN, said Evelar.

He did not mention the fact that we would soon reach the extent of the mental probe we had conducted at the Sacred Halls.

IS THERE ANY HOPE THAT YOU WILL FIND NAALI SOON?

THAT'S HARD TO SAY, I said.

THE CLUES ARE FEW AND FAR BETWEEN, Evelar concluded.

NETTA, HAS LEENA BEEN ABLE TO LOCATE HIM?

NOT AS YET, AUNT. YOU SEEM ANXIOUS. WHAT HAS HAPPENED?

IS IT THAT OBVIOUS? The Regent sighed. *DELSI HAS LOST CONSCIOUSNESS. I FEAR OUR TIME IS RUNNING OUT.*

OH DEAR, said Netta worriedly.

WHAT ARE YOUR PLANS? asked Averil.

FROM HERE, said Evelar, *I SUSPECT WE WILL CROSS THE MOUNTAINS TO ZELONA.*

HOPEFULLY WE CAN PICK UP THE TRAIL AGAIN FROM THERE, I said, completing the thought.

YOU SOUND UNSURE...

WE KNOW THAT NAALI CROSSED THE MOUNTAINS NEAR HERE, I said.

BUT WE CANNOT BE SURE EXACTLY WHERE HE WAS TAKEN, said Evelar quietly.

OH DEAR, said Averil, unconsciously echoing her niece.

BE ASSURED, Your Highness, said Atwin. *WE WILL FIND NAALI IN TIME.*

I HOPE YOU ARE RIGHT.

Early the next morning Netta awoke with a scream, startling us all awake.

"They are coming!" she cried, clutching at the amulet at her neck.

At that moment, there was a scratching at the canvas door flap of the cave and Netray himself entered.

"My scouts have had an encounter. Kalkar are nearby and we have to move the village. They closed in just before dawn, but now they are dormant so we must get away while we can. We are heading to our winter camp down by the plain."

"It was time we moved on anyway," said Evelar.

"We thank you for your kind hospitality, Sir," said Atwin.

Netray smiled. "My son will lead you as far as Zelona."

"Thank you, Sir."

TWENTY

During our stay with Netray and his people Gliss, the mythical beast which had carried Netta, had disappeared into the wilderness. But within a few minutes of leaving the camp she came trotting up out of the trees. With a little cry of delight, Netta jumped from her borrowed horse and ran to the gleaming animal.

I had noticed on our journey that Gliss would allow none but Netta to lay hands on her and now the girl had her arms wrapped about the animal's neck.Geltray, Netray's younger son, had accompanied us as guide and now he sat on his horse watching in awe. He dismounted and began to walk slowly toward the pair, one arm outstretched as if to touch the mythical beast. With a nervous whinny, Gliss backed away.

Netta looked around to see the young tribesman advancing. She placed herself in front of Gliss protectively. Still, Geltray advanced, mistakenly thinking that the animal would react in the same way as the horses he spent so much of his life with.

Gliss let out a piercing cry and Windfoot, the black stallion, clattered angrily toward him, carrying Atwin along with him on his back and placed himself firmly in the path of the intrepid tribesman. Geltray tried to step around the stallion dismissively, but Windfoot blocked his path again, nipping at him warningly. Geltray looked at Atwin.

"Would you care to control your horse?"

"Windfoot is not mine to control, I fear. He carries me because it is his wish to do so."

"He's only a horse, My Lord," said Geltray derisively.

"I would not tell him that. He is very protective of our fabulous friend there and I cannot shield you from the consequences if you continue in your present design. I suggest you drop it. She will not allow anyone but Netta to touch her, so there is no real point in trying, is there?"

Geltray grumbled under his breath.

"I am glad you see the light, My Lord," said Atwin. "Gliss will be travelling with us and we would not want any foolishness along the way, now would we?"

Geltray grumbled again.

"Do not take it too hard, Geltray," said the Prince companionably. "You know that creatures like that bow not to the whim of man. Oh and by the way, Gliss will carry Netta, so we will not need that horse we borrowed. We are not that far from camp, so we will wait here while you return the horse to your herds."

"What will I tell my father?"

"Why tell him anything?"

We were made uncomfortably aware of the extent of Netta's naiveté some three days into the journey through the mountains. Geltray tended habitually not to join us about the camp-fire in the evenings, preferring rather to scout the nearby woods for signs of kalkar. On this particular night Netta decided to find a nice secluded spot by the stream to wash. She had been gone some ten minutes when we heard a muffled cry. Then the Princess called out in panic.

"Atwin!"

The Prince jumped up and ran into the woods. Worried by the anxiety in that cry, Evelar and I followed. From the trees ahead we heard a startled exclamation, followed by a fleshy crack and a heavy thud. We hurried in concern toward the sounds. What we saw stopped us in our tracks.

Netta had stripped to her petticoat and chemise and her dress was draped over the lower branch of a tree. She stood now huddled in Atwin's comforting embrace, her face buried in his chest. The knuckles on Atwin's right hand were grazed and Geltray was sprawled on the ground, one hand pressed gingerly to his jaw.

Atwin looked across at us, his eyes blazing. He pointed an accusing finger at Geltray.

"That man has to go!" he said vehemently.

"I didn't touch her!" said Geltray defensively. "I swear I never touched her!"

I admit I was inclined to believe the poor man. From what I had learned of Netta lately, all he really would have had to do was look at her the wrong way. And the fact that the Princess had not been properly dressed at the time would have added to her panic. Netta would not tell us what had happened, but from what I can gather the tribesman must have stumbled across her accidentally and things went downhill from there. I had to give Geltray the benefit of the doubt. Perhaps Evelar was right. Netta was too innocent for her own good.

The last two days of travel were tense and, as if to reflect our tension, the sky above was dark and there was a blustery wind. Evelar had tried to smooth things over between Atwin and Geltray, with only moderate success. They rode as far apart as possible, Geltray far to the front and Atwin trailing along behind us. Netta rode beside me in a nervous silence.

With a storm building overhead we rode the last few miles through the foothills toward Zelona. Geltray stopped some way from the city gate. He would not enter with us into the city. We parted in an uneasy friendship and the young tribesman turned back the way we had come. Gliss, too, refused to enter the city.

Netta watched sadly as she trotted off, hoping she would find us later and reluctantly joined Atwin on the stallion's back. As the storm broke over our heads, we rode down into Zelona. The storm beat down on us as we headed for the nearest inn. As we rode into the courtyard Evelar stopped. I turned back to look questioningly at him.

"Not here," he said in a quiet voice.

"But it is wet out here," said Atwin. "We may not find another inn on this side of town."

"Not here," said Evelar again. He turned his horse and rode out of the courtyard and off down the street. With a shrug at the others I followed and the three of us rode through the dripping rain after the revealer. I had learned to trust Evelar's judgment and if he wanted to go somewhere else, I was willing to get wet.

Some ten minutes later we splashed our way into the courtyard of another inn, outwardly identical to the one we had just rejected. We stabled the horses and made our way inside. The proprietor came bustling over in that manner common to inn owners everywhere and ordered us good naturedly to stop dripping on his floor.

He led us to a large table near the fire and took our drenched cloaks from us. For some reason he decided not to try to take Evelar's revealer's cloak. Perhaps it was the stern look of warning Evelar sent his way. Or maybe it was the hand resting negligently on the hilt of his sword. Evelar is rather attached to his cloak.

We dried ourselves gratefully by the fire.

"You'll be wanting a room, then," said the inn-keeper, setting up a rack on which he draped our cloaks to dry in front of the fire.

"That would be nice," said Netta. "As would a bath, for that matter."

"That can be arranged. But it will cost extra."

"Of course," said the Princess primly.

"I'll see to it then."

"In the mean-time," said Atwin, "we will have some ale and something to eat."

"Right away, My Lord."

As the inn-keeper bustled away, we sat on the bench at the old oak table and watched the activity of the tavern. A group of young hot-heads looked at us coldly from their drunken corner.

They were obviously itching to pick a fight, but the presence of the revealer in our midst put a damper on their enthusiasm. We ourselves were suddenly unassailable and the prospect of having a trained warrior on hand to prevent them meant that they could not turn their predatory intentions on another target. They were understandably unhappy.

The inn-keeper brought ale for Atwin and the revealer, but Evelar waved it away with a grimace of distaste. The inn-keeper's wife brought steaming bowls of stew. She was a cheerily round woman, eager to please.

"When you're ready," she said to Netta and me, "I'll take you upstairs where you can bathe in private."

"I thank you," said Netta.

"It's a pleasure. We don't get much gentlefolk here, you know. If there's anything you might be needing, My Lady, don't you be hesitating to ask. Just send your maid down to me and I'll do the rest."

"Maid?" Netta looked at me in surprise.

"Oh dear," said the woman. "Did I get it wrong?"

"No matter," I said with a chuckle.

"Mym is a dear friend," said Netta. Then she smiled a

little mischievously. "And she is married to Evelar."

"Who?"

"The revealer."

"Oh!" The friendly woman looked Evelar up and down appraisingly. Evelar looked up at the woman scrutinizing him. "Nice catch!" said the woman with a broad wink at me.

Netta gasped. Evelar looked at me quizzically and I couldn't help laughing. He raised an eyebrow.

'Never mind, Dear,' I said mentally.

After the meal, Netta and I made our way upstairs.

"You boys should probably think about washing too," I said archly.

"Later, my love," said Evelar. "I need to nose about a bit first."

When we came back downstairs, Atwin was sitting in conversation with an old man in the corner. The tavern was quiet. The hot-heads were gone, no doubt to find a tavern with less dangerous patronage. When Atwin saw us he excused himself and met us at the old oak table.

"Find anything interesting?" I asked.

"Not really. The most unusual occurrence in the last fifty years was the day the inn-keeper bought this old table."

"Oh?"

The Prince chuckled. "Some old peddler came into the tavern selling old wooden utensils. When the inn-keeper said he was not interested, the old man became determined to sell him something. Finally, he mentioned an old oak table he had in pieces in his wagon. The inn-keeper pricked up his ears and became immediately intrigued. So the peddler took him outside, and the next thing you know they were assembling this heavy old thing."

Netta sighed. "So it seems that Naali never passed through here."

"I would not be so sure," said Atwin. "I think we just found the clue we have been looking for."

"What do you mean?" I asked.

"Something struck me about the table story. My old friend over there claims to remember seeing something strange. He was a young man at the time, so unless his memory is playing tricks on him he probably did see it."

"See what?"

"As the table was being assembled, he swears that he saw the wood glowing."

"Glowing?"

"A blue nimbus."

"Naali!" cried Netta.

"It would appear so."

"Why don't you see if Leena can pick up anything," I suggested.

Netta nodded. Silently, I reached out with my mind and told Evelar what we were doing.

'I'm on my way,' he said tensely.

Netta laid a hand flat on the table and took Leena in the other. She concentrated and immediately began to glow blue. The old man in the corner tottered over curiously, seemingly pleased that his memory was working after all. The glow increased and flowed down Netta's arm into the hand on the table.

The inn-keeper came over, drawn by the strange glow. "What the crock?" he mumbled under his breath.

The blue nimbus grew to engulf the table. Within the glow, tears could be seen flowing down Netta's face. At that moment, Evelar arrived and stopped in surprise. He approached slowly, not wanting to disturb Netta. He came up behind me and we watched in silence. Finally, Netta relaxed. The glow faded from about her, but it hovered eerily over the table.

"What did she say?" I asked.

Netta took a deep breath. "This table was made from a piece of an ancient tree which is the home of Leshma, an ageless spirit. Naali rests within that tree."

"Where is the tree?" asked Atwin.

"She cannot tell. Naali is somehow shielded, so though she can tell that he is in the tree, she cannot find where that tree is."

Atwin cursed. "Another dead end."

"Maybe not," said Evelar. He stepped up to the table. "Mym," he said, holding out his hand for me to take. I opened a mental channel and gave him the energy he needed. With his right hand he made a slow pass over the table and the blue nimbus acquired a golden tone.

The inn-keeper's eyes widened. The other old man crept closer in wonderment. Evelar closed his eyes and concentrated. He began to trace a glowing design on the table. As his index finger moved over the ancient oak surface, the gilded blue glow coalesced and followed the path he traced on the wood.

As he worked, a part of my mind remained separate and I wondered at this new power. Yet again my revealer was performing an amazing new talent and I could not help wondering what this might lead to. This was the third time he had done something so amazing as to fill me with wonder. Surely these things were preceding something, why else would they occur in such unexpected magnificence? Perhaps it will become clear in time.

My revealer opened his eyes and looked at the shimmering design he had made. The shape was of a triangle standing on its apex. Across the top and down the left-hand side were what looked like clouds in the shape of bearded old men. At the right side lay the long undulating body of a serpent. And in the middle stood a fiery dragon.

From the apex, at the lower end of the cloud-like figures, came a straight line, stretching from there into the very heart of the dragon. At that point, one shining leaf sprang from the dragon's chest.

"What does it mean?" asked Atwin in a hushed voice.

Evelar studied the design for a long moment. Then he looked up in sudden comprehension.

"Mym, would you find my map?" he said.

"Of course."

I hurried upstairs, found the map and brought it back down. Evelar took the map from me gratefully and positioned it on the table over the glowing design. As we watched breathlessly, the blue-gold glow burned its way through the map, until we could all see exactly what it meant.

The old cloud-men were the mountains - the Dragons to the west and the Heights to the north. The serpent was the coastline. And the dragon was the Barren Wastes in the middle.

"What means that line?" asked Netta. "And the leaf?"

"The line is a pointer, stretching from here, Zelona, into the heart of the desert," said Evelar.

"Where it meets the tree," I said, completing Evelar's interpretation.

He grinned at me. "It looks like we've found Naali."

TWENTY ONE

We sat about the old table, planning the next leg of our journey.

"I hope you all realise we can't stay here," I said quietly.

"Why?" said Netta then. "We have seen no kalkar for days. I thought we had lost them."

"We had, while Gliss was protecting us. But she's not with us right now."

"But she was not with us in the mountain camp, with Netray's people."

"No," I said, hesitating. I would have to tell them what I knew from my dreams.

"What's bothering you, my love?"

"When I was ill I dreamed and I learned."

"What are you talking about?" said Atwin.

"The kalkar can hear Leena," I blurted.

"What?" said Netta.

"When Netta uses Leena in some way, the kalkar hear and are able to find us. When we were with Netray, Leena was quiet and we were safe. Previously, Gliss was shielding us, so they could hear Leena but not locate her."

"And you think they will find us now?" said Atwin.

"How can you be so sure?" said Netta.

"Because when I dreamed, I was with the kalkar, in their collective mind, looking at the world from their point of view. I know how they think."

Atwin whistled. "I believe you. This whole journey has

followed that pattern. Every time Leena did something they found us soon after. I am surprised we did not see it before."

"What do we do now?" said Netta.

"We rest while we can and we leave at midnight," said Evelar firmly.

Atwin nodded. "We had best head upstairs then."

"I'll keep watch, in case we have to move in a hurry," said Evelar. "I can rest and absorb in the saddle."

Netta and Atwin stood to head to our room, but I hesitated.

"Are you coming, Mym?" said Netta.

"Ah... I'll be up in a moment," I hedged.

With a wave and a shrug Netta went upstairs, followed closely by the Prince.

'What's wrong, my love?'

I slipped in under his arm. *'Do you think we could be on watch somewhere... quieter?'*

Seeing the others leave, the landlady bustled over to us and sat across from us at the table. I sighed and Evelar pulled me closer. *'It was a nice idea, my love.'*

"Can those two be trusted without a chaperone?" she winked. "Or are they a couple too?"

"They will be soon enough," I replied. "But for now all they'll do is sleep."

The woman laughed and leaned in close. "Not what you two would like to be doing right now," she said suggestively. "You look like you need some privacy. Been travelling a while have we?"

I felt my cheeks grow hot and she laughed again. Evelar looked blandly at her, face carefully expressionless.

"Oh you can hide behind that revealer face all you want, but I know what's going on in that handsome young head of yours."

She leaned in even closer with a conspiratorial grin. "I

remember what it was like to be young and in love, though you wouldn't know it to look at me." She gave a gleeful cackle. "Follow me," she whispered.

Curious, we followed, and she led us behind the counter and through a door to the back room, where there were crates of ale bottles and a small kitchen area. The woman signalled for us to follow. She led us through another door to find a cosy little room, a fireplace welcoming us with warmth and light and a large low couch by the fire.

"This is our private sitting room, but you can use it tonight. Stay as long as you like, I'll make sure you're not disturbed."

Evelar smiled at the woman, his mask dropping now that we were in private, and she beamed.

"Now that's better," she said. "You're stunning when you drop that revealer act. No wonder she loves you. Oh I know, you have to keep up appearances, but you should smile more often."

I could not help giggling at his nonplussed expression. The woman winked at me and bustled her way from the room, closing the door firmly behind her.

We stood looking at each other for a moment in bewilderment. I felt suddenly shy and embarrassed, but then he stepped forward and slipped his arms about my waist.

"I suppose we should make full use of the facilities," he said archly.

I giggled again at that.

"That's more like it! I've missed hearing you laugh."

Much later we lay snuggled together on the couch, watching the flames dance and enjoying the quiet, but we both knew this moment had to end. The raucous sound of patrons drunk on ale in the inn drifted to us, muffled but jarring nonetheless.

"We should wake the others and get moving," I said sadly.

"I know."

A particularly loud cry from the inn broke our mood. Someone was calling, closer now, as if they had come through into the kitchen room and we could hear the landlady protesting.

"That's Atwin's voice," said Evelar then. "Time to go, my love."

We reluctantly gathered ourselves and prepared to leave. Evelar placed a gold coin on the mantle for the landlady to find, our thanks for her discreet understanding. Then we exited the cosy room and faced the commotion. Coming up behind the irate woman, I put my hand on her arm and she turned, calming when she saw us.

"It's alright, mistress," I said. "Thank you for your diligence."

"There you are!" Atwin exclaimed. "We have to go. Netta says they are coming, fast."

Evelar nodded. "Then let's move."

Gliss rejoined us almost as soon as we left the city, her magical shield enclosing us once more, and by midday we were through the fertile farm lands and could see the flash of sun on sand ahead. The vegetation became stunted, less virile, as we neared the edge of the Barren Wastes.

In the mountains we had been isolated, but we had always been close enough to other people to be able to buy supplies and information about the path ahead. But now we would be leaving civilization far behind.

The rolling countryside flattened and the soil grew lighter, less rich. Trees gave way to shrubs and grass gave way to bare earth. The lighter earth, mostly sand now, drifted into dunes, difficult to climb and unstable under the hooves of our mounts. Finally, some hundred meters or so from the invisible line that marked the edge of the desert, Evelar called a halt.

We stood at the top of a dune and looked out over the Barren Wastes. Ahead, four or five dunes rose and fell, before one final rise gave way to that wide expanse of flat, infertile sand, which stretched as far as the eye could see.

Netta urged Gliss forward and made her way to the top of that final hill. Though Atwin called her back, the Princess went on, eager to see that view from the very edge of the desert. Atwin was gathering himself to ride after her but, on impulse, I stopped him.

"I'll go," I said.

I spurred Cheena forward and rode out to the edge of the desert. As I came up beside Netta, intent on bringing her back to the others, my gaze was caught and held.

I drew in my breath softly. From my previous vantage point the view had been arresting, but separated by those final hills of sand. Now, with nothing between us and that inhospitable expanse, I was mesmerised.

Nothing but sand and a few dried out shrubs, stretching on forever. It was breathtaking and very sobering. I sat on my horse and drank in that sight. Finally, Evelar called me to with a chuckle.

'Three days out there and you won't think it so glorious, my love,' he said in my mind. *'The desert is a killer. She's breathtakingly beautiful but still a killer, infinitely powerful.'*

'The beauty of any predator is in the sleekness which gives it the power to kill,' I replied.

'Come back, Mym,' he said then. *'There's much we must prepare if we are to conquer the dragon.'*

"What are they for?" asked Netta. Evelar had spent

some time searching the countryside and returned with three long staffs of wood and several shorter ones.

"It's hot out there," he said. "Especially in the middle of the day. We'll need to shelter the animals and ourselves, while the sun is high. We'll travel early in the morning and late in the afternoon, resting in the heat of midday. It also gets very cold in the middle of the night. We'll need shelter then too. It would be easier if we had camels, but we don't."

"Camels?" asked Netta.

"They're rare and very valuable. The nomads use them."

"Nomads?"

"People who have adapted to life in the desert. I lived with them once."

"They live out there?" Netta said incredulously.

"The camels help. They ride them instead of horses."

"Why?"

"Because they can survive for some time without water. Speaking of water," he said, rummaging about in the packs for water containers. As well as our canteens, he had picked up somewhere several oilskins. "There's a well some ways back," he said to me. "Take the others and fill these, all of them, as full as they will go. There's a trough, so take the animals and see they drink plenty of water. You'd better drink your fill from the well also."

"What about you?" I said.

"I'll be along in a while. I have to find the direction. We wouldn't want to miss our target."

As the sun began its slow descent, we gathered ourselves and struck out into the desert. The worst of the day's heat was past, but we still were soon sweltering in our heavy cloaks. At one point Netta made to remove hers, but Evelar stopped her.

"That's not a good idea," he said.

"Why?"

"Would you rather be hot or burnt?"

"Oh," Netta said, shrugging back into the cloak.

"You'd better put up the hood too."

We stopped late and rose again well before dawn. It was hard going and the poor animals laboured in the heat. Though we were rationing water severely, the horses could not survive without it and our meagre supply dwindled rapidly.

As the sun rose steadily to its zenith we paused and set up the shelter; a large blanket held down with stones at one end and propped up with the three long staffs at the other, slanted away from the blistering sun.The horses sank gratefully to the sand in the dubious shelter.

Gliss was a wonder. She lay protectively among them, her wings outstretched over them, fanning slowly to form a cooling breeze. Netta and Atwin slipped under the shelter behind the animals and were soon dozing peacefully, a great way to escape the heat. But I could not sleep.

After a few moments I slipped out of the shelter and joined Evelar where he sat quietly on watch. He had his cloak propped up over himself with one of the shorter staffs he had brought with us. My revealer widened his little tent with another of his staffs and invited me to join him. Very cautiously, I slid in under the cloak and leaned back against his chest.

"What troubles you, my love," he said, wrapping his arms about me.

"How far do you think we have to go before we get to the tree?"

"I have no idea. The centre of the desert is pretty much untouched, even by the nomads."

"We only have enough water for another day or two at

best, since the horses need so much."

"I can find water if necessary."

"How?"

"There are ways, signs to look for."

He said it calmly, in a voice that was almost a whisper. He was more relaxed in that moment than I had ever seen him, almost serene. It was as if he had somehow come home.

"How long did you live with the nomads?"

"The last time, three months, I think. Quite a few years overall. Why do you ask?"

"You know the ways of the desert so well. You seem to belong here."

He laughed softly. "How very astute of you, my love."

"You love being out here," I said.

"It's more than that, really. You could say the desert is in my blood. I was born here, you know."

"No, I didn't know that. So you literally are at home here. No wonder you fit so."

"My home is the College now. I was so young when I left here."

"Is that why you were given the name Sand?"

"I suppose so. I come back here when I need to recharge. But it's hard to hide in the desert. The nomads always find you."

"I should think you would want them to find you."

"Have you ever had to face kin who don't understand what it is that drives you?"

"Yes actually, I have," I said, thinking of my father.

"Then you know why I avoid them." He sighed. "Of course, it's not my choice of career that bothers them."

"Oh?"

"It's the fact that I took my sister with me. She was promised to the chief's son, but we are twins. She wouldn't let me go without her."

"What made you decide to go to the College?"

He chuckled. "We discovered our power early. As children we would play mental tricks on each other. It was fun, just a game. We never knew we could turn it into a career. Then we had an encounter with a lone revealer, an artisan on a secret mission. He came across us in the middle of one of our games and was impressed. So he told us all about the College and how we had to go there as supplicants at age ten. We were nine at the time, and from that moment we couldn't wait to go. Our father was furious, but we went anyway."

I snuggled in closer, feeling immensely happy that he had taken that path. I wondered what had made him reveal so much. Members of the College liked to keep their little secrets. It made life more interesting. But I had learned more about my revealer in those few moments than I had in all the months I had known him.

On the third day, Evelar started to look for water. I know not what signs he found, but when we stopped for our midday siesta he allowed us to sleep longer than usual. I woke after an hour or so and joined him on watch. I have never learned how to sleep in the daylight hours. When Netta and Atwin awoke some two hours later, Evelar told them that we would be moving no further that day.

"Why?" said Netta.

"We wait till dusk," Evelar replied. "Then we dig."

It was treacherous. The sand filled our well almost as quickly as we could dig it. We worked in shifts, alternately digging and resting huddled in a blanket. But we were getting nowhere. Finally, Netta decided to ask Leena for help. She supported the sides, so the going was easier after that. As the hole got deeper, Evelar rigged an elaborate apparatus which could carry the sand out of the hole and double as a way of getting in and out ourselves. But ten feet and several hours later we still had not found water. Atwin climbed out of the hole and sat down in disgust.

"Keep digging," said Evelar from down the well.

"But it is hopeless."

"Keep digging."

Reluctantly, Atwin returned to the task. Finally, at fifteen feet, we hit mud.

We continued our journey with newly filled water-carriers. After the back-breaking work of the night, we all fervently hoped that we would find the tree before we ran out of water again. But we weren't to be so lucky. We had to dig twice more before we reached our goal. At the end of the twelfth day in the desert, Netta saw something on the horizon. Heedless of our warning she galloped on ahead. We caught her as she stood stock-still in the middle of nowhere. Atwin gasped and made to join her, looking in wonder at absolutely nothing.

"I don't see anything," I said.

"Look with your mind, not your eyes," Evelar replied.

I closed my eyes and saw it, the most enormous tree in the world. Then we moved forward to join our companions. The animals immediately found an invisible trough of water and drank thirstily. We looked up with our minds at the glorious branches overhead. When I looked with my eyes I saw nothing, but my instinct told me that my eyes were lying.

"How do we find Naali?" asked Atwin.

Netta placed her hand on the invisible bark and instantly began to glow.

"Naali is inside the tree," she said in a hushed voice.

TWENTY TWO

Netta put both hands on the trunk that was not there and began to explore, guided by the glowing amulet at her neck. Finally, she found what she was looking for and traced a square, creating a glowing blue outline. Then, she gathered herself and pushed.

A door opened onto darkness. When looking with bare eyes, it looked like a hole of nothing standing in mid-air in the middle of the bright yellowness of the desert. When you moved around to behind the hole it was gone. Of course, when you agreed not to trust your eyes, it was merely a door in the trunk of a thousand foot oak tree.

Netta peered inside cautiously. Then, as she raised a foot to step inside, there came a strange, high pitched... sniggle from the invisible branches above.

* * *

"Sniggle?" said the Maestro incredulously.

"You know," said Miyam. "A kind of a cross between a snicker and a giggle."

"You can't be serious."

"Well," said Sand from the darkness beside the fireplace, "I suppose that's what it was. Good word, my love."

"Thank you, Dear."

* * *

We looked up. A curious little creature clambered down from the branches, chattering delightedly.

"It gladdens me at last to see that arrived hast thee," it

said.

"Ex... cuse me?" said Atwin.

"Waited long for thee have I."

"What did it say?" said Netta.

"Come, My Children. For thee one doth await."

With that, the weird little creature led the way into the dark heart of the invisible tree.

"You would be Leshma," said Atwin.

"Ah, that I be, My Child." He sniggled again.

The dwarf-like gnomby creature led us chatteringly down a steep dark flight of stairs. Soon we emerged into a cheerful little room lit by the golden bodies of thousands of glow worms.

Even before we entered, Leena began to glow once more. As we stepped further into the room our eyes were drawn involuntarily to, of all places, a bookshelf above the tiny bed. There, perched incongruously amongst a clutter of trinkets, stood a large crystal, pulsating softly in a blue light, which emanated from the golden amulet within.

"Naali!" Netta cried out, and ran across the room.

She jumped up onto the bed and reached out with both hands to take the glowing crystal. The glow at her neck engulfed her and joined the blue of Naali. Then she sank down onto the bed with a little cry of grief, cradling the lump of crystal in her lap and crying broken-heartedly.

Atwin went to her and sat in front of her on the bed. He reached out to brush the wisps of hair from her eyes. When he touched the crystal in her lap, it flared blue in response, and she looked up at him tearfully.

"Is there no way Leena can break the spell?" he said.

Netta shook her head dejectedly, and Atwin cursed vehemently.

"To come so close," he said bitterly, "And be unable to complete it."

As the two of them sat together dejectedly, glowing faintly, Evelar slowly crossed the room to them. Both jumped as my revealer knelt by the bed and reached out with his left hand to touch the crystal which encased Naali. The glow took on a golden tinge as Evelar concentrated briefly. Then he stood up quickly and strode from the room, catching my hand on the way out and pulling me with him.

Once outside, he whistled for Lumen and the two of us mounted quickly. He kicked the horse into a ground-eating canter and we rode away from the invisible oak tree. At a point not appreciably different from the rest of the surrounding desert, some few hundred meters from the tree that was not visibly there, Evelar reined in and swung from the horse. He reached up to help me down and, taking my hand, he led me away from the horse to a blistering spot on the crest of a rise in the sand.

He bent then and picked up a handful of hot yellow sand. He closed his fist and told me to place my hands about it. Then he put his other hand over the top of mine and began to concentrate. Realising what he wanted, I opened a mental channel through which he could draw energy.

He looked at me and held my eyes for a long moment. Then he removed his hand. I released his fist and he opened it, showing me what he now held. A perfect diamond, clear and uncut, catching the late afternoon sun with a light that was blinding.

He grinned then and led me back to where his stallion waited patiently. We remounted in silence and rode quickly back to the tree that we could not see. We re-entered the cheery little room where the others waited expectantly. Several times in the past Evelar had succeeded where Leena had failed and we hoped that this time would be no different. Evelar strode purposely to where Netta and Atwin sat.

"Lift the crystal up," he said quietly, "and hold it between you."

With a look at each other they did so. Evelar held the diamond in his right hand and reached out to place his left flat on top of the crystal. I came up behind him and offered my energy once more. The blue nimbus brightened to gold and Evelar himself actually began to glow with the power of it.

The gold light slowly began to permeate the crystal. Fine cracks began to form. The light increased steadily. Naali glowed his heart out inside his encasement, a blue spark within the gold, seemingly trying to add his strength to Evelar's, desperate to escape. The crystal could surely not contain such forces. But it did. Beads of sweat began to form on my revealer's brow.

From behind, I wrapped my arms about his waist, hoping that the contact would strengthen the channel. With a little shrug of effort, he harnessed the stronger flow of energy. The crystal began to vibrate. Netta and Atwin held it fast between them as it resonated violently.

The energy force from inside and out was implacable. Still the crystal would not break. It was riddled now with hairline fractures, visible as a series of brighter lines within the energy field. Finally, when none of us could have handled the pressure any more, Evelar gathered in a huge amount of energy.

He raised the diamond in his right hand, drew in his breath and, in a sudden movement, slapped it down on the side of the crystal, simultaneously releasing the built-up energy in a sharp burst of power.

The crystal shattered in an immense explosion, and as it did so the fragments dissolved into nothing, even as they rained down on us. A triumphantly glowing Naali fell into Netta's waiting hand. Evelar and I crumpled to the floor, our energy drained.

I felt very grey. All we could do was lean against each other and watch the very welcome sight of Naali resting in Netta's wondering hand. The little goblin creature, Leshma, tottered up behind us and tapped me on the shoulder. He offered a large mug.

"Drink, My Children," he said.

I took the proffered cup and smelled it suspiciously. My nose shrivelled. I looked doubtfully at Leshma. He sniggled.

"Drink," he said.

Tentatively, I took a sip. My tongue exploded and I pulled a face. I sat gagging as a strange feeling of warmth began to overtake my body. Almost against my will, I took another, larger sip.

The taste was fractionally more bearable this time. The warmth made its way into my very bones. I took a third sip, almost controlling my shudders. This time, I felt remarkably good.

I handed the cup to Evelar, who looked at it with considerable distaste. He made to hand the cup, untouched, back to Leshma, who merely sniggled and pushed it back.

"It's rather disgusting," I said with a laugh, "But it's remarkably effective, Dear."

He sniffed at it. Then, taking a deep breath, he closed his eyes and downed the horrid liquid. He gasped. Then he spluttered a bit. Then he smiled as the warmth took over.

"It's almost worth it," he said.

Now that I had regained my senses, I thought back on what Evelar had just done. He had created a diamond crystal and used it to break the spell holding Naali. That was crystal channelling on an immense scale. For the fourth time since starting this journey he had done something monumental, outside the sphere of College training. There was obviously something building here that was more important than anything I could fathom.

* * *

"This strange idea you keep mentioning intrigues me, my dear," said the Maestro. "What is it?"

"I don't know, but has something to do with Sand, I think."

"Me?" Sand interjected. "What event of such significance could possibly involve me?"

"I'll let you know when I figure it out," said Miyam.

* * *

Netta and Atwin were sitting staring into each other's eyes. Evelar stood up carefully and offered his hands to me, helping me rise. We looked at the pair sitting motionless on the bed.

"Come along, you two," I said.

Netta looked at me rather absently and she slid unresisting from the bed. Atwin followed, equally dazed.

"Wait," she said then, in a soft voice that seemed to come from far away.

She was glowing furiously. She turned to face Atwin. She lifted the chain which held Naali between her hands and without ceremony placed it over Atwin's head. The explosion of blue light was blinding and was accompanied by a trembling of the earth and a clear, bell-like note that hung sustained in the air.

Then, of a sudden, the glow and the sound and the tremor of the earth, all stopped. All was painfully still. After several intense moments we came to, and made to leave. As Netta turned away from Atwin she was pulled up short.

The amulet about her neck was pulling her back, hovering in mid-air at the end of the chain, straining to reach Naali, who was similarly pulling Atwin forward. The two amulets, the long lost spirit of King Rexa and his beloved wife, were desperately trying to reach each other.

As Netta involuntarily turned back, the minute distance between them was closed and with a little clack the two amulets fused together.

In that instant, the blue glow returned to engulf Netta and Atwin. They resisted the pull, Netta quite frantically, but the influence of the amulets was far too great and the two were thrown together in a passionate kiss.

Netta, with her hands flat on his shoulders, struggled against the compulsion. Finally, they pulled apart, Netta giving a gasp of shock. They stared at each other in consternation. Netta's jaw dropped.

"W... we have to what?" she said in a horrored whisper.

Netta and Atwin were drawn together again and this time there was no escape. Leshma sniggled and trotted from the room as they fell back onto the tiny bed.

I looked at Evelar, who raised an eyebrow suggestively.

"What a nice idea," I said archly.

With a shameless grin, he took my hand and we hurried from the room, closing the door after us. The blue glow seeped out from under the door as we climbed the stairs.

Riding together on Lumen, we headed out into the desert evening. Cheena nickered at me as we left, but I heard Evelar send a thought for her to stay with Gliss and Windfoot, offering rest and shelter under the tree with plenty of water in the trough.

I was glad to be heading out alone with my revealer. Riding together like that was so intimate and we had both missed it. I leant back in the warmth of his arms and closed my eyes, drinking him in and listening to the absolute silence of the desert.

We set up camp atop a high dune and sat watching the sunset. We had no need of words, our bodies talking for us, sharing our pleasure long into the night, until finally we slept in each other's arms.

I raced in a frenzy of fear. The packs were gathering, a huge collective ready to run. Each new group joined us in the great mind and our terrible fear spurred us onward. Soon we would be a mighty army and we would go, streaming out across the sand to where the great killer had finally shown herself.

He had come! All subterfuge was gone, the mist swept away, and the one who kills had risen from the shadows to mock us all. She had found him and now we were all dead. Naali the mighty murderer was free, and reunited with Leena the terrible. The group mind screamed in silent terror, with one thought. Naali is found! Catch them now! Stop them before they kill us all!

I sat up with a gasp, my heart racing and my blood cold. Beside me Evelar was sitting in stunned silence, gasping for breath.

"They're coming!" I cried.

"I know."

TWENTY THREE

As the white desert sun rapidly burned off the cool of the night, my revealer and I rode back toward the invisible tree. It was with disappointment that we hurried to get back to the others. Being on the road with so little privacy for so long, it had been a relief to be alone together. But when we crested a hill and looked to where the tree was we pulled up short.

The invisible tree was no longer invisible. Evelar spurred the stallion forward, and we soon found ourselves under the spreading leaves of a now perfectly visible giant oak tree. It was glorious. Evelar slid down from behind me and reached up to lift me down.

We gazed up, and I let out a little joyous laugh. Leshma trotted over and handed us a cup each. We sniffed at it suspiciously, remembering the concoction he had served us before, but it turned out to be a nourishing stew.

"What happened to the tree?" I asked.

"When freed was Naali, broken was the spell," said Leshma.

Somehow we had not noticed the change when we rode away from the tree the evening before, but of course we had been a little preoccupied then.

"Were you two not cold out there all night?" asked Atwin in a peculiar voice.

We shared a lingering look. "No," I said.

"Not appreciably," said Evelar thickly.

"I see," said Atwin.

At the strangeness of his tone, we looked to where Atwin was sitting at the base of the tree and saw a stranger. His eyes flicked about nervously as he chewed at his fingernails.

"Are you alright?" I asked in concern.

"No... not really," he said absently.

Concerned, we moved closer. The Prince looked at us briefly and dropped his tortured eyes, unable to let us in. Evelar knelt beside him.

"What ails you, my friend?" he said gently.

"Fear..." said Atwin with a catch of breath.

"Fear? Of what?"

The Prince looked sideways at Evelar, and snatched his eyes away again. "She was... so pure," he blurted in a strangled voice, his eyes darting about. "So very... pure..." Then he looked at Evelar, finally meeting his friend's eyes. "It scares me to think what this may have done to her," he said earnestly. Then he dropped his eyes again, shifting his gaze about erratically. "She should never have been pushed like that," he whispered brokenly.

"Where is she?" asked Evelar.

Atwin moved his head slightly, indicating that she was still inside the tree.

"I'll go," I said quietly.

In the little room I found Netta lying in a tangled heap of blankets, her tousled hair spread out about her. She was awake, but her eyes stared blankly as she nibbled at one thumb-nail. She had been crying.

I knelt by the bed, but she refused to look at me. I sighed. There was no quick way to heal this. She would need time to come to terms with it. But I could help her find her dignity.

"Would you like me to help you get cleaned up?"

She nodded ever so slightly.

*

When we emerged from the tree some time later, Netta had reached some semblance of her old self, but her regal bearing was shattered. She had not spoken a word to me and she refused to look directly at any of us, especially Atwin. She avoided him entirely.

The Prince watched her with tormented eyes. She had decided, totally out of character, to leave her hair unrestrained, as if the long golden tresses could somehow shield her from the world. With her head held bent, her face was hidden, so she did not have to look at us, and we could not look at her.

The situation worsened when we decided it was time to go. Netta livened up, looking eagerly about for her fabulous mount. But the winged unicorn was gone.

"Where is Gliss?" she asked in a voice that was barely audible.

We looked at each other in consternation. How could we tell her that the mythical beast had been attracted by Netta's innocence and had now left us?

"She's gone," I said finally.

"Why?"

There was no easy way to say it. "You can no longer touch her," I said.

"Why?" she asked again.

I hesitated and looked at the others for help, but what could they say? The last thing she needed was to feel tainted by what had happened. I think maybe she already felt that way. When she felt our tenseness, she knew without me having to say it.

"Oh," she said in a small voice.

A single poignant tear spilled down her face. Atwin reached out a hand to comfort her but stopped as she made to pull away. His face twisted in pain and he ran a nervous hand through his close-cropped hair. His other hand clenched into an impotent fist at his side.

When Evelar suggested that she ride with Atwin, Netta actually looked at the revealer, her panic overriding her sense of shame. I coughed delicately.

"You can ride Cheena," I said, offering the reins of my mare. I cast a reproachful look at Evelar, surprised by his lack of tact. Netta smiled wanly in relief. Then she withdrew again into herself, hiding behind her hair.

After a cheery farewell from a sniggling Leshma, we rode north away from the giant oak tree. Evelar and I once again rode together on Lumen, his faithful stallion. I knew that I had done the right thing by giving Netta my mare, though Evelar was not so sure.

"I won't have you forcing her the way the amulets did," I said firmly. "Let her take her time. She'll come around eventually."

"How can you be sure?"

"Let's just say I have a feeling. When she sees how happy we are..." At that he tightened his arms about me, bringing a soft giggle to my lips. "She'll want something like it for herself. She'll feel better about herself once she realises there's no shame in love."

"I hope you're right, Mym."

"Have you ever known me to be wrong?"

Three days from the tree it was time to look for water again. But as we rose in the early hours of the evening to begin digging, Netta raised her head and stared west, out over the blackness of the desert night. Atwin gave a grunt of surprise, clutching at the amulet about his neck, but Netta stopped him from removing it with one gentle hand.

"What is it?" said Evelar.

"Kalkar," they said together.

"How did they find us?" Netta asked.

"They must have felt the noise the amulets made back in the tree," said Atwin quietly. "And we no longer have Gliss to hide us."

Netta withdrew again at the reminder of those events, and Atwin cursed under his breath. Evelar cast about and pointed to a rising dune in the distance. We made our way to the summit and prepared as best we could for attack.

At least from here we could defend from above as they came up the hill. The amulets could not tell from which direction they would come, so we stood at the top waiting. We did not have to wait long.

Staring out into the darkness we watched, barely breathing. The desert sands shone and glimmered in reflected moonlight, and we could see almost to the distant horizon. The sand under our feet was still warm from the heat of the day, but the cold night air frosted with our breath. A light breeze blew, bringing a faint warm tang of sulphur.

The chill of the desert seemed less the longer we waited and then it hit us, a gust of warm air tainted with smoke. I felt rather than saw the first of the enemy, a dark smudge in the distance as it crested a rise. The force emerged from the darkness, first a few with numbers rapidly growing, rank upon rank, clustered in groups.

It looked like our dream had been made flesh, as if many packs had joined together. We could never hope to combat such an army. The packs came on, filling the sand for miles in every direction, surrounding us.

The sand no longer reflected the moonlight, but the kalkar force hiding the light did not smother it. Instead, it seemed even brighter as the creatures themselves shone. With their cloak of skin thrown back and the full moon shining down, the markings on their skin picked up the light, glowing with eerie phosphorescence. Every one was different and every one was breathtaking.

Together, the assembled mass of fluorescent colour all around was at once beautiful and disturbing. A million splotches of colour shining in the moonlight like a massive swarm of large nocturnal insects, punctuated by the red glowing eyes of the kalkar, all trained on us.

"Well, goodbye my friends," said Atwin fatalistically. "It has been fun."

From out of the assembled horde boomed a thought, implanted directly into all our minds. *Give us the one who kills. Give us Leena and her mate. We will melt them with our fire. We will spare the human bearers. Surrender them now!*

"Never!" Netta and Atwin cried in unison.

So be it!

With that, the first rank began to move forward. The rest of the horde hung back, standing motionless and humming, a weird ululating back of the throat kind of sound. The first rank was enough to strike fear in our hearts as it sped forward, rapidly closing in.

"Can't the amulets do something?" I said.

Atwin looked pointedly at Netta, who was steadfastly ignoring him.

I sighed. "Netta," I said.

She turned her head in my direction but did not raise her eyes.

"Please," I entreated.

She looked out at the advancing kalkar, their bright colours flickering with movement. Lowering her head in defeat, she walked over to Atwin. She raised her tragic eyes to his tortured ones and lifted her hands for him to take. Then the amulets began to glow.

As the blue glow grew to engulf our two friends and as

the kalkar closed in, Evelar and I prepared to fight. Since Atwin was otherwise engaged, I took his sword in my right hand and my knife in the other. Then we mounted up and waited, one either side of the pair as the kalkar circled.

The wild black stallion reared up and screamed his challenge and the fight was on. The kalkar army threw itself on us. We tried only to keep them away from the couple in the centre, to give them time to do whatever it was they were doing.

The wild stallion proved a formidable fighter. He spun and reared, he kicked and bit, oblivious to the burns he sustained. We rode in a circle, felling the enemy as quickly as we could. They held no weapons but their touch was weapon enough.

We slashed at them, but although our blades inflicted pain, a killing blow barely slowed this enemy. Their blood steamed out, boiling and causing blisters where it sprayed our skin. Its acid touch melted the sand where it fell, forming beads of glass that crunched under our feet.

I wondered what the amulets were doing. It was taking more time than we could give them; the assault was too great. Two mounted people and a wild horse cannot hope to hold off an inhuman army. We fought in sheer desperation.

In a sudden blinding flash, the blue glow from the amulets spread out over the dark army, stopping them in their tracks. Those that were not instantly frozen by the wave hurriedly backed out of range. Then the light condensed and formed a large ball about us. With a sharp detonation the ball rocketed skyward, stretching into a great crackling beam shooting up into the stars.

Every eye on the field stared upward, following the line of blue light in terror. The weird humming began again. As we watched, there was a rustling and a wave of movement. Each individual in the leading rank of enemy appeared to grow as with a slow rising movement the fleshy cloak spread wide becoming firm and taut.

Then with a reverberating swooping sound the front rank pushed, the membranous wings forcing the air down against the ground and lifting them off.

"Atwin!" Evelar yelled. "Whatever you're doing, now would be good!"

"Netta!" I cried at the same moment. "Hurry!"

Then a piercing battle cry rang out across the desert, and the dark horde paused in its advance as it was attacked from behind. The nomads had finally appeared, and a small force was battling its way through to us.

The group advancing on wing continued its relentless progress, huge wings beating slowly in unison, and we readied for an aerial attack.

When they reached us they hovered just out of reach, focused only on the column of blue light and the two figures within. A few creatures continued into the light, drawn in like a moth to a lantern. I blocked the mental screams as they hit the glowing blue column and fell, their fire snuffed instantly, hitting the ground with a sickening thud.

The relief force had reached the inner circle of the horde, running up the hill to meet us ahead of the next wave. Without comment they pushed us into the centre of their circle and faced the enemy.

Exhausted, my revealer and I dismounted and stood beside Netta and Atwin, who were oblivious to the battle raging about them. We looked up at the small force in flight above, but they showed no interest in us, circling about the column of light but making no further attempt to reach the amulets and their bearers in the centre.

I massaged my right arm, the still-weak muscles aching from the strain of wielding a sword. I did not realise I was shaking until Evelar smothered me in his embrace, murmuring soothing words of comfort. Then I heard the low rumbles of thunder and realised what Netta and Atwin were doing, and why it was taking so long.

We looked up to see storm clouds forming, with lightning flickering within. The blue glow spread out across the sky, bringing more thunder clouds and lighting up the night. They were bringing rain to the desert!

We watched with bated breath. As the party of nomads held their own against the horde the clouds overhead grew darker, blocking out the stars. A fierce wind grew up, bringing more clouds to roil and twist as they filled the heavens and snuffed the moon.

The nomads eyed the storm with suspicion, but they fought on. The kalkar grew nervous and the less valiant broke and ran. Not that it did much good. In a violent crash of thunder the clouds burst above us, dropping their load of deadly water on the army of kalkar.

The first to fall were those in the air above, their whole bodies exposed to the torrential rain. This was no ordinary rain, which would have run off their slick skin membrane and into the sand.

The wind whipped fiercely at the thin folds of skin that we now knew were wings, pulling them away from their bodies despite their efforts to clutch at them and spreading them wide like sails, allowing the driving rain in underneath. As their bodies were exposed the tender flesh began to steam and ooze. Amid guttural screams of agony, the dark horde melted slowly into the sand.

We watched dumbfounded, oblivious to the rain bucketing down on us. Netta and Atwin had broken their link once the storm broke, satisfied to let it run its course. The nomads gazed in awe, catching the rain in their upturned faces. I lifted my arms into the air and spun about in front of Evelar. I laughed with joy as he joined me in the dance, the rain soaking us to the skin.

Our companions watched, Netta covertly and Atwin clapped in time as we spun, twirling about each other in complete abandonment. When the dance finished we stood wrapped tight in each other's arms.

"What was that one?" asked Atwin.

"The D'onara," I murmured.

"The dance of celebration," said Evelar.

"Appropriate," said Atwin.

Netta said nothing from where she stood, head bent, by the horses, but she looked sideways at us in envy of our happiness. The leader of the nomad warriors stepped forward and introduced himself in the common tongue, his striking accent similar to Evelar's familiar tones, though much stronger.

"I am Ontaro, second son of Old One. My brother, Chief Entranos, bids you come and meet with him."

Evelar pulled away from me slightly. "We will come," he said.

Ontaro hesitated. "I have noticed that you carry very little water. One wonders how you came to be so far into the desert?"

Evelar laughed. "We've been out here for over two weeks."

The man seemed surprised. "But how is that possible?"

Evelar smiled benignly, and said something in the language of the nomads. He translated mentally for me. *'I am Evelar, son of Shevron, who is nephew to Old One.'*

Ontaro smiled and spoke. *'Then welcome, Cousin,'* Evelar translated.

"My friends speak not the words of the desert," Evelar said then.

"Then we will speak so that they may understand. How is it that we have not met before?"

"We have, but not for many years. I have not lived with the people since boyhood and I return but rarely."

"Ah. Then we must make haste. Come."

Evelar faced me then. "Take Lumen. I'll ride ahead with Ontaro. The warriors will guide you."

He and the nomad climbed onto the backs of two kneeling camels. The beasts stood up and the cousins struck out over the sand. We three mounted up and rode out amongst the warriors. We picked our way through the battlefield, careful to avoid the steaming puddles of goo that had been kalkar.

The nomads slowed their desert beasts to match our less versatile horses and by the time we reached the tent city of the nomads the sun had peeked over the horizon and begun its steady climb. I gazed at the camp, stretching out over the sands, hundreds of tall conical tents.

The sides of each tent were rolled up high off the sand and I could see the tall central post from which the canvas stretched, held out in a circular form by many long ropes attached to pegs driven deep into the sand. As we made our way through the camp I saw they were made of some kind of animal skin, probably camel.

Inside the tents, rugs covered the ground and possessions hung from the thick central post. Many people sat outside the open entrance to their tents in little groups. Eventually I saw Evelar and Ontaro sitting with another man outside what must have been the chief's tent, sharing a pipe.

Evelar excused himself and came to meet us. At his request, the horses were taken and cared for.

"Entranos wants to meet you," he said, leading us to where the men sat.

"Chief Entranos, may I introduce Prince Atwin of Drasmil, bearer of Naali and Princess Nettayna of Shirall, bearer of Leena."

Entranos bowed his head with respect. "Welcome to our camp," he said solemnly, voice thickly accented with lilting vowels and rolled R sounds. "I am told you have achieved a monumental feat, bringing the amulet Naali back into the light. My congratulations."

"Thank you, Sir," they said together and Netta ducked her head again.

"Sir," Evelar continued. "I would also like to introduce Miyam."

Entranos took my hand and bowed over it. "Welcome Miyam. Please be seated."

Before we could join them in the circle, a man stepped out of a nearby tent and looked in our direction. He froze, staring at Evelar. The revealer looked up to meet the man's eyes and smiled.

"Excuse me, Sir. I must speak with my father."

He took my hand and we made our way to where the man waited, dumbfounded. The two looked at each other for a long moment. When Shevron spoke it was in the language of the desert, but Evelar sent a running translation in my head.

"How's your sister?" Shevron asked.

"She's well, Father."

"It's five years since you last visited, boy, since the death of the one you called Mist."

"Yes."

I looked at Evelar in surprise. *'You knew Mist?'* I asked mentally, remembering only then how he had called her name when I was injured.

'Briefly,' he sent back.

"It's been a long time," said Shevron. "Your visits are too rare, My Son."

"I'm sorry, Father."

They embraced then and the ice was broken.

"And who's your... friend?" said Shevron, looking at me.

Evelar took my hand again, speaking now in the common tongue. "Father, this is Miyam." He looked at me and smiled tenderly. "My wife."

"Ah." Shevron smiled. "I welcome you as a daughter, Miyam."

His accent was similar to Evelar's speech but heavier. My revealer had retained only a ghost of the intonation I now heard from his father and I had grown so used to hearing it that I no longer noticed it.

Then Shevron winked at me. "Perhaps you can control this rogue son of mine."

My face went hot and I ducked my head, suddenly shy. Glancing about I saw that Netta had witnessed the little exchange and now sat with head bent watching us from underneath her hair as we sat with Shevron outside his tent. What I saw concerned me greatly.

She seemed to be having trouble coping with her conflicting emotions, withdrawing even further into herself as she tried to deny what she was going through. She needed help.

I saw Netta raise her head to stare, and when I followed her gaze I saw an enormous woman, short but as round as she was high, her great body hidden by a large shawl, with eyes locked on Netta. The men had fallen silent and watched the woman with a reverence that suggested she was a person of consequence.

'Who's that?' I sent silently to Evelar.

'Sand Mother', he replied.

'Your mother?'

I felt his chuckle deep inside my mind. *'No, that's her title. She's a holy woman, keeper of women's business.'*

Netta stood up then, and went to the woman, drawn by

her eyes. With an arm about the girl's shoulders, the fat woman led Netta toward her tent. Then the woman stopped and I felt her connect with me.

She turned to look at me and I knew that she wanted me to come to her as well. With a little nod of assent I followed. I saw the woman give a signal to a young girl sitting at the entrance and the child hurried to let down the sides of the tent, enclosing the interior in darkness and privacy.

As my eyes adjusted to the dimness I noticed all manner of paraphernalia hanging from the central post, and enigmatic images decorated the camel hide walls. Mats and cushions were strewn on the floor around a brick hearth and the smoke from the fire smelled of fragrant herbs and incense as it circled the room and wafted up through a gap at the top of the post. The woman told us to sit and offered a cup filled with sweet nectar.

"I am Sand Mother," she said. "And I am here to help."

TWENTY FOUR

Two nebulous days we spent sequestered in Sand Mother's tent. From what I remember, the first day passed in almost total silence. But, in the care of Sand Mother, Netta slowly rose out of her personal seclusion, and began to act more like her old self. Perhaps she felt safe in the purely female environment. Time in Sand Mother's tent had no meaning. The outside world did not intrude on her domain.

The only other soul we saw was the young girl who had enclosed the tent as we entered. She was either a daughter or an apprentice, but Sand Mother never enlightened us. She brought food twice each day, brought fuel for the fire and emptied the chamber-pot.The fire burned day and night, and during the heat of the desert day the tent was stifling.

Sand Mother stripped down to her underclothes and instructed us to do the same. The girl kept the water jug topped up, even when Sand Mother tipped its contents over the fire to make steam. On the morning of the second day Sand Mother encouraged Netta to talk.

Sand Mother did not need to be told what had happened, but Netta needed to tell it, so that we could sort out the root of what was troubling her. She needed to air her thoughts, instead of letting them fester in her mind.

"Do you feel violated?" asked Sand Mother carefully.

"No," said Netta uncertainly. "Maybe a little..."

"How do you feel?"

"Betrayed."

"By whom?"

"Leena."

"Ah. So you do not blame Atwin?"

"No!" she gasped. "He had no more choice than I."

"Yet he troubles you?"

"Yes."

"Why?"

Netta hesitated. "We were both forced," she said. "I realise that."

"But?"

"But he knew what he was doing," she blurted.

"It bothers you that you were not his first woman?"

"No..."

"Perhaps you feel uncomfortable because he was your first man?"

"Yes... No... I suppose..."

Sand Mother nodded then in satisfaction. "Do you love him?" she asked gently.

Netta looked up at her. Then she lowered her eyes dejectedly and nodded.

"Then what's the problem?"

Netta looked up in surprise. "I..." a single tear spilled over.

"You are afraid that he does not love you?"

Netta nodded forlornly.

Sand Mother turned to me. "Does he love her?"

I smiled. "With all his heart."

"How do you know?" blurted Netta.

"Do you trust this woman?" Sand Mother asked.

"Yes," said Netta, but she sounded uncertain.

"But she troubles you?"

"Yes."

"Why?"

Netta hesitated. "She..." She blushed furiously.

Sand Mother smiled. "She has a lover? Who better to advise you, child?"

Netta looked sheepish.

Sand Mother looked back to me. "How do you know, Miyam?" she asked.

I smiled more broadly. "Just look in his eyes."

Sand Mother laughed delightedly. "Precisely. The eyes are the mirrors of the soul, child," she said to Netta. "The face and the muscles around the eye, they can lie. But the eye itself cannot show anything but the truth."

After lunch on the second day, I emerged bleary-eyed from the tent of Sand Mother. She wanted to spend a little time alone now with the Princess. I needed to reacquaint myself with the real world. As I cast my eyes about the camp, Evelar sent a thought.

'Is Netta healed?'

'Not quite,' I replied. *'But she will be.'*

'Will you join us, my love?'

I glanced about and finally located him sitting with his father and Entranos outside the chief's tent.

'In a little while. I need to walk about for a bit. You can join me if you like.'

'I like very much!'

I saw him excuse himself, and watched as he came toward me, disconcerted by the unexpected absence of his cloak. Even the red head sash was gone. I drank in the sight of him, appreciating his tall athletic form, shivering in anticipation.

"I've missed you, my love," he murmured as he took me in his arms and kissed me. "Let's go somewhere more private."

A happy little laugh bubbled up and escaped me as he took my hand and led me away from the camp.

When we eventually returned to the tent city, I was surprised to see a crowd of people gathered to greet us.

"What's going on?"

"My father wants to welcome you," Evelar replied with a smile.

"I don't understand."

"It's a tradition amongst the desert people. We don't have a marriage ceremony as such, but the parents of a newly paired couple will perform a welcome. My father is acknowledging you as my wife and welcoming you to the family tent."

I felt a lump in my throat as I looked at him and my vision blurred. "You mean we will be married?"

"In the eyes of my people, yes," he grinned.

A warm glow of happiness spread from the centre of my soul, and I threw myself into his arms.

"It holds no meaning in the College of course," he said. "It won't be official there, but at least here it will be."

He took my hand and led me through the crowd to Shevron's tent. As we passed, the women pressed little glass beads into my free hand.

'The beads are for you to make into a necklace,' he explained silently.

'Where did they come from?'

'They're made right here, and are traded all over the known world.'

I opened my hand to look at the beautiful beads, each one different, with colours weaving in intricate patterns within the glass. As we neared the tent, I realised the walls were down and had been painted in elaborate patterns just like those in the beads.

The ground all around had been decorated with beautiful swirling designs in coloured sand. Our path was decorated too, and I felt a pang of sorrow as our feet scuffed the amazing artwork.

Shevron was waiting at the door of his tent, face a picture of pride and happiness. He beamed at us as we approached.

"My son, I welcome you home," he said and turned to me. "My new daughter, I welcome you home. You are one of the people now and will always find a home with us."

With that statement, Shevron invited us into his tent, where a simple meal awaited and herbal incense flavoured the smoke from the fire.

Early the next morning we prepared to leave. Atwin appeared from the tent of Old One, where he had been counselled and healed. He appeared a little subdued but happy, and helped us load the horses. Entranos gave us food and water and offered to send an escort.

"I know the way," said Evelar. "But thank you for the offer."

As we completed our preparations, Netta finally emerged from Sand Mother's tent. The wise woman stood at the flap, giving last minute advice and encouragement. Then Sand Mother embraced the girl, and Netta made her way toward us, eyes forward in a plucky reminder of her old self. She moved to where my mare waited patiently for her, took the reins and led her to me.

"Thank you for letting me ride Cheena," she said softly. "You can have her back now."

Then the Princess walked to where Atwin was standing by the black stallion, watching. She stood in front of him and lifted her chin, looking him straight in the eye.

"May I ride with you?" she said.

Atwin was tongue-tied. "Ah... sure," he said in bewilderment.

Netta reached up and took gentle hold of Windfoot's mane, pulling herself up without Atwin's help. She sat regal and tall. She locked eyes with Sand Mother, watching from outside her tent, and gave a smile and a nod.

"Come on, then," Netta said to Atwin imperiously.

"Ah... alright." He clambered up onto Windfoot's back behind the Princess. Uncertainly, he reached his arms about her and wrapped his fingers in Windfoot's mane.

We struck out northward across the desert, safe in the knowledge that the extra water bags given us by the nomads meant we did not need to dig again.

"The kalkar have left us alone since the rainstorm," said Evelar as we set off. "But we need to get moving."

Atwin nodded in agreement. "Every mile further from our last known position makes it harder for them to find us."

"Are they close? Is there any indication from the amulets?" I asked.

"No," said Netta. "But they are coming."

"And we have no fabulous beast to hide us," said Atwin.

"I'm sure they can only track us if we make some sort of psychic noise," I suggested.

Evelar nodded and finished my thought. "We'll have to keep quiet and hope it's enough."

In four days we rode safely into Tellemot. We did not wait in town, but went straight to the dock to find passage to Shirall. We boarded immediately and by dusk were headed out of the harbour on the evening tide.

As night fell, we gathered in the little cabin we shared and spoke quietly.

Ella Mortimer

"We should send a message to Averil," said Atwin. "They will be wondering how we are progressing."

"Yes," said Netta. "We need to tell them we are coming. Mother needs us!"

"I'm not sure that's a good idea," said Evelar then.

"The kalkar will hear," I said.

"But did you not say that they would not attack over water?" said Netta then.

"I know I said that before, but I think this is different."

"They're desperate now. The amulets crushed them in the desert," said Evelar.

"And they'll be more anxious to stop you now," I finished.

"I don't think fear of water will blunt their vengeance," Evelar concluded.

"You may be right," said Atwin.

"But they need to be told we are on our way!" said Netta.

"Is it worth the risk?" I asked.

Netta pouted. "I just want to know that Mother is alright. What if we are too late?"

Atwin sighed. "Netta, I know you are worried, but what if they are right and a communication brings the enemy down on us?"

"We defeated them once," she said in defiance. "We can do it again!"

I shrugged. "Alright, Netta, if you want to risk it."

We stood in a circle and joined hands. Netta and Atwin spoke the words, and soon we heard an anxious voice in our heads.

THERE YOU ARE, said Averil. *WE HAVE BEEN SO WORRIED!*

I AM SORRY AUNT.

WHERE ARE YOU? HAVE YOU FOUND HIM?

WE ARE ON OUR WAY HOME. NAALI IS WITH US.

OH, THANK THE GODS.

HOW IS MOTHER?

SHE IS NOT WELL, DEAR. SHE HAS NOT WOKEN FOR MANY DAYS.

OH. Netta sighed.

WE WILL BE THERE SOON, AVERIL, said Atwin.

PLEASE HURRY. AND BE SAFE.

Atwin closed the link and Netta sank on to the bunk, tears falling. The Prince went to her and took her in his arms.

"We should prepare," said Evelar.

"If the kalkar heard they'll be here soon," I finished.

"Sleep while you can," said Evelar.

Atwin nodded. "We will be ready."

Sailing north from Tellem Cove as the night deepened, we settled in for a tense vigil. I sat snug with my revealer in a hidden corner over the rail, and together we scanned the sky. Staring out over the sea, with the moon shining on the water, we watched for the first sign of kalkar on wing.

The mental scream hit us first, a thousand minds in unison crying out for justice. *Catch them. Stop them. Get them now.* Then we saw them, glowing colours glinting on the far horizon, reflecting moonlight as they flew.

We climbed out of our cosy spot to find Netta and Atwin already on deck. As we hurried to them they joined hands and began to chant, the blue glow springing up about them. The enemy sent a wave of triumphant thought as the glow served as a beacon in the night. *There! Get them. Go now!*

One sailor cried out at the sight of the enemy approaching like fire, eyes glowing and heated air slamming our faces ahead of them.

"Get water!" Evelar yelled at the men. "Now!"

The sailors milled around, reluctant to listen to a stranger, but the Captain emerged from his cabin.

"Do it!" he ordered and the men jumped to obey.

"And get those sails down!" Evelar suggested loudly.

The sailors grumbled but set to work. The foremost kalkar were upon us. One headed straight for the highest mast and perched there, setting the topmost sail alight.

The sailors hurried to get the rest down before we lost them all. The glow about Netta and Atwin grew to engulf the ship, freezing the closest creatures. The remaining kalkar hovered close by, reluctant to touch the deadly aura.

They transmitted their frustration and anger in a solid wave of thought. Desperate to get to the amulets, the creatures buffeted the shield in an attempt to break through, oblivious to the instant death it brought.

Then the water around the ship began to roll and swirl. It rose in a wall about us, sucked up into the blue light until it formed a swirling bubble of water encasing the ship. The kalkar continued to throw themselves at the shield, but now instead of freezing and falling with a splash they melted, the liquefied flesh falling like rain.

I ducked, expecting the ooze to fall about me, but the shield was still in place within the wall of water and the remains of the enemy were deflected into the sea. Still the kalkar came, trying with sheer numbers to break in on us.

"Come on," Evelar said, grabbing my hand and leading me to where the others stood.

Standing either side of the couple, we each took their hands in ours and joined the circle without breaking it. I concentrated on letting Evelar use my mind for whatever he planned. He took the power and directed his thought upward into the dome of water above.

As the blue glow took on a golden tinge, the water bubbled and steamed. The blue shield drew more water from the sea and thickened. Then with a sudden crash of thunder it began to rain, upwards.

The water coating the shield sprayed up into the enemy force, hitting them full on their exposed bodies, the protective membrane of their wings useless. The bulk of the enemy fell in agony, landing in the sea in a cloud of steam.

The remaining kalkar finally broke and fled, the final thought of utter defeat hitting us in a wave as their shock drove them away, their anguish and despair floating back on the wind.

TWENTY FIVE

Sailing on into the Gulf of Shira we arrived four days later in the port of Shirall. With autumn slowly deepening into winter, we looked out over a city blessedly free of kalkar, and rejoiced. As we rode up the hill toward the ruin that was the upper palace a crowd was gathered to watch us.

Ordel stood beside the Princess Regent, eagerly awaiting our arrival. Behind the pair, but in front of a gaggle of servants and courtiers, stood a petulant Kandina. Her face as she noted that Netta and Atwin were riding together on one horse was a study in amazement. As we rode closer I saw her jaw drop and her bottom lip begin to tremble.

I sent a mental caution to Evelar. *'Keep your eye on Kandi,'* I said. *'We left only a few weeks before her birthday celebration, and she's likely to be a bit sour.'*

'Especially since Atwin was a fellow offender,' said Evelar wryly.

The crowd gathered about us, eager to help us down from our mounts. As Atwin helped Netta dismount, Kandi positioned herself behind him, arms folded haughtily in front of her. When the Prince took Netta's hand and turned to make his way to where Averil waited, Kandi was there to block his passage.

"Hello Kandi," said Atwin mildly.

He brushed past her, and Netta gave her a little smile as she followed, Atwin's hand clutched in hers. Kandi spluttered and stared after them in astonishment.

"Well," she said finally.

She watched as Netta embraced her aunt and Atwin planted a kiss on Averil's cheek. Then Netta threw herself into her father's waiting arms. Ordel took the Prince's hand in a greeting that hinted at the familial bond shortly to be shared by the two men. Kandi cried out in horror and sobbing brokenly, turned and fled.

The Queen lay comatose on the four-poster bed and Netta stood sadly at her side. She placed a hand on her mother's brow and felt the faint whisper of life, which I heard in my own head when I searched. She was close to death.

If we had arrived just a few days later Delsi would have slipped away beyond all hope of recovery. Atwin stood at the other side of the bed, waiting for Netta to prepare herself. When the time came to revive Delsi, the amulets would take over again. Finally, Netta reached out across the bed to Atwin with both hands.

The Prince took her hands in his and the pair immediately began to glow. The blue nimbus spread to engulf them and laid itself gently over Delsi's prostrate form. After a few moments they began to chant in the ancient language. The spell came haltingly at first from their lips, rusted from centuries of neglect as the amulets formed the words in their minds.

The spell slowly worked its magic and Delsi began to stir. The pair raised their hands higher and the glow grew more intense. Delsi tossed fitfully on the bed. The glow above her took on a reddish tinge and stretched upward as the evil charm was dragged out of her body.

The angry red formed a spinning ball beneath their hands, hovering above the Queen as the last of the charm was pulled away. Then it was sent upwards to hover above the room. Delsi continued to glow, blue and clean, as the amulets did their work on her damaged body.

Then the aura cleared and Netta and Atwin raised their hands above, sending the blue shooting at the ball of red, merging with it and turning it purple. The red slowly faded as it was neutralised and when the ball was completely blue they drew it back, shrinking it until it was fully merged back into the aura of the amulets, and as they lowered their hands the blue glow dissipated.

Delsi's eyes fluttered and then slowly opened. Her once glorious blue eyes had faded to grey, and she stared blankly. She opened her mouth to speak, but was too weak to make the sounds. Ordel went to her side and took her unresisting hand in his.

"I am here, love," he said softly.

She turned her head toward the sound, but could not focus her eyes on her husband. She tried to speak again, her voice a cracked whisper. Averil brought a glass of water and urged her to drink. After a few sips she tried again.

"I... cannot see... Ordel," she whispered. She tried to raise a hand to his face but could not lift it more than and inch or so off the bed.

"Rest, love," said Ordel. "You are very weak. Perhaps you will regain your sight as your health improves."

"Perhaps..." she whispered, though she sounded unsure. "Netta?" she said then.

"I am here, Mother." Netta took her mother's other hand.

"So you found Naali then."

"Yes, Your Majesty," said Atwin.

"Ah. We must celebrate his homecoming."

"Not until you are rested, love," said Ordel. "There will be plenty of time to celebrate when you are fully recovered."

With the spiritual poison that had almost killed her

removed at last from her body, Delsi recovered quickly. We watched as the Queen walked slowly through the underground gardens on her husband's supporting arm.

"Mother is getting stronger every day," said Netta happily. "I just wish her eyesight would return."

"I don't think it ever will return," I said.

"The effects of the poison were too long eating away at her body and her eyes are permanently damaged," said my revealer from the shadows.

Atwin smiled. "It does not worry her. She walks with confidence despite that."

"She's happy to be alive," I said.

"That's all that matters," said Evelar from where he stood in the dimness beneath a tree.

"Will you come and sit?" said Atwin. "You know you do not have to keep up the pretence with us."

Evelar shrugged. "It's what I'm used to, my friend. It's just how I'm trained."

"Delsi cannot see you, and Ordel sees only her," said Atwin.

"Come and join us," said Netta. "Sit with your wife!"

Evelar chuckled. "If I do that I might not be able to control myself. I wouldn't want to embarrass you, Princess."

Netta blushed. "I am over that now!"

"Oh really?"

"He's just protecting his image," I teased. "Heavens forbid someone should see, and realise that revealers are human too."

"Our marriage is not yet public knowledge," he said defensively.

"Well, we are alone now," said Netta.

"If someone comes, I give you permission to melt back into the shadows if you must," said Atwin.

Evelar stepped away from the tree and gave a mock

bow. "I hear and obey, Your Highnesses!"

With that, he came and sat, pulling me into the circle of his arms.

"What shall we do now?" asked Atwin then.

I snuggled in close, enjoying the quiet. "Be happy that the danger is past, and we can sit here with no reason to rush off."

"Actually, my love," said Evelar. "I should be getting back to the College. I need to report to the Maestro."

"I have not released you yet, my friend," said Atwin. "You are going nowhere!"

"My mission is complete."

"Mother is planning a celebration," said Netta. "You must stay."

"As you wish, Your Highness," he said.

"I do wish," she said. "Face it, Evelar, you have friends now!"

"Not to mention a wife," said Atwin. "Your life has changed forever. You can no longer hide behind that revealer face and pretend you are not human."

"All our lives have changed," I said.

"For the better," said Atwin with a smile for his princess.

The first I knew we were no longer alone was the absence of my revealer at my back. He had melted into the shadows just as Atwin had said he would.

"Kandi!" cried Netta, jumping up to run to the younger princess. "Where have you been? I thought you might be avoiding me."

Kandi just glared at her. Worried by that look, Atwin got up to follow.

"What have I done?"

"You have taken my prince," she snarled.

"Your what?"

"You knew he was mine. I told you! He was going to marry me."

"What are you talking about?" said Atwin from behind Netta.

"She wanted you for herself," I said quietly. "Until Netta came, she firmly believed that you would marry her."

"You must be joking!" said the Prince, shaking his head. "I had no idea!"

Kandi rounded on him. "How can you say that? Why did you come here so much if not to see me?"

"Kandi, I came here because I am meant to be here, not because you are here."

"You lie! You loved me!"

"We were friends, Kandi that is all."

"That is not true!"

"Kandi, I'm sorry," I said. "But you were never meant for him. Naali and Leena have made sure of that."

"I will not allow it! I will stop it!"

"Kandi, it's none of your business," I said. "You can't do a thing to prevent it."

"I can and I will!" she cried, storming off.

Netta stood gasping for a moment.

"What was that all about?" said Atwin.

"Would you have married her?" asked Netta. "If I never came here?"

"Of course not! I never saw her that way."

Evelar came up behind me. "Well, it looks like I'm staying for a while. Who knows what she'll do now."

At the royal table, Atwin was seated between Netta and her cousin Kandi. The younger princess took avid advantage of the situation by monopolising Atwin's attention. She was so intent on her efforts to win the Prince for herself that she quite neglected to note that Atwin was holding Netta's hand firmly in his all the while.

As the meal came to a close, Delsi stood regally to make her speech.

"My friends," she began. "As you know, I have of late been rather ill. The illness was such that certain of our number were obliged to undertake a gruelling journey in search of a cure. As you can see, I have at last recovered from my... indisposition, hence our celebration tonight. But there is another, more glorious, cause for celebration."

There was an expectant hush as the court hung on her words.

"The cure I mentioned could only be effected by obtaining and using a certain lost artifact. I speak of Naali, the ancient talisman of the Kings of Shirall, the residence of the spirit of Rexa and mate of Leena."

The crowd began to murmur.

"At some point, long in the past, the King was lost in battle and his amulet disappeared. Since that time the Queen's Amulet, Leena, has continued to keep watch over us, calling forth in each generation a boy to become mate to her new infant heiress. But, without Naali, the boy could never be king."

There was a flurry of whispering throughout the gathering.

"My friends," the Queen continued, "I am alive. This means, of course, that our intrepid travellers have succeeded in their quest. Leena has been reunited with her long lost mate. Naali has returned. And, for the first time in thirty generations, Shirall will have a king!"

The murmurs became a roar and the crowd rose as one with cheers and applause. After a few moments, Delsi raised one regal hand in a call for silence.

"My friends, this brings me to one final revelation. Would you like to meet your new king?"

There was a roar of assent from the crowd.

"Before I reveal him to you, dear friends, there is one last fact of which you must be made aware."

The crowd hushed.

"Everything, as we all know, happens in its correct time. It is my belief that this has shown itself to be true once again. After eight hundred years, our beloved Shirall could never accept just anybody to be her king. The man destined to wield Naali must be of a certain calibre. He must be a man of courage and honour and enduring faithfulness, a man who can lead us unerringly into a new age."

A rumble of chatter rippled through the gathering.

"I believe Leena has chosen well. Our new king not only has these qualities and more in abundance, but he has also proven himself to us time and again. He has long been accepted as one of us and is loved as a true son of Shirall. He is, in addition, already destined to become a king in his own right. Surely this is an omen. It is a sign of things to come as our two houses merge into one. My friends, the one who will be king is none other than our dear friend, Prince Atwin of Drasmil."

The court roared out anew and the applause was deafening as Atwin slowly rose from his chair.

"For many years," he began, "I have looked on Shirall as my home, even more so than my poor afflicted Drasmil. Whether this was brought about by the call of Leena, or by the distress inherent in my ambiguous position in my father's court, I cannot say. But I sincerely hope that the love I hold for the people and places of Shirall shall, one glorious day, be reciprocated. I place my trust in you and hope that you may learn in time to return my trust."

The audience let out a collective sigh.

Atwin lowered his gaze to meet Netta's eyes, raising the hand he still held to his lips, lifting the Princess from her chair to stand graciously beside him.

"Leena has chosen to give me her blessing, allowing me to be the bearer of her mate, Naali. It is my greatest hope that Leena's bearer might accept me also."

Netta looked deep into his eyes. Then she smiled radiantly. "How can I refuse when you ask so very nicely," she said.

She reached up with one hand to touch the side of his face. Then she drew him down to her and kissed him gently. The crowd burst out in a fit of unbridled joy as the two amulets engulfed the pair in a radiant blue glow.

Kandi looked on in utter shock. With a little angry moan of pain she stood hurriedly and stalked her way toward the great staircase. From his vantage point in the crowd, however, Evelar planted himself in her path. Quietly, I slipped up behind her.

"You wouldn't be thinking of leaving, would you?" I said softly.

She spun to face me. "I do not see how that can be any of your business," she declared.

"True," I assented. "But perhaps you should look around you."

She hesitated in her angry retort. "What are you talking about?"

"People are watching you, Highness."

She looked about nervously.

"They're noticing that you're displeased."

"I care not what they think," she sniffed.

"Perhaps not. But if you don't start showing some pleasure in the joining of Netta and Atwin who are, after all, predestined to be together, you'll soon find yourself surrounded by enemies."

"Is that a threat?"

"Of course not. It's a warning. Court politics can be

a dangerous game, Highness. One in which you're still a little out of your depth. You have just shown all your cards, which makes it rather difficult to bluff."

She looked nervously up to the royal table, to find Netta watching her.

"Is there a problem, cousin?" asked Netta quietly.

"Not at all," said Kandi, after the briefest hesitation. She forced a smile. "My congratulations."

"Thank you. Will you rejoin us, then?"

"Of course."

TWENTY SIX

Another round of chaotic preparation began. This was the most important royal joining in centuries and attendance would be huge. Prince Atwin called on his brother and the armies of Drasmil and Shirall, to begin refurbishment of the above ground palace as lodgings for visiting dignitaries and courtiers from all the far flung kingdoms of Sharné.

I came upon Kandi in the tower room, watching the men as they worked carting stone and climbing scaffolds.

"Who is that?" she asked, pointing to the man leading the troops.

"I believe that's Prince Calib, Atwin's brother," I replied.

"Prince? But he is a soldier."

I nodded. "He's the commander of the army of Drasmil."

"I like soldiers, did I ever tell you?"

"Yes, you did."

"I wish Atwin was a soldier."

"He may not command the army, but he's as well trained as his brother. All kings must be able to lead an army."

"I never knew that!" she smiled a secret smile. "I am glad. When I win him back I will be sure to appreciate him all the more."

"Now Kandi, don't start that again."

"I will win him," she said with a stubborn frown.

"Kandi you can't still believe you can stop the joining?"

"I will find a way."

I frowned. It appeared Kandi was going to hang on to

her hopeless crush until the very last. I hoped she would see sense once the joining was over.

'If she doesn't come to terms with it soon, she'll find herself sorely disappointed,' said Evelar, hidden somewhere nearby.

'That's an understatement,' I replied.

I stood stripped to my chemise in a riot of coloured fabric, once again at the mercy of the head seamstress and her army of assistants, watching as Netta argued with her.

"No, she cannot wear white again!" Netta said to the woman. "I am the bride, I wear white, nobody else.

"But Your Highness white is the best colour for her. I was going to put you in pink."

"For my joining?" Netta was livid. "You will do no such thing!"

"Your Highness, I'm the professional here, I know what I'm doing."

"How dare you! I am the Princess here! It is my joining and you will do as I say!"

The woman bowed. "As you wish, Your Highness."

I sighed with relief.

"Now," Netta mused as she looked at the fabrics strewn about. "You and Evelar are standing as our witnesses, you have to match."

She picked up a bolt of shimmering satin, a deep blood red. "But it has to be the right red. Where is he, Mym?"

I shrugged. "He's always close by, he has nothing else to do. Since Atwin insisted he stay for the joining he follows me around like a lost puppy," I teased, knowing he could hear me.

"Stop lurking, Evelar and come here," said Netta then.

He appeared as if by magic on silent feet and the head seamstress gasped, face livid.

"What do you think you're doing, we have a woman half naked in here, get out!"

Netta gave her a look of distain and waved her away. "Leave him alone, they are married," she said.

"Netta!" I cried. "You're not supposed to just tell people that!"

"Why not? It is nothing to be ashamed of."

"But it's a secret!"

Netta made a dismissive noise. "Come here, Evelar, I want to check this colour."

With a face devoid of expression he came across the room, boots eerily silent on the stone floor, the revealer image untarnished by Netta's irreverence.

"Stop that," she said. "Now I assume you intend to keep your cloak on?"

He said nothing, eyes staring out of a perfect revealer mask.

The seamstress started to protest. "If he's standing with the Prince, he must be dressed…"

Netta hushed her. "The cloak is part of him, he would not be our dear friend without it."

"But it's torn and filthy!"

"So clean it, mend it and press it!" said the Princess in exasperation. "And you let her do it," she said pointedly, eyes shooting daggers at him.

She held the cloth up to compare it to the red border of his revealer's cloak.

"Let me see if this is the right red." Then she smiled in satisfaction. "Perfect! This is the one."

She held it out to the flustered seamstress. Evelar quietly slipped back out of sight, noticed only by me. The woman shrugged as she examined the fabric.

"It's rich enough I suppose. With a few frills, a pink underskirt and petticoats it should serve well."

"Enough with the pink!" cried the Princess. "She is a warrior, not a princess. No frills, no underskirt, no petticoats. Something simple and plain and short like her tunic."

The seamstress gasped. "Bare her legs? You can't, it's unseemly!"

"She can wear hose and boots like she usually does. I want to see my friend standing with me, not some stranger."

"Not short!" said the woman. "The whole world will be there, Your Highness, you must observe some propriety!"

Netta sighed. "Alright, make it long. But no frills! Simple and sleek, like the fighter she is."

"As you wish, Your Highness."

"Now," said Netta. "At some point, Princess Kandina will be seeing you. You can put her in frilly pink."

Netta motioned to me. "Get dressed, Mym. We have to find Kandi and convince her to stand up with Calib."

"I don't like your chances," I said as I quickly dressed.

"I will not give her a choice."

She strode from the room ahead of me.

"You too, Evelar," she said to the room as she left.

We found her in the garden, standing forlornly on the little footbridge over the pond, staring down into the water.

"Kandi?" Netta said carefully.

"What do you want?" she spat.

"I want you to stand with Calib at the joining."

She looked up, face a picture of astonishment.

"Why? You know I do not approve of this joining, why would you want me there?"

"Because I still love you and I want you beside me. You may not like me right now, but I know deep down you want me to be happy."

Kandi shook her head, tears falling unheeded. "I do not

Ella Mortimer

believe you. I will not stand with you. I refuse!"

"Nevertheless, I want you there."

"You came here, you pretended to be my friend and you stole my prince. I hate you!"

"Do you hate Atwin too?"

Kandi sobbed. "How can you ask that?"

"Because if you love him as you say you do, you will come and you will stand and you will wish him well."

"That is not fair!"

"If I have to speak to your mother to make you be there, I will."

"I do not care what you do! I will kick and scream and cry havoc. I will not stand there quietly and watch you marry my prince."

"Then you will lose him forever."

"I hate you!" Kandi screamed as she fled.

Averil had sent for the Princess with no explanation, and Netta pulled me with her as she hurried to the audience chamber. When we entered we saw Delsi sitting on the main throne with Averil next to her and Ordel standing behind. Evelar slipped unnoticed into his accustomed place behind Averil. On Delsi's lap sat a small jewelled box.

"Netta," said her mother, knowing without seeing that the Princess had arrived. "This came for you."

"What is it?"

"It is a gift, from my father," said Ordel. "Your grandfather."

"My grandfather?" she whispered. "I have a grandfather?"

"I am sorry, angel," said Delsi. "But with our dangerous situation we could not allow him to meet you before. That will change soon I hope."

"But who is he? Where is he?"

"I am not at liberty to say, my dear," said Ordel.

"Why?"

"Because that is what he wishes, for now. When he is ready, you will meet."

"But..."

"There is a note," said Delsi.

Netta took the note and read aloud.

> *My Dear Nettayna,*
>
> *I regret that I have not been able to see you grow and become the beautiful princess I know you are today. I remember happy visits with you when you were a small child, before the invasion that sent you into exile. I loved you then and I love you still, even if you do not remember me.*
>
> *I would like to offer my heartfelt congratulations on your coming nuptials and the wondrous event that has led to it, the rediscovery of the King's Amulet, Naali. I cannot be there in person at this time, but I hope to soon remedy that.*
>
> *I would like to offer you this gift. It belonged to your grandmother and was passed down through many generations before that. I hope it pleases you, and just maybe you would like to wear it on your special day.*
>
> *My love and best wishes are forever yours,*
>
> *Miradel, known as Thoy,*
>
> *Your loving grandfather.*

* * *

"Why do I know that name?" said Sand from the darkness.

"Maybe you heard it somewhere?" The Maestro shrugged with a quiet chuckle.

* * *

Netta looked up at her parents, eyes glimmering with unshed tears. Delsi held the box out to her. Taking it and opening it carefully, Netta gasped. With one hand she lifted out a beautiful gold necklace, set with countless sparkling diamonds and rubies. She held it up and stared at it in wonder. Looking again into the box, she replaced the necklace to bring out matching earrings and bracelet and then a small, elegant tiara.

* * *

"Did she wear the jewels?" said the Maestro eagerly. "How did they look?"

"I'm getting to that, Sir," said Miyam with a bewildered look. Why was the Maestro so interested in the jewellery?

"I'm sorry, my dear," he said. "Please continue."

* * *

"Very pretty," said a sarcastic voice.

Netta dropped the gems back into the box and spun to see the newcomer.

Haughty demeanour with a sneer crossing his face, dressed in gold doublet under a sable coat with crown lopsided on his head, stood King Gerard of Drasmil.

"Your Majesty," said Averil mildly. "You are welcome to Shirall."

"Welcome, am I? I think not!"

"I assure you, you are most welcome."

The King snarled. "As I am here to put a stop to this lunacy I am sure that is not the case. I do not approve of this joining, I give no blessing on this alliance and I resent being bypassed in this marriage treaty. I am here to bring the traitor to heel and have him transported back to Drasmil for judgement."

"I am truly sorry you feel that way," said Averil with a smile. "I am afraid I cannot allow that."

"You cannot allow it? How dare you!"

"Oh I dare, Your Majesty. This joining has nothing to do with you or your precious kingdom. This is a Shirall matter, a monumental historical event, involving the return of a legendary relic. Nothing you say will prevent this from taking place."

At that moment, there was a commotion at the door and both princes came stumbling in.

"I am sorry, Your Highness!" Atwin began. "I had no idea…"

"You!" the King exploded, rounding on the Prince. "You have made yourself a very cosy alliance behind my back. You have set yourself up very nicely, taking control of my household, winning away my army in readiness to seize my throne. Now, setting yourself up here to win yet another crown. Is there no end to your traitorous intent?"

"Father, please," Calib stepped forward. "There is no such intent."

"And you!" the King sneered. "Allowing yourself to be seduced away from my side by this traitor, helping him in his evil design. I thought you had more sense."

"Father, if you would just see reason," Calib tried again.

"No, Calib, there is no reason besides the power building machinations of this snake who betrays me at every turn."

"Stop!" Netta cried and the King made a strangled noise mid tirade. "You have no right to treat your son this way. He has given you nothing but respect and love, even in the face of your accusations, and he deserves better from you."

The King rounded on her. "Now you keep out of this, little princess and leave the politics to the grown ups."

Netta reeled back a step at the vehemence of the King's attack and Atwin hurried to her side, a hand on her arm, standing as a shield before her.

"Netta, leave it he will never see reason," he said.

The King gave a disdainful laugh. "Look at you, all in this together. The plot goes deep, I see. How long do I have? When will you come for my crown, or my life?"

"Your Majesty," said Delsi then. "I assure you there is no such plot. This joining is not an alliance, and it is not a prelude to a coup. When I am no longer able to perform my duties as queen I will stand down and Netta will rule in my place."

"With the traitor as king," grumbled Gerard. "If this joining goes forward, I swear I will remove all rights the snake has to my kingdom and Calib will be my heir."

"I wish you would reconsider. Atwin will only be king in title, not fact. You know as well as anyone that Shirall follows the female line. Atwin has nothing to gain from this marriage but happiness and a home that accepts him."

"Ready to plot my removal, you mean!"

"I should think you would be pleased that he will not be resident at Drasmil to feed your fear of betrayal. Put aside your paranoia, Your Majesty."

"I..." the King went silent, breath catching in his throat as his illness took hold. His eyes rolled back into his head and Calib and Atwin jumped forward to catch him between them as he fell.

Netta sank to the step at her mother's feet. I hurried to her as Atwin saw the mad king carried away to his hastily assigned quarters and a medic called for treatment.

"Why do so many people object to this joining?" she whispered. "What is it I have done to deserve this?"

"Netta, it's not you," I replied, putting an arm about her shoulders.

"Oh, Mym, but it is," she cried. "Kandi hates me, Atwin's father hates me. Maybe we should call it off."

"Netta, that's exactly what they want, but it's not what we all want. We want you to be happy."

"But I am not happy, Mym," she sobbed. "How can I do this if it means losing a friend in Kandi, and Atwin losing his father?"

"I lost my father long ago," said Atwin from the doorway.

Sobbing, Netta ran into his arms. "What if he carries out his threat and removes you from the succession?"

He smiled. "Calib will never allow that. He works every day on my behalf, controlling my father from within his trusted circle. I will never have a greater ally."

"Netta, my dear," said Averil then. "I promise you, we will all support this joining. We are your family and we love you. Kandi is a silly girl who will do as her mother says. King Gerard will see reason, even if it is his own twisted logic that wins him in the end. All will be well."

TWENTY SEVEN

White satin, pearlescent and shimmering in the candle light, overlaced with sprays of tiny silk flowers of every colour, tripping and scattering from waist to hem in beautiful abandonment. White silk lace, smothered in pearl beads, peeking out at the front from beneath the voluminous skirt. No less than seven silk petticoats held the skirt out to more than a metre in diameter. Beads and flowers intertwined over the entire bodice, swirling in splashes of colour and shine.

Long blonde hair hung loose to her waist, threaded with thousands of tiny live flowers of every colour. Gold tiara studded with diamonds and rubies sat at her brow, the matching necklace sitting perfectly just above her amulet and the earrings accentuating her lily white neck where they hung from her ears. Sprays of flowers laced her arms and the jewelled bracelet lightly embraced her slender wrist.

I lounged in an armchair in the corner, watching the Princess as she was primped and pampered by an army of handmaidens. They would start on me soon, and I was not looking forward to it. My dress hung nearby, long flowing sleeves, bodice covered in beading and skirt so long it seemed to go on forever. But at least it was not pink.

The hairdresser had already finished with Netta's floral sprays and was calling me over when there was a knock at the door heralding the Regent Averil and her daughter

Kandi. The younger princess was pouting and red eyed, but she entered the room without protest and stood calmly as her mother left the room.

Netta smiled with relief. "Kandi, I am so glad you came."

"I am not doing this for you," she replied. "I am doing this for Atwin, because it will make him happy."

"If you say so," said Netta.

"Thank you for coming, Kandi," I said with a smile.

The hairdresser worked quickly with nimble fingers as my hair was filled with flowers to match Netta's. Looking in the mirror she offered I realised the sprays stood out much more prominently in my dark hair. I sighed. It was for Netta, and I had to admit the effect was rather pretty.

'Are you free to join me, my love?' said a voice in my head.

'Absolutely,' I replied, eager to get out of that room for at least a short time.

"Netta, do you mind if I step out for a while?" I said.

"I thought he was with Atwin?" she replied, eyes twinkling.

I gave her an exasperated look.

"Alright, Mym," she laughed. "But behave! No playing, you will mess up your hair!" she called after me as I hurried out.

In the garden, I stood quietly under a tree. When my revealer finally arrived, I gave him a look of exasperation. He stopped and stared at me, his mask gone and eyes drinking me in.

"What?" I said.

"Your hair! It's grown so long." He came to me and slipped his arms about my waist.

"It's the weight of all those flowers," I joked.

"You look amazing," he murmured as he kissed me.

"What's going on?" I said when he released me.

He put a finger to my mouth. "Shhh. You'll see. Close your eyes."

I laughed. "What is this?"

He waggled a finger at me. I sighed and closed my eyes. I felt him put something about my neck. Only when it was fastened did he let me open my eyes and I looked down. It was a large, faceted diamond on a necklace of fine glass beads. I took it in my hand and looked up at him.

"The diamond you made from sand?"

He nodded, grinning.

"I thought it was destroyed when Naali was freed from the crystal!"

He shook his head. "I kept it and I had the palace goldsmith cut it and set it for you, along with the welcome beads."

I looked down at it, eyes filling with unshed tears. "It's beautiful," I said.

"As are you," he murmured. He lifted my chin with one finger and kissed me gently.

Walking in procession, we made our way along the dark corridors of the underground palace, heading toward the surface. Kandi was in the lead, her pink frilly gown covered in beads and flowers accentuating her youthful beauty, chin lifted proudly, tears in her eyes.

I followed, treading carefully to avoid stepping on my long red dress. Netta had been full of praise when she saw it.

"Oh, Mym," she had said. "It hugs in all the right places. His eyes are just going to pop out of his head!"

The bodice was a mass of beads, tight and low cut, leading seamlessly into the long skirt that flowed and moved when I walked. The head seamstress had restrained herself to only one petticoat which gave just enough volume to hold the skirt out slightly as it fell shimmering to the floor.

Behind me, Netta walked slowly and carefully, maids fluttering about her, and the rest of the household staff followed. Stepping out into the sunlight I saw the crowd, thronging to welcome us on our road to the temple in the palace grounds.

Every spare inch of the courtyard was filled, and every patch of grass from there to the temple was a mass of people, cheering and throwing flowers. We made our way slowly through the gardens, Kandi walking stiff and proud ahead of me and Netta following in a flurry of excited activity. It seemed an eternity.

Finally I saw the small stone building ahead, people surrounding the place. I longed to get inside where it would be quiet. The square building had been renovated for the occasion, with new cobbles laid around and new plaster on the walls.

The three men would be already waiting on the far side of the building, and we heard the cheers from all around as we arrived at the near side. Then all went quiet, and out of the hush a lone flute could be heard.

It played a long lilting melody, trilling to the air like a bird in flight. Then a drum began to mark time, a slow heartbeat. Walking in time to the beat we moved slowly along the near wall of the temple, past the closed door.

At the corner the drum let out a reverberating roll of beats, before continuing its slow march as we began moving along the next side. Directly opposite, unseen by us, the men would also be walking.

Three times we completely circumnavigated the temple, turning a corner at each drum roll and walking in time to the slow rhythmic beat, until eventually we returned to the original side for the third time to find the door finally open.

The drum stopped and the flute was heard again, its trilling notes proclaiming the next phase of the ceremony. And the drum began again. Kandi was first to enter and on the other side of the temple, through the other door, Calib would enter at the same moment.

After the third drum roll it was my turn, and Evelar's from the other side. I entered the temple. It was dark, no lanterns or candles. A blank wall faced me and I turned to the right, following the corridor as the faint sounds of the drum guided me on. At the next drum roll I turned left and rounded the corner.

I could see light shining out of the doorway to the left in the middle of the corridor. In the dim light of the far corner I could see my revealer ready to meet me. As the drum beats continued we walked slowly toward each other, the light growing as we approached the doorway.

There we stood bathed in the light streaming from the interior cella as we waited for the next drum roll, staring deep into each other's eyes as the magic of the moment overcame us. I felt happy, enthralled, overwhelmed and as breathless as if it were our own joining.

'You look incredible, my love,' he said in the privacy of my mind. We barely heard the drum roll as we joined hands and entered the cella.

In the small room a woman, the priestess of Aphris, joiner of hearts, dressed entirely in cloth of gold, bowed in greeting from where she stood behind the stone altar. She signalled with both hands and we moved to the two corners nearest the door. Kandi and Calib already stood in the far corners, Kandi stone faced and staring blankly, and Calib staring at her, entranced.

We turned in our corners to face each other, eyes locked across the small room as the final drum roll sounded, heralding Netta and Atwin. Then all sound ceased. Both radiant, eyes only for each other, they stepped up to the altar and the private ceremony began.

The altar contained a small fire pit in its top which was laid ready. The priestess lifted her hands and began to sing.

"We call the spirits to give their blessing

For the achievement of this joining

Where heart and mind, soul and body

Combine with love and life."

As she sang the last line, the priestess brought her hands down with a clap and a spark, lighting the fire. The Prince and princess sang the response.

"My love is keen."

In my head a voice echoed the response.

'My love is keen.'

I felt a bubble of laughter and suppressed an involuntary smile. Looking across the room his eyes were twinkling as he smiled suggestively.

'Behave yourself!'

'I'm perfectly serious,' he replied.

The priestess stoked the fire, adding kindling as she sang the next verse.

"We call the east wind's blessing

For the beginning of this joining

Where heart's ardent fire blazes forth

At the coming of the sun."

The royal couple sang the response. "My heart is warm."

'My heart is warm,' I whispered silently and he smiled more tenderly this time.

The priestess sprinkled fragrant incense over the flames and sang the next verse.

"We call the north wind's blessing

For the enchantment of this joining

Where minds soar with the clouds above

In the bright azure sky."

The royal couple responded. "My mind is true."

And we responded together silently. *'My mind is true,'* smiling together, holding each other's gaze.

The priestess dipped her hands into a bowl of water which stood by the fire pit, lifting a double handful and allowing it to dribble over the flames reducing them to glowing coals.

"We call the west wind's blessing
For the conclusion of this joining
Where soul sinks with the setting sun
From whence the rivers come."

The response came. "My soul is pure."

And our response followed in the intimacy of our minds. *'My soul is pure.'* My vision blurred as my suppressed happiness brought tears to my eyes.

Now the priestess reached into another bowl, at the other side of the fire pit, and pulled out two handfuls of soil, which she sprinkled over the embers of the fire as she sang.

"We call the south wind's blessing
For the fulfilment of this joining
Where bodies meld with life's arousal
On the bones of the earth."

Netta and Atwin sang the response. "My body is strong."

And we sang our own silent response, Evelar adding a suggestive raising of the eyebrow. *'My body is strong.'*

The priestess tipped the last of the water and earth into the fire pit and mixed it with her hands. Then as she sang the final verse she drew magic symbols with the muddy ash mixture on the royal couple's face, chest and hands.

"We call the spirits to give their blessing
For the stability of this joining
Where heart and mind, body and soul
Combine with love and life."

In hushed voices, the couple sang the final response.

"My love is firm."

And my revealer and I sang the same response, silently and with an overwhelming rush of emotion. *'My love is firm.'*

With the ceremony concluded, the priestess signalled and the newly married couple turned together to exit through the doorway. Evelar and I came together and joined hands, following Netta and Atwin, and I sensed Kandi, sobbing softly, and Calib falling in behind.

Sitting between Evelar and Calib I looked out over a sea of people milling about at the open air joining feast. Kandi sat at the end of the long table at the other side of Calib, and beside Evelar's other hand sat Netta and then Atwin. Down the opposite side of the enormous table sat the few kings who had made the journey, and Ordel the Prince consort, with Delsi at the head and Averil at the foot. Opposite Kandi sat the mad king.

Evelar had his stony revealer face on, but under the table he clutched my hand, and I wondered what was troubling him. When I asked, he shook his head and smiled before settling the expressionless mask back in place.

I had thought the sumptuous feast at Netta's welcoming banquet had been lavish, but this left it far behind. Countless whole beasts roasted on spits all down the side of the field. In front of those a second row of fire pits contained all manner of root vegetables baking slowly in the coals that had been raked to the front, and thousands of linen wrapped mystery items boiled in huge pots hanging over the flames behind.

While we waited for the meal, the wine and ale flowed freely and the crowd was supremely merry. All except for Princess Kandina laughed and smiled and made a lot of noise. So it was that only those nearest could hear the conversation going on between Kandi and King Gerard.

"You seem unhappy," said the King with a smirk.

Kandi gave him a look of pure disdain, her eyes brimming with tears.

"My daughter is entertaining a silly crush that will soon pass when she realises there is no point fighting fate," said Averil.

The King chuckled. "Ah, I am glad to see I am not the only one who objects to this joining."

Kandi almost smiled at that.

"Leave it be, Father," Calib warned.

"No, Cal, if everyone else can play politics and form alliances then so can I." He fixed his gaze firmly on the young princess. "What is it you most object to?"

Kandi sobbed. "It should have been me."

"Now Kandi, we talked about this," said her mother.

"It is true!" she cried. "If Netta had not come this would never have happened, and in the end I would be sitting there beside him."

"Kandi, you must stop this."

The King chuckled delightedly. "Now that would have been a great match. Much more to my taste, anyway. No empire to build with you!"

"Father!" Calib exclaimed.

Kandi was openly sobbing now, the tears falling freely unheeded. "I wish she had never come here! I wish she would just go back to where she came from. Everything would be how it should be if she was gone!"

"Kandina!" her mother snapped.

The mad king laughed delightedly, his expression reminding me of some criminal plotting his next escapade. "I like your attitude, young lady. Perhaps we should talk more."

"Father, that is enough," said Calib.

*

Some time later, after the food had been consumed with great enjoyment and accompanied with enthusiastic carousal, the last formality of the day was performed. The joined couple danced, followed by their witnesses. Evelar led me out willingly, but he still seemed distant and distracted.

I missed his usual irreverent mental comments, but he gave me no explanation for his mood. Kandi I understood as she stepped out with Calib, face a picture of dejection, oblivious to Calib's adoring gaze.

Immediately following the dance, the royal couple retired to many cheers and congratulations and suggestive comments. They were not expected to attend the rest of the celebration, and once they left the noise shifted up a notch, echoing out over the town.

Soon after, Kandi begged permission to leave and was escorted to her chambers by her favourite handmaiden. Pulling me in close and enclosing us in a mental shield, Evelar finally met my eyes, his mask down. His gaze was troubled, his brow furrowed, and that grin I had been hoping for did not light his face. He kissed me with an urgency I did not expect, and in my mind he sent an erotic thought.

'Let's head downstairs. I want to get you out of that magnificent dress.'

At any other time that comment would have made me blush, and I would have admonished him for his irreverence. But there was a seriousness to his tone that stopped my mirth. His eyes held a deep sadness that caught my breath, and his mental touch was at once tender and melancholy. I allowed him to lead me silently away from the thronging crowd.

TWENTY EIGHT

I awoke early the next morning to find an empty space beside me. Not concerned, I reached out sleepily with my mind and searched the palace. Evelar was nowhere to be found. I sat up in bed, worried now.

Evelar would have told me if he needed to leave the palace. I searched again, but he was definitely gone.I dressed quickly and made my way to the audience chamber where I found the Queen and her sister. Behind the Queen, Ordel stood where he could whisper advice. The absence of my revealer gave the scene a certain surreal quality.

"Where's Evelar?" I asked peremptorily.

"The revealer?" asked Averil. "Why he has left, Dear."

"Left?"

"Early this morning," said Delsi. "He has returned to Eeasto."

"What?" I said incredulously.

"He said something about reporting to the Maestro."

"What?" I said again.

"Is there a problem, Dear?" said Averil.

"Ah... No, of course not," I said, forcing a smile.

My mind was racing and my heart beat painfully in my chest. Averil, along with Delsi and Ordel, did not know about Evelar and myself, and could not know what I was going through at that moment.

He must have a reason for running off. He would never do anything to hurt me. Without another word I strode from the throne room. I did not want my revealer to get away without an explanation. I yelled a thought at the man.

'What do you think you're doing?'

He ignored me, though I knew from his mental wince that he had heard.

'Don't you dare leave me like this!' I screamed.

He ignored me.

I raced to the stables and cast about for a suitable mount. I stopped at Cheena's stall and gave her an apologetic pat.

"I'm sorry, girl. He's too far ahead, we'd never catch him. I can't take you."

I noticed Kandi tightening the cinch on her bay gelding. Perfect. I came up behind her and commandeered him.

"I need to borrow your horse," I said as I jumped into the saddle.

Kicking in with my heels I left Kandi with no time to answer. She spluttered a little and watched helplessly as I rode away. Spurring the horse to a gallop I rode north away from Shirall.

I spent the first several minutes cursing under my breath. Full of self recrimination, I told myself I should have seen this coming. His strange behaviour at the joining feast was suddenly, startlingly explained. His mission had been to get Netta and Atwin together. He had succeeded. He must have known even then what he planned to do.

I rode on. I had no idea how far he had already travelled, but I planned to catch him. I pushed the poor horse to the limit.

Finally, I saw a mounted figure in the distance, riding at a gallop, his cloak billowing out behind him. I leant forward and gave the gelding his head.

Kandi's horse was young and a racer. Evelar's older stallion, though a fine horse, was slower. When I caught him up, I did not try to pull him to a stop, nor to overtake him and block his path. I was angry. I simply ran him off the road.

He was forced to pull up short or slam into a tree. I said nothing. He gathered his composure and looked at me, a little sheepishly. I stared him down.

"Don't look at me like that," he said finally.

I continued to stare.

"I... I thought it would be better if I... slipped away."

I continued to stare.

"I'm sorry," he said petulantly.

"Better for whom?" I said then.

"Well..."

"It was a cruel thing to do," I said in a harsh voice. "What were you thinking?"

He hung his head. "I couldn't bring myself to say goodbye..."

My heart melted. "But you don't have to. I'm coming with you."

He looked up. "You can't," he said. "I can't take you to Eeasto."

"Why ever not?"

"Because I can't get you into the College."

"Of course you can."

"No, I can't. You're not a member."

"But my mother was. Do you really think I've never been there before?" I laughed at him. "Don't you know who my mother was?"

"I have no idea who your mother was."

"Oh, that's right. I've been waiting for you to work it out. Sometimes, my dear Sand, you're too brilliant for your own good."

He blinked. "Excuse me?"

"You get so involved with all those deep convolutions of fact and fiction that you miss the things that are staring you right in the face."

"What has that got to do with anything?"

"There you go again," I said in exasperation. "My mother was a revealer, I can get in."

"Your mother is dead, it no longer counts, and you have no familial tie with me."

"I'm your wife, damn it!"

"Not officially..."

"You poor foolish man," I said then. "Do you really think that matters?"

"I can't take you to Eeasto," he said stubbornly.

"In that case..." I said, and slid down from Kandi's horse.

I walked to his side and looked up at him innocently, reaching out to touch his hand. Then, before he could throw up a mental shield, I ripped the energy from him and materialised a quill and paper. He clutched at his temples with a groan of pain.

"Did you have to do that?"

"Sorry," I said as I wrote a quick note. "I've never done that before and I wasn't sure I could."

I tied the note to the bridle and turned the horse toward Shirall. I gave his rump a good whack and he bolted. Evelar looked incredulously after the rapidly disappearing horse.

"What did you do that for?"

"To force you to give in."

"I can't leave you out here, miles from Shirall."

"Exactly."

He sighed. "I'll have to take you back to the palace."

"Don't you dare!"

"I thought it would be easier for you if I left you with friends," he said defensively.

"I'm not going to stay here without you!"

"I'm not going to leave you sitting outside the gate of the College."

"Then I may as well sit here in the middle of the road and wait for the next carriage to come along and run me over!"

I walked away from him and splonked myself down in the dust of the road, my back to him. Mean, I know, but I wanted to shake him up a bit and it worked. He sprang from the saddle and came up behind me.

"Mym, please don't do this."

I ignored him. I couldn't trust myself to speak. My anger was fading and I felt about ready to cry. He knelt behind me.

"I'm sorry, my love," he murmured. "I didn't mean to hurt you."

"What hurts is that after all this time you still don't trust me!" I said with a catch in my voice.

"Of course I do," he moaned.

"Then let me come with you!" I wailed.

"You really think you can get in?"

I nodded. *'I need to get in,'* I sent silently through my tears.

He sighed. "Then we'll give it a try."

So he helped me up and we settled ourselves together on Lumen's back. His arms went about me as he clicked to his horse and we started out on the long journey north.

* * *

"And that, my dear Maestro," said Mym. "Is how we came to be here together."

She let out a long sigh and fell silent, letting her conclusion hang in the air.

"Sand was right," said Maestro. "It was a long story. But well worth it, my dear."

"Well told, my love," murmured Sand from his dark corner beside the hearth.

The Maestro rounded on him. "My dear boy! You

astound me!"

"Excuse me?"

"What have you been doing to get so powerful all of a sudden? I swear if there were another colour above artisan you would be wearing it! My goodness boy, your report told me nothing of this!"

"What are you talking about, Sir?"

"Sir, please," Miyam broke in. Bathed in the soft orange glow of the flames that danced merrily in the fireplace, her young brother Domyn had fallen fast asleep in her lap.

The Maestro went to the door and called for an apprentice to take the boy to his dormitory. When Domyn had gone, guided sleepily away by the Apprentice, the Maestro went to get something from his desk.

"Now, Mym," he said. "I have something for you."

He brought to her a small metal box, secured with a little silver padlock.

"When you left, we were all terribly disappointed. But I felt certain that you would one day find a way to return to us. In anticipation of that day I kept these things for you. Everything here is yours by right."

He held out the box to her in both hands. She stared at it, her face pale, and she slowly reached out to take it from him. Sand was drawn from the darkness in curiosity, seeing the pain in her face. She looked up to the Maestro and met his gaze, and her eyes were filled with grief.

* * *

The King lounged, one leg draped lazily over the arm of his throne, foot kicking absently. In one hand he held a large goblet filled to the brim with deep red wine. The flagon lay on its side on the flagstones, side smashed from the casual drop when it had been emptied. Lifting the cup to his lips the King drank, slopping the liquid down his straggly beard. His lopsided crown slipped as he tipped his head back, but he caught it clumsily and righted it over one ear.

Harsh laughter escaped him as he remembered the pretty little princess at the snake's joining feast. He had spent so long searching for a way to prevent the empire building machinations of that traitor, and the little miss had given him the perfect solution without even realising what she had done.

He chuckled to himself. He could not wait to bring his plan to fruition. That girl was perfect. He could handle her as a daughter-in-law. She had no power, no title to inherit, in fact no value whatsoever, yet she had a spunk that would control his rogue son and hobble him so that his crown would never be threatened again.

Through the fog of his celebratory flagon, he heard a commotion, and glanced toward the door. There were sounds of a struggle and a sudden thud, followed by the entrance of a tall scruffy man dressed in dirty grey tunic and trousers with a torn and filthy cape to complete the ensemble.

"You really need to train your guards better," said the stranger with a sneer. "Too easy."

The King sniggered. "Oh you are perfect!" Then he turned serious. "But never forget to whom you speak, spy. I can have you killed faster than you can reach for your sword."

The spy bowed. "Point noted, Your Majesty."

"Now, down to business. I have a… person… I need to get rid of. Alive, mind you, I would not want to be accused of murder as well as madness."

* * *

TWENTY NINE

Sand paced the floor of his artisan's quarters in an agony of worry. Whatever the Maestro had given her, it had made Mym draw into herself in a way that he had never thought possible. When he had guided her unresisting to the armchair she had sat slowly, as if in a daze, and had drawn her legs up under herself, curling up into a tight ball and hugging the little black box tightly to her chest.

Tears glistened on her cheeks and her face was so stricken that he had looked worriedly to the Maestro for explanation. He thought back on what he had learned when the Maestro had drawn him aside to speak quietly.

"Six years ago, Miyam was withdrawn from the Art by her father."

"Why?" Sand asked.

"It was after Mist was killed," he said carefully, bringing a frown to Sand's face. "He was worried that something similar might happen to her. Miyam resisted, of course, but I have no control over the whim of the parent in these cases. There was nothing I could do." He sighed. "In less than a month she would have been made apprentice. She had already passed the exams at the top of her class."

"What have you given her?"

"Only some things that were left behind. I think we should leave her here alone."

Now, late in the evening, Sand paced. What was the connection he was missing? Why had her father been so worried when Mist died? It was a dangerous business, being a revealer and sometimes members of the College died or were killed on duty. Surely he understood the risk a revealer faces when active outside the College. Perhaps it had something more to do with the death of her mother.

Sand paused at the window to look out. The moon was high and the Apprentice on hall duty had still not brought Mym home to his rooms as he had asked. He paced again, but his worry would not ease. Perhaps he should return to the Maestro's study, to see if she was still there. Yes. His concern drove him back to the small room.

When he entered on silent feet the girl was sitting on the hearth rug, staring into the embers of the dying fire. The metal box sat unopened on the Maestro's desk. Sand picked it up and carried it to her, placing it on the floor in front of her.

"Why don't you open it?" he asked softly.

"Because I already know what's in it." Her voice was flat, without emotion. It worried him.

He knelt and took her hand. "Mym, what's wrong?"

She sighed sadly. "It brought back memories."

"The box?"

She nodded. "If I open it," she whispered, "I'm afraid I might lose myself in... things I had pushed away until they were forgotten."

He moved her hand until it rested on the metal lid of the box. "Open it," he said gently.

"I can't!" she said in anguish.

There was a long silence.

"Sand..." she said then. "You said once that you knew Mist..."

He hesitated. "For a short while, a long time ago."

Miyam hurried on. "I never found out exactly how she died. No-one would tell me. All I know is that she was on an assignment with a journeyer when it happened."

Sand rose quickly and went to the fireplace. He felt her look up and watch as he busily stoked up the fire, feeding in more wood.

"Sand..." she said. "Were you... that journeyer?"

He drew in a sharp breath. He kept his back to her, unable to hide the tension in his shoulders.

"Were you?"

He sucked in a deep shuddering breath. "If she had been with anyone else," he said finally, "she would be alive today."

Miyam rose and went to him, placing a gentle hand on his arm.

"Tell me what happened."

He moved away from her, his back stiff.

"Sand, please," she said with a catch in her voice. "I must know."

He turned to face her and their eyes met. He was surprised by the pain in her eyes. His own guilt was nothing compared to her grief. Again he wondered what he was missing. He did realise that the telling was important to her and that the deeply buried trauma of six years was coming to the surface, not only for her but for him also.

Perhaps he too would be helped by the telling.Silently, Sand took her hand and led her away from the fire. He settled himself down in the soft chair and Miyam knelt on the cushion at his feet. Then, in a voice that was barely audible, he began to talk.

"I was twenty-one, barely a year out of the brown," he began. "It was my first major mission. It was already a success. We were on our way home. Then we were set upon by a force of mercenary spies determined to prevent the information from reaching the council. There were ten of them. We killed two each before we were forced to fight back to back. We were surrounded and we fought desperately.

"Mist killed two more to my one before I found myself on my knees. She rendered another unconscious before turning and forcing back the other two. One more died by her hand before I regained my feet and dispatched the other. But neither of us had noticed the one behind us regaining his senses.

"Before I could react he had crept up behind and run her through. Mist crumpled at my feet and I killed that last enemy, but I was too late to save her life. I knelt to help her but she was already dead."

His voice had been low and monotonal, but now it faltered and he fell silent, his head bowed in grief as he relived those moments. Miyam sat at his feet, crying softly. Haltingly, Sand continued, compelled now to finish the tale.

"I carried her body back to the College and delivered the report to the Maestro. Then I requested dismissal from the Art. My request was overruled because Mist had written a journal, in which she recommended me for master." He fell silent again momentarily.

"From that day forward," he said in a stern voice, "I vowed to become the best there is. Just to ensure that I could never again be the cause of someone's death." This last was bitter.

"It wasn't your fault," said Miyam.

He reached out to touch her tear-stained cheek, astonished by her sorrow. "Would you trust me with your life?" He said then.

"You saved my life," she said and turned over her right arm to reveal the long white scar.

He traced the line with one forefinger and smiled.

"You surprised me that day," he said.

"Oh?"

"The way you fought. It was so like her."

"Mist?"

He nodded. "The style was the same." He looked at her then. "Now I realise how much you remind me of her in other ways. You even look like her."

"Did you love her?"

He laughed. "At the time, I suppose I thought I did. But most of what I felt was hero worship. I was young and impressionable and Mist was the perfect role model."

He stood up, still holding her hand, and moved to where the little metal box lay forgotten on the rug. He stooped to pick it up and handed it to her.

"Open it," he said quietly.

Together they sat cross-legged on the rug, facing each other. The girl fingered the padlock almost reverently. There was a little silver key tied to the handle and she used it to open the lock. The hinges creaked faintly as she slowly lifted the lid. She stared at the contents for a long moment.

"Is it what you thought?"

Miyam nodded slowly. She reached in and brought out a small dagger. Sand had a vague idea that he had seen it before. The double sided blade was honed to a fine edge. The hilt was made of hard wood, polished to a fiery red. Into the pommel was carved an elaborate symbol the rune for the letter 'V'. She passed it wordlessly to Sand and he examined it closely.

"A fine blade. What does the initial stand for?"

"Veroni," she said.

"Wasn't that Mist's real name?" he said in surprise and she nodded.

The next item was a sturdy leather belt, varnished to a fine sheen that matched the red of the knife. It was stamped with an elegant design along its length. The buckle was small but ornate, and again Sand felt a vague stab of recognition. The next piece made him gasp.

It was so unusual that he recognised it immediately. It was a wristband, designed to cover the back of the hand and the forearm almost to the elbow. It was a strange silver colour with shimmering panels on the top side. Silently, Miyam slipped it onto her right arm and it fitted perfectly.

"That belonged to Mist!" Sand said in surprise.

The girl nodded. She drew out the tiny sheathed blade that belonged with it, holding it flat on the palm of her left hand. With a small movement of her right wrist the knife leapt out of its sheath and hovered in the air.

The Artisan watched the deadly instrument as Miyam skilfully sent it darting about the room. The little blade had no handle, but a point at each end. Along the sides it was sharpened to a deadly edge. The whole thing was the size of her little finger. Sand had seen that very blade and armband used by Mist.

"Did you know her?" he asked.

"Very well," she said with a sigh. As she played with the tiny blade the tears brimmed over, spilling into the hand that rested in her lap.

Finally, Sand caught her wrist in his hand and the mote knife fell to the floor. She refused to meet his eyes and he touched the box with his other hand. The girl looked down.

"What else is there?"

She reached in and clasped something small. "Only this." She held out her hand and opened it for him to see. She held a tiny wooden box.

Sand took it from her and opened it. His eyes widened and he glanced quickly at her. Inside was an Art name badge and on its coloured surface, hidden in a design that could only be deciphered by an Art member, was the rune for Mist.

He looked up and caught her eyes. Taking the badge from its box, he placed it in her waiting hand, closing her fingers over it. She hung her head and a small sob escaped her as her hands fell into her lap.

"Tell me what all this means," he said quietly.

She was silent for a long while, but Sand knew she would answer. She drew in her breath slowly.

"Haven't you worked it out yet?" she said in a voice choked with grief.

She raised her tragic eyes to meet his troubled gaze. She dropped them again to her lap and let out a tortured sigh.

"Mist was... my mother," she whispered.

Sand watched her for a long moment. It made such perfect sense, and he finally realised what she had meant when she accused him of missing the obvious.

He rose and crossed the room. He bent to pick up the little mote knife from where it lay on the rug and brought it back to her. He took up the silvery sheath and carefully inserted the knife with a click. Then he reached out to the girl and drew her hair from her eyes.

The sheath held a powerful clip on its underside, and this he used to secure her hair. When he had finished, the weapon formed an attractive and apparently harmless ornament.

* * *

THIRTY

Kandi huddled in the stall, her beloved horse snuffling at her hair. She loved coming here and sitting in the quiet with only Swiftly for company. She loved smelling the hay and that horsey smell. Just sitting here was enough to calm her when she thought too long on her shattered life.

This stall was the only place she could wallow in self pity without interruption. Swiftly never judged, never told her she was a silly girl, and never assumed that she would get over it. Every time she thought about it, the tears came unbidden. The pain was as strong now as the day her prince had married another.

How could she have read the signs so poorly? She knew she had made a mistake and that she had wronged her only friend, but a part of her still hoped the Prince would one day realise she was the one he really loved. She knew it had not been his fault, and she even admitted that Netta was probably no more guilty than he. It did not make it any easier to accept.

Curled up in her corner, listening to the quiet noises of the stable, she suddenly held her breath. There was a faint scraping of feet on the dirt floor and she carefully moved over to the stall door to peek over the top. Netta! She ducked down again and listened.

"Hey my little Glimma," Netta was saying. She was talking to her new horse, Kandi realised, the beautiful white mare that had been a joining gift from the King of far off Nella Fillenga, who had been unable to travel to the celebration.

"Shall we go for a ride, girl?" Netta murmured.

There was a jingle of tack as the Princess prepared to saddle the horse. Then Kandi jumped as she heard a gasp and a heavy smack and a thud. Her blood went cold as Atwin's wild stallion screamed, and she cowered down in Swiftly's stall, terrified.

Something had happened and she knew she should run for help, but what if someone else was there, someone who had hurt Netta and would hurt her too? Trembling in fear, Kandi peeked over the stall door again. The stable was empty but for the horses. Kandi could hear the wild horse crashing about, screaming his rage.

She carefully opened the door and slipped out of the stall, creeping to look in on Glimma. She sidled past the angry stallion, keeping her distance as he glared balefully from his stall, nostrils flaring. The white horse was still there, sniffing at something on the ground. Moving closer, Kandi saw it was the saddle, dropped carelessly in the straw.

Kandi ran from the stable, hoping to get help, but stopped with a gasp. There, across the courtyard, was a cloaked figure on a grey horse, with a limp form slung across the saddle in front, hooves clattering as he galloped away.

"No!" Kandi cried. "Not this! This is not what I meant!"

Desperate to catch them now she ran, but the rider had already passed unchallenged through the outer gate. By the time she reached the gatehouse the kidnapper was down the hill and rapidly disappearing down the road. She cried out for the guard but there was no answer. Only then did she see the poor man, killed by a blow to the head.

* * *

When Miyam and her revealer were summoned to the Maestro's study, they found him standing by the window, tapping his foot impatiently.

"Ah, Mym," he said in a business-like voice. "Happy birthday."

He pointed to a parcel on his desk. She looked at him questioningly.

"You're a little early. My birthday's not for three months."

"Perhaps I'm late. Are you going to open it?"

Carefully, Miyam unwrapped the parcel. She found, folded neatly, a cloak with the brown border of an apprentice. She looked up at Maestro uncertainly. She fingered the fabric reverently.

"Well?" said the Maestro.

"Well what?" she replied.

"Aren't you going to put it on?"

She gathered it up and cushioned her face in it. Then she looked up again. "But..."

"Perhaps I should explain," said the Maestro then. "You had already qualified for apprentice when you left. I hoped that you would come back some day, so I took the liberty of neglecting to record your withdrawal. So, technically, you are still an apprentice."

Miyam looked to Sand and back again. "You mean..."

"If you're willing, you can step back into classes right away."

"I..." she hesitated.

"Surely you don't need to think about it?"

"Of course not, but..." she looked at Sand again. She didn't want to be left behind when he went out again, as he inevitably would.

"Don't worry," said the Maestro. "It won't be for long. The examinations begin in a few weeks. I've already marked you down."

Miyam looked a bit panicked at that.

"From what I've heard of your activities over the past

few months I'm sure you won't have a problem," he said reassuringly. "After all, if you had stayed you would have been tested a year ago and would now be working as a journeyer in the field. How can I keep one of my best trapped here in the College by a technicality?"

She looked at Sand again, her face stricken. The Artisan took a step toward her.

"Oh, I see," said the Maestro in comprehension. Then he smiled. "What if I were to declare Sand on vacation until you gain the green. Then you can go out as journeyer with him as your teacher."

It was Sand's turn to look a question at the Maestro. "Is that legal?"

"It's an executive decision. I do that on occasion. The council doesn't usually object."

Sand nodded, a little dubiously. Then he took the apprentice cloak from Miyam's limp grasp and shook it out. He placed it over her shoulders and fastened it with the nameless badge handed to him by the Maestro. Tears of wonder stood in her eyes.

As Sand pulled the hood over her head and secured it in place with the matching brown sash the tears spilled over. Sand gently brushed them away and she gave a sudden smile. Then she buried her face in his chest and he closed his arms about her.

But Sand's 'vacation' was not to be. After the midday meal that afternoon, as the Maestro sat in his cosy armchair by the fire dozing off, he was woken by an incoming psychic message.

FATHER?

The Maestro sat up straight in his chair. He stifled his pleasure at hearing that mental voice. It had been far too long.

WHAT IS IT, SON? YOU SOUND UPSET.

THOY, WE NEED YOUR HELP! A woman's voice, his son's wife.

WHAT'S HAPPENED?

SHE IS GONE, SOMEONE HAS TAKEN HER, she sobbed.

HUSH, LOVE, the Maestro heard the gentle comforting tone through the link. *FATHER, WE NEED EVELAR BACK HERE, NOW.*

OF COURSE, I SHALL SEND HIM RIGHT AWAY.

PLEASE, THOY, TELL HIM TO HURRY, she cried through the fading link.

When they arrived at the Maestro's office, concerned by the urgent summons, they found him pacing in agitation. He looked very worried.

"I'm sorry, Sand," he said. "But I'm afraid you are going to have to go out again."

Mym shook her head and slipped her arms about Sand's waist. "But you said…"

"I know what I said," the Maestro stated as he paced the floor. "But I can trust no other with this case."

"What is afoot?" asked Sand.

"I have just received a message from Shirall. I really am sorry, my boy, but I need you there."

"Has something happened?"

The Maestro took a deep breath. "Princess Nettayna has been kidnapped."

* * *

Four Zjobock Dhort stood on the bluff by the entrance to the great hatching cavern, staring at the fast retreating force heading for the horizon. The latest group of warriors had just set out to join the new pack alliance, winging their way south, riding the great thermal currents that rose off the rocks of the plain.

Twelve Suppreck Asfar travelled with them, and Four supposed she would never see him again. She reached out to the pack mind, hoping to catch an echo of his essence, but the prevailing thought was of the journey south and the other packs waiting at the gathering place.

She wished she could have gone with him, but she was unmated and so not yet made adult by her mate's knife. She could not go to war. More distressing, was the male who stayed behind, the one she did not want, the one she would be forced to mate in a few short moons.

Four shivered, her internal fire guttering in her distress. When this war was finished, how many warriors would return and how many packs would be destroyed forever? She reached out again with her thoughts, the pack mind ever present, but the beautiful mind of Twelve Suppreck Asfar was hidden beneath the group.

Many such groups had already joined the gathered, and as they did the great group consciousness took over, guided and controlled by the Leader. She wondered, not for the first time, who this Leader was. There had never been a Leader before. There had never been a joining of packs on this scale before. There had never been anything like this before.

She followed the warriors, allowing the great mind to pull her along. She stood in the same spot for three cycles of the sun, sleeping where she stood and waking at night to continue her vigil. Finally, she felt the gladness as they arrived at the meeting place. Now they would wait for their turn to begin a longer journey, flying in short hops from island to island heading west, toward the land of the humans.

THE END

Ella Mortimer

The Race of Fire
Book Two: Awakening Sand

The King's amulet, carrying the immortal soul of King
Rexa, is reunited with his beloved queen.

The dark horde of kalkar, who burn everything in their
path, have been defeated.

An even darker, more malevolent force is now in control
and the free world is set to burn.

As the kalkar prepare for a new invasion, the Princess is
kidnapped and the battle begins again.

From the secretive world of the revealers a hero will
emerge, who will risk life and love to take the battle
to the next level.

Sand must find his power and rise above his own
humility, to break the will of the terrible god Kayus, who
holds the invading enemy in thrall.

But will he survive death itself and escape the afterlife to
fulfil his destiny as the Awakener?

Ella Mortimer

The Race of Fire
Book Three: Rekindling Truth

Evelar, known as Sand, is the Awakener. Legend says the Awakener will bring truth to the world, but what is that truth and what is he supposed to do with it?

As Sand begins his predestined task the minds of those around him seem to fill his head. But underneath it all is another voice, carrying the long dead memories of a forgotten past.

Where are these memories coming from and what do they have to do with the strange amulet that belonged to his sister, an amulet so like those warn by the King and queen of Shirall?

As Sand's new memories bring to light the ancient history of the people who settled this world, our friends must embark on a new quest, to find and neutralise the great spirit who nearly destroyed them all.

Sand is about to discover that the truth is more amazing than he ever dreamed.

APPENDIX

CHARACTER SKETCHES

MIYAM

EVELAR

NETTA

ATWIN

MIYAM & EVELAR

NETTA & ATWIN

KANDINA

KANDINA

AVERIL

DELSI & ORDEL

GLISS